I0557156

Dear Teddy

by KATE BRIDGER

Redfern House Publishing
Nelson, BC Canada

Copyright © 2016 Kate Bridger

All rights reserved. No part of this book may be repro-
duced or transmitted in any form by any means without
prior permission in writing from the publisher, with the
exception of reviewers who may quote brief passages in a
review.

Book & cover design by Kate Bridger

dba Redfern House Publishing
Nelson, BC Canada

Characters and locations within this story are fictional. Any resemblance to real persons or places is probably inevitable, but not intentional.

Prologue

'Exile'
25 Champlain Street,
Cobden, Ontario,
Canada

April 14th, 1959,

My dear Teddy,
I can't believe I'm here. It's just so awful thinking about how far apart we are. The aeroplane flight was dreadful. Father kept saying what a great adventure it all was and how lucky we were to be on a jet plane and not stuck on a ship for ten days together … small blessing. It was horribly noisy and uncomfortable and all I could think about was that, with each passing mile, I was that much further away from you. I cried the whole way. Will I ever run out of tears? I even thought about what it would be like if we crashed. Would I really care? And then I remembered our promises to one another. Besides, I wouldn't want my parents to have the satisfaction of thinking they'd won.

We spent the first night in a 'motel' (that's American for a hotel where you can bring your motor car even though we didn't have one!) in Montreal. Daddy insisted on putting a coin in a slot at the head of the bed to see what would happen and then the whole thing started shaking and making a terrible noise. Mum and I just stood and watched while he knocked himself out laughing like it was the most wonderful invention ever. I couldn't see the point of it myself.

Then some really annoying people showed up to welcome us to Canada. We didn't know them; they were friends of some friends of Daddy's cousins in Winnipeg, I think. They talked non-stop in their lazy American-sounding voices. They brought me a box of horrible sugary poo-brown sweets that were supposed to look like maple leaves and a couple of tea towels for Mum that also had maple leaves on them. Then they dragged us out for supper. I was too tired to eat and Mum kept telling me to sit up straight and smile and that it wouldn't be much longer until we could fall into bed. I don't really remember much about it.

I miss you so much; it hurts.

The next day, Mr. & Mrs. Bentley came back to drive us to Cobden in their gigantic American 'station wagon'. It was an enormous tank of a car called a Chevrolet, but it only had two doors so it was really hard to get in and out of and I felt horribly trapped in the back seat squished between Mum and this Bentley woman. We drove for hours and hours on the wrong side of the road until we got to Cobden and our new house. We'd only stopped once and that was for lunch in Ottawa. Then it was just more of the same forest and bushes and nothing much else until we got here. They kept telling us to look at all the 'beautiful scenery'. I didn't bother.

The house is horrible. It doesn't even have a name.

Perhaps I'll call it 'Exile'! My room has a bed, a chest of drawers and some diabolical wallpaper with flowers all over it. Our own things won't be here for a couple of months.

Oh, Teddy, I wish I could wake up and discover this is all some terrible dream. I love you so much and I don't know how I am going to survive without you. You've got my address now, so please write soon (but don't put 'Exile' on the envelope!!). I'll write every day but I need to be sure you've received this first. I wouldn't put it past Father to have told Miss Frobisher to destroy any letters that come from Canada addressed to you. Teddy, I need your letters more than anything right now … no, I need your kisses more.

Missing you, love always, Gillian xx

P.S. Haven't met any lumberjacks yet! (And I hope I never do!)

~ ~ ~

Chapter 1 - Six Months Earlier

"Mummy, where'd you put my satchel? It was right by the door. Why'd you have to move it?" screamed Gillian who, as usual, was just minutes away from missing her bus.

"It's right where you left it, dear. Use your eyes, not your voice," replied Mary Mathers with all the patience she could summon first thing in the morning. This was the normal daily routine because Mary's daughter, Gillian, was always running behind. Secretly, Mary wondered if her daughter would ever get organized, or if her entire life would be spent looking for things that were exactly where she'd left them in the first place.

Gillian moved her father's heavy duffle coat aside and retrieved her loaded satchel. She swung it onto one shoulder and tore out of the house, slamming the door behind her. She ran down the drive, along Oak Road, passed Postlethwaite's Ironmonger's shop and arrived, panting, with only seconds to spare at the corner of Sycamore Road and Ambleside Drive. The red Ribble bus was just pulling up to the kerb.

Gillian boarded the bus and took her favourite seat in the second row beside the window on the left side of the vehicle. She shrugged off her satchel, dumped it on the seat beside her and waited for the conductor.

"Mornin' Gillian." Fred, the conductor, greeted her as

he strode up the aisle towards her, "looks like you left the house a little late again today, but you made it."

"Yes, I couldn't find my bag. Return to Kendal please."

Gillian loved the sound of the conductor's ticket machine as it printed and spewed out her little yellow paper ticket.

"Put it somewhere safe, love, you'll need it to get home," added Fred. They shared this same exchange every day.

The next twenty minutes were the best minutes of Gillian's day. She loved the slightly stale air of the cosy, overheated bus with its stained, but comfy, plush red seats. She surrendered to the predictability of the familiar journey and gazed out of the window hypnotized by the regular rhythm of the passing telegraph poles. If you thought hard enough about it, you could convince yourself that it was the poles that were marching by, not the bus that was moving.

At Lakeview Cottage, Gillian's best friend, Julie Burgess, hopped on the bus. Although Julie's arrival put an end to Gillian's private thoughts and daydreams, she was happy to see her and immediately moved her cumbersome satchel from the adjacent seat and set it on her lap so her friend could sit down beside her. As always, Julie was pressed and dressed immaculately; her school beret perched on her head at precisely the correct angle, her tie knotted flawlessly and her Clark's shoes buttoned and polished. By contrast, Gillian looked as if her beret had landed randomly on her head after falling from a great height, her shoes were scuffed, and her unwieldy leather satchel was wrinkled and ink-stained, nothing like Julie's brand new bag with its gleaming buckles.

"So, did you get your Maths done?" asked Julie.

Julie and Gillian attended Kendal High School for Girls

and were both in Mrs. Pratt's Maths class. They were good pupils, although Gillian preferred English and Composition to Algebra and Geometry.

"Yes, I pretty much finished it. I didn't get around to my homework until after tea. I saw Teddy in the village on my way home and we bought licorice pipes and sat in the square for a bit."

"So, do you *like* him?"

"You know I do," replied Gillian for the umpteenth time.

"No, I mean, you *really* like him," Julie persisted.

"Yes, I *really like* him … whatever that's supposed to mean."

"You know perfectly well what I mean," continued Julie. "So spill … do you kiss and things like that? Does he put his hand down your blouse for a feel? Do you have a secret meeting place where you go to snog?"

"Good God no! Nothing like that! What have you been reading lately? We just spend time together and talk about things. Sometimes, if I can sneak away, we go for bicycle rides up into the Fells. He's not like other boys."

"So, he's never tried anything … is that what you're saying?" Julie persisted.

"I don't have to answer that," replied Gillian sternly, suddenly wishing their bus journey was over.

"Aha! Then he has tried to kiss you. Good. One day you'll have to tell me what it's like when a boy sticks his tongue in your mouth."

"Ugh!" replied Gillian, genuinely shocked. "Look, it's our stop. Get up Julie, we've got to get off."

Never one to give up on anything, Julie assured Gillian that their conversation would be continued in the very near future. Julie had managed to sneak a copy of the forbidden *Lady Chatterley's Lover* from her mother's beside table and, like most school children of her age, found certain passages exciting and intriguing. Now her mission was to find someone she knew who had experienced some of the things written on those pages—like the 'queer vibrating thrill inside the body' described by Lawrence's Connie. Was it like that tickly feeling that happens 'down there' when you ride your bicycle over cobblestones? Julie, with absolutely no experience or exposure to boys, reckoned she was going to have to learn these things from her friend, Gillian, who, so far, was the only person she knew who was in love with a real live boy.

Meantime, Gillian spent much of the school day wondering about Julie's questions. Could there be something wrong with her if Teddy hadn't tried to cop a feel? What if one day he really did stick his tongue in her mouth … would she gag? Would that spoil everything? He'd held her hand once; that had been nice. They were crossing a stream and Teddy was helping her keep her balance on the slippery stones. She often thought about it afterwards and wished she'd fallen in so that he could gallantly save her. Maybe next time. They spent much of their time walking together. Teddy usually brought his fishing rod along and Gillian would be a good sport and sit patiently while he showed off and pretended he was going to catch their supper. Usually he caught nothing. Of course, there was the day he cast too far and his fishing hook snagged on the feathers of a duck on the opposite bank. Despite the duck's apparent distress, Teddy and Gillian had laughed until they were both rolling on the grass. Eventually, after Teddy pulled himself together, he was able to cross over and retrieve his hook. The duck waddled off angry but unharmed.

Gillian was not a particularly graceful child and Teddy always found it very amusing to watch her struggling to climb over farmers' gates, or stone stiles in a lady-like fashion.

"Are you trying to look up my skirt?" shrieked Gillian on one occasion.

"You know I am!" replied a cocky Teddy, "why else would I bring you this way where there are eight gates and three stiles when we could have just walked along the lane?" he added, chuckling to himself. "C'mon Gill, don't be such a prude."

Am I a prude, thought Gillian as Mrs. Pratt drew a perfect parallelogram on the blackboard? Gillian was well aware that the boys who attended the village school where Teddy went were always whistling at girls and making lewd comments. Was Teddy like that when she wasn't around? Sometimes she felt he treated her like a child even though he was only a year older than she. Would he soon tire of her and want to be with the girls who wore lipstick and suspender belts and sat in the back row of the cinema on Friday nights?

Gillian's father, Harold, never missed an opportunity to remind her that the Postlethwaites were 'just shopkeepers', barely literate and common. Teddy's father, Henry, owned Postlethwaite's Ironmonger's in the village and it was generally assumed that one day the sign above the shop would be repainted to say: Postlethwaite & Son. Harold Mathers, on the other hand, had a respectable job as the headmaster of Kendal Grammar School for Boys and Gillian's mother, Mary, was also employed there as a school secretary. Needless to say, the Mathers were determined that their daughter would receive a proper and complete education in a reputable school. Harold, in particular, regarded the village school and its attendees as lesser beings and wasn't reticent about saying so.

"You don't want to spend your whole life stuck in a little country shop like that boy, Teddy Postlethwaite," Harold cautioned over and over again. "Henry's grandfather opened that shop, then Henry's father ran it. Now it's Henry's turn and soon it will all go to Teddy. Not much ambition in that family, if you ask me. We're not like that, Gillian. Your mother and I have worked too hard making better lives for ourselves so we won't sit by and let you squander yours."

Harold had, indeed, made a reasonable life for himself. He was born the son of a Welsh coal miner and decided as a youngster that mining was not the life for him. He always claimed that the War made a man out of him and, as soon as it was over, he resumed his education and obtained a university degree. Immediately after graduating, he began teaching at a private school in Windermere and, just a few years ago, took up his current position in Kendal.

Mary had grown up in Sussex. Her parents were moderately well off, largely due to funds they had inherited. She was an only child and her parents had insisted that after she finished school she should acquire some employable skills and so she was packed off to secretarial school. Although it was never with the intention that she become a career woman, it was agreed that, if all else failed, at least she could support herself. As it turned out, she met Harold while she was still taking her courses and, even though they married shortly after, she'd had a taste of independence and had no intention of letting her skills go to waste. Except for the first few years after Gillian was born, she had always gone to work. She was well ahead of her time in that respect.

Teddy and Gillian had planned a picnic for Sunday afternoon. Teddy always worked in the shop on Saturdays, so Sunday—after he'd dutifully attended church with his father—was usually the only time they could get together on the weekend. Gillian decided that this excursion would provide the perfect opportunity to talk to Teddy about their future together. Coincidentally, Teddy had plans of his own for this outing. He, too, was thinking about their relationship. Were they just pals, or were they boyfriend and girlfriend?

Teddy remembered the first time they'd spoken to one another. It was on a cold, wet October afternoon. Teddy had been strolling along Repton Lane on his way home when he'd spotted Gillian pushing her bicycle along the lane towards him. Her head was down but he could tell by the rise and fall of her hunched shoulders that she was crying.

"Hello," he said. "Are you all right?"

"No," Gillian sobbed, "I've got a puncture and I'm going to be late for tea and Daddy will be so cross."

"Hey, cheer up," said Teddy, "I can fix that in a jiffy. My dad owns the ironmonger's shop in the village. We can go over there and put a patch on it if you like," he added.

Gillian nodded and began to follow him.

"I'm Teddy, by the way," he said after a few moments.

"I know," replied Gillian, "I've seen you in the shop before."

After Teddy had expertly applied a John Bull bicycle patch to the wounded tyre, he invited her out for an ice cream. They both shared a Knickerbocker Glory. Gillian had never seen anything like it before … it was huge with layers of strawberry and chocolate ice cream, whipped cream, fruit, nuts, syrup, raspberry jelly and even a maraschino cherry on top which Teddy graciously insisted Gillian enjoy.

During that first afternoon they fell into easy conversation and chatted about all sorts of things … their families, their favourite music, books they'd read (although Teddy didn't have much to contribute there), sports they liked (Gillian had even less to contribute there) and so on and so forth. This was the first of many such encounters. They were both a little shy and awkward at first but, over time, they became one another's bestest friends. Before long, they both began changing their after-school habits, hoping to run in to one another 'accidentally on purpose'. Teddy loitered around the shop after school and Gillian, hoping Teddy would magically appear, always made a point of looking in the shop window on her way home while pretending to be fascinated by some new gadget or garden tool. Conversation was rarely difficult for them and it was a comfortable secret they both cherished. It wasn't that they deliberately chose to keep their friendship hidden but, both Teddy and Gillian knew instinctively, that to tell anyone about it could open it up to misinterpretation and spoil it forever. Teddy didn't want the lads at the village school teasing him about his little girlfriend with the chunky woollen knee socks and plaited hair. Gillian didn't want her friends looking down their noses at her for consorting with someone they might consider common.

Eventually some of his mates learned about his peculiar friendship with the headmaster's daughter and, of course, teased him mercilessly.

"Going fishin' again with little Gillian, are you?" they'd jeer, implying that the fishin' he was doing with her had nothing to do with trout. Teddy would just shrug it off but, deep down, he wished they'd just shut up! And, secretly, he wished he and Gillian really were doing more than just fishing when they were alone.

Things were changing. Teddy and Gillian were both growing up and Teddy was aware of new feelings and urges developing. It was time—he thought—time to tell her how much he liked her and that she was more than just a convenient friend who obligingly carried jars of worms in her bicycle saddlebag for him to bait his fishing hooks with. In truth, he was very fond of her and could only imagine how lonely his life would be without her. She made him laugh.

She listened to him and, in turn, he loved to listen to her prattle on about this and that. He didn't always pay attention to what she was actually talking about; he simply enjoyed the sound of her voice sprinkled with her funny self-conscious giggles.

She was certainly different from the other girls he and his friends hung about with. None of those girls in their kitten heels and mohair twin sets would want to sit by a stream in a drizzle hour after hour watching him cast flies. None of those girls would have sat at the back of the shop with him and patiently helped him with his English Composition. Teddy was not an unintelligent lad, but he had more of a mathematical and logical mind than a creative one and he found writing stories and poetry both painful and pointless. With Gillian's help, he'd managed to get a reasonable mark on a poem he'd written about dirigibles—although Gillian secretly thought it was dreadful. He wasn't a fan of novels and fiction; he preferred books and journals about science and mechanical things. It took him almost six weeks to plow through *David Copperfield* when they'd been assigned it at school. Gillian, on the other hand, loved to exercise her imagination. It was a form of escape for her. Sometimes she would read out loud to him from her favourites, like C. S. Lewis' *The Lion, The Witch And The Wardrobe*, or Arthur Ransome's *Swallows And Amazons*. He barely remembered, or even heard, the stories, but he revelled in her close proximity and the reassuring cadence of her voice.

"I'm going to be a writer someday," Gillian told him. "I'll write stories for children. I might even draw pictures to go with them. What do you think of that, Teddy?"

"I think it's a super idea, Gillian. I think you'd be very good at it," he replied indulgently.

"And what will you be, Teddy?"

"Oh, that's easy," he said, "I'll be a shopkeeper just like

my father and like his father before him. I've never thought of doing anything else."

"But if you could … what would you want to be?" Gillian persisted.

"I dunno, Gillian. People like me don't get to choose. I just want to be happy. Someday I'd like to have a wife and a family and we could live together above the shop if I fixed it up a little. I don't have big dreams like you, Gillian. They're a waste of time for me."

And that, thought Teddy, as his mind snapped back to the present, was their one and only problem. They came from different stock. Besides, Gillian's parents couldn't stand the sight of him.

He'd been to Gillian's house only twice during the time he'd known her. The first time, he'd dropped by to return a book she had left at the shop after one of their informal tutoring sessions. Gillian's father had answered the door, snatched the book out of Teddy's grasp and, without even offering to call Gillian to the door, slammed the door shut and that was that.

The next time Teddy went to Snowdrop Cottage, he'd been officially invited for tea. Gillian had had to work very hard to get her parents—her father in particular—to agree. That catastrophe had occurred only a few weeks ago and was still a fresh wound in his memory. It had been a dreadful ordeal and he knew he wouldn't have put himself through it for anyone but Gillian. They'd all sat at the dining room table, eyes cast down at their plates and no one spoke for a painfully long time.

"How's your father these days?" asked Mrs. Mathers, eventually.

"He's well, thank you," Teddy replied politely.

More silent minutes passed. All that could be heard was the ticking of the grandfather clock and the irritating clicking sound of Mr. Mathers' jaw as he chewed.

And then Harold—Mr. Mathers—cleared his throat and launched into his topic for the evening.

"So, Edward, what are your plans for the future?" he asked.

"For the future … well, er … for the future my plans are to finish school, I suppose," Teddy answered awkwardly. He could just see Gillian out of the corner of his eye. Her head had dropped and she was staring helplessly at a wayward crumb on the damask tablecloth beside her.

"Yes … and then what?" Harold volleyed back.

"Well, I'll be working then, won't I? I'll be working with my dad."

"It's a shame," replied Harold, "it's a shame a young man like you doesn't want to get ahead … raise yourself from having to serve all day in a little village shop. There's no real future in that, is there, son? It's a bloody shame there isn't a war on. That would set you young people straight. There's nothing like a war to turn little boys in shorts into men in long trousers …"

"Or, corpses," mumbled Teddy.

"Or what!" exclaimed Harold, spittle flying in all directions. "How dare you speak of our soldiers like that? You wouldn't be sitting here enjoying Mrs. Mathers' splendid steak and kidney pudding if they hadn't given their lives for you."

"Given?" Teddy challenged, "given? Beg your pardon, sir, but I don't think those 18-year-old lads 'gave' their lives. Their lives were taken. They were forced into it. I see no glory in war, Mr. Mathers. I never will."

That had marked the end of the teatime conversation and the rest of the meal passed in excruciating silence but for a few 'please-and-thank-yous'. Poor Gillian sat hunched up, red-faced and on the verge of tears for most of it. If not for her, Teddy would have got up and left immediately but he wanted to protect her as best he could from across the table.

"Lovely sponge, Mrs. Mathers," he said as he poured rich creamy custard over the generous slice of Swiss roll with its perfect jam spiral that Mrs. Mathers had placed in front of him.

"Thank you, Teddy."

"I love a good sponge, me" he added.

"Yes, it's Gillian's favourite too," replied Mrs. Mathers. "It's your favourite too, isn't it dear?" she asked, raising her voice slightly and looking directly at her mortified daughter. Gillian managed a shrug in response and lifted her eyes just a fraction, enough to give Teddy an apologetic look.

"Well, there's something I never knew before," remarked Teddy with a grin.

"What?" shouted Harold, suddenly feeling that he might be missing out on something, "what didn't you know before?"

"I know a lot about your daughter, Mr. Mathers, but I never knew she liked a good sponge," he replied.

Gillian couldn't help herself … all of a sudden her shoulders were quivering as she fought to hold back the giggles. Teddy caught her eye and smiled. It was the warmest smile Gillian had ever seen. For the first time in her life, she felt safe and worthy and ever so slightly less of a child and more of a woman than she had only hours before.

"Well," exclaimed Harold slapping his over-starched linen serviette down on the table, "I don't know what you two find so amusing, but I think I've had just about enough of this nonsense. Time you went home young man. Now!"

On Sunday afternoon, the day of the picnic, Teddy and Gillian met at the end of Gillian's lane. As usual, they both brought their bicycles. Gillian had her unfortunate satchel with her as well because she'd told her parents she was riding over to a friend's house to do some homework. Instead, they rode straight to Postlethwaite's shop where Teddy let himself in through the back door and stashed the satchel out of sight in a storage cupboard. Then they headed out of the village along Repton Lane, passed the corner where Teddy had first found Gillian pushing her disabled bicycle, and continued for a couple of miles until they reached 'Newtless Pond', so named because it contained no newts. 'Newtless' had also become a secret word the two of them shared when talking about anyone lacking guts or personality. Miss Frobisher, the village Postmistress, for example, was considered 'newtless' … even though she was quite friendly with Teddy's father. "She's so plain," remarked Gillian one day. "And 'newtless'," added Teddy with a chuckle.

Teddy threw down a waterproof for them to sit on beside the pond. It was a cool, late spring day that looked like it might dissolve into a rain shower at any moment, but Teddy and Gillian didn't care.

"Where's your fishing rod, Teddy?" asked Gillian.

"I didn't bring it," he replied, "I want to focus on you today." He smiled at her. "Here, have a sandwich …"

Teddy unwrapped the greaseproof paper packages containing the meat paste and Marmite sandwiches he'd made for the occasion. No surprises there … he always made the same sandwiches. Gillian's contribution was usually a couple of chocolate biscuits discreetly filched from the pantry at home and, using her pocket money, she always provided the drinks: dandelion and burdock for Teddy and fizzy lemonade for herself.

They ate in companionable silence until, finally, Teddy spoke:

"You know I really like you Gillian, right?"

"Yes, I s'pose so," she answered warily. Was this the opening to a break-up speech, she wondered?

"And you know that sometimes I go out with the lads and some of the girls from the village, right?"

"Yes," replied Gillian again.

"They mean nothing to me, Gillian. We just have a few laughs. It's you I really like. I know your parents don't approve, but I need you to know you are very important to me, Gilly-girl. I mean … er … what I am trying to say is, do you like me too?"

"Oh gosh, yes!" exclaimed Gillian without restraint, "I love spending time with you. We're not children anymore, we don't have to pay any attention to what my parents think. Please don't break up with me, Teddy, I don't know what I'd do."

"Break up with you?" asked a genuinely surprised Teddy, "I didn't even know we were officially going out together, so how can I break up with you? Look, what I'm trying to say is that I think we've been pals long enough. Let's change all that, Gill. Would you be my girlfriend?"

"Oh, yes, Teddy! I'd love to be your girlfriend."

"Well, I'm glad that's sorted then," said Teddy, raising his dandelion and burdock bottle to Gillian to clinch the deal.

After that, a silence hovered between them, thick as the encroaching mist and unbroken until, all of a sudden, Teddy quickly packed up the remnants of the picnic and then slowly inched himself across the waterproof to sit closer to Gillian. He put an arm around her shoulders and tilted her face towards his. Gillian felt as if a flock of butterflies had been released in her lower abdomen. Teddy leaned in and kissed her very softly on her lips.

He leaned back momentarily and looked directly at her, "how was that?" he asked.

But, before she had time to respond, his lips were on hers again and his tongue was working its way between her lips and slowly and ever so gently exploring the inside of her mouth.

It was a new and very strange, but not unpleasant, sensation Gillian thought.

"And that?" Teddy asked, "how was that?"

"That was strange," admitted Gillian coyly, "but not in a bad way," she added hastily.

"We just need practice," replied Teddy as he moved towards her once more.

How long they 'practised', Gillian couldn't tell but, after a while, they both realized that the light mist that had been lurking over them when they first arrived was now a full on rain shower.

"Oh my, Teddy, we're getting soaked. We'll have to head back. Look at the water just dripping off you! Come on," challenged Gillian, as they rapidly rolled everything up in the waterproof, "I'll race you to the bikes!"

Gillian walked on air for the rest of the afternoon and into the evening. When she'd arrived home, dripping wet, her parents couldn't understand why she'd chosen to ride home from her friend's house while the rain was at its heaviest, but even their disparaging remarks couldn't touch her. It was not until the following morning, Monday, when Gillian, running late as usual, bellowed to her mother that she couldn't find her satchel.

"I'm sure it's right where you last put it," replied Mary Mathers. "Why must we go through this every single morning?" she moaned.

And then Gillian realized that, this time, her satchel really wasn't in the front hall and that her mother was absolutely right, it was, indeed, right where she'd left it. It was still stashed at Postlethwaite's where she and Teddy had put it before they went on their outing.

Gillian didn't know what to do. But, after a brief hesitation, she decided it would be best if she left the house as usual and tried to sort it out on her way to the bus stop.

"Found it! Bye Mummy," she called.

She walked down the lane and towards the ironmonger's. She could hardly go in and ask Mr. Postlethwaite if she could go to the back and grab her satchel because he'd probably think it was a bit odd and, besides, who knew who he'd tell. She also knew that Teddy would already be on his way to school, so she couldn't ask for his help until later. She daren't go to school without any of her books and notes but she couldn't just loiter around the village until four o'clock either. Eventually she decided the best plan would be to get on the bus as usual and hope Julie, who was far more creative than she when it came to devising devious plans, would help her come up with a plan. If not, she'd just have to wander around Kendal for the day and prepare to face the consequences of her truancy when she returned home.

Julie hopped on the bus, cheerful and smartly put together as usual.

"Gill, how was the weekend?"

"Oh good," replied Gillian tentatively.

"I went over to Liz's house. Her brother was having a few mates over. It was really fun. We played Ludo and Liz's mum made toasted cheese for everyone. You should've come, Gillian. Maybe you could bring your 'boyfriend' next time," Julie teased.

"Look, Julie, I'm in trouble," said Gillian, interrupting Julie's chatter.

"You're not … you know …" exclaimed Julie in mock horror while stroking an imaginary belly with her hands.

"Of course not, silly, it's nothing like that! How could

you think such a thing? It's just that Teddy and I went on a picnic yesterday and I had to keep it secret from Mum and Dad, so I told them I was going to Hilary's to do some homework. I had to take my books and stuff with me to make it look good and we dropped everything off at Teddy's dad's shop and I forgot to pick it up on the way home. My parents will kill me if they know I was out with Teddy and that I lied to keep a secret from them," explained Gillian grimly.

"Must run in the family," replied Julie.

"What?" Gillian asked.

"Keeping secrets … that's what."

"What do you mean by that?" demanded Gillian.

"Oh, I'm sorry. You know nothing about what's really going on, do you Gill? I mean about your mum and Mr. Hopkins," Julie added with an exaggerated sigh.

"Mr. Hopkins? You mean the history master at Daddy's school? What's he got to do with anything? What's he got to do with my mother?"

"Oh, it's nothing," replied Julie, trying to back pedal as fast as she could. "It's just some silly story my brother told me … something about your mum and Mr. Hopkins having a bit of a 'thing', if you know what I mean. It's probably just talk … forget I said anything, Gill."

The bus pulled up at their stop. Gillian and Julie stepped onto the pavement and automatically began walking toward the school entrance.

"What are you going to do?" Julie asked.

"Oh, I suppose I'll just go in. I'll pretend I left my satchel on the bus. Is it true, do you think?"

"No," replied Julie, giggling, "of course it isn't true. You told me yourself you left it at Postlethwaite's."

"Not that, you idiot! Do you think it's true what your brother said about my mum?"

20

"I dunno really," Julie replied lightly, "but I wouldn't worry about it. It seems hard to believe that your mother would be snogging Mr. Hopkins in the boys' school staff room, doesn't it? I mean, your dad's the headmaster there. I'm sure it's just gossip, that's all. Well, I'll see you later, Gillian. You'd better start rehearsing your lost satchel story."

Julie walked away and Gillian headed towards the school office.

She delivered her story convincingly and was briskly reprimanded for being careless enough to leave her belongings on a public bus. She assured Headmistress that her satchel was properly marked with her name and address so it would likely be on the return bus waiting for her at the end of the day.

It was a very long day for Gillian. She couldn't help but worry about what Julie had told her that morning, in part because it wasn't the first time she had heard similar rumblings. In the middle of an exceptionally tedious Algebra class, Gillian's mind wandered back to something that happened over a year ago. Her mother, along with a few teachers from the Grammar School, had volunteered to accompany a group of upper sixth form boys on a weekend trip to Morcambe to celebrate the end of term. They were all expected to return on Sunday evening but Mary came down with some tummy troubles—she thought it might have been the clams she'd eaten at lunchtime—and felt too ill to travel that day so she decided to stay an extra night. Mr. Hopkins offered to stay behind too so that she wouldn't be left on her own. Gillian remembered her father was livid about it and, at the time, she thought that was pretty mean of him considering her mother was feeling poorly. But, thinking about it now, she had to admit there might have been more to it. Certainly her mother had looked unusually hale and hearty when she finally returned the following evening.

Then, only a few weeks ago Hilary Bates—who confessed to dawdling on High Street on her way back to school after a doctor's appointment—claimed she'd seen Mrs. Mathers in a café with some bloke who definitely wasn't Mr. Mathers. Hilary told Gillian—and half the school probably—that the couple had been leaning across the table gazing into one another's eyes and laughing at some private joke. How she'd managed to discern all that through a fogged up café window, Gillian didn't know and, until now, hadn't given it another thought. But, could it be true? In which case, it was another bit of information giving credibility to the stories.

If her mother really was carrying on with another man, what would dear Harold do about that, she wondered? Maybe he'd heard the rumours too. That might explain why he'd been extra grumpy over the past few weeks. He'd been brisk and stern for as long as Gillian had known him, but lately he seemed much more irritable and quick to snap at even the most trivial things. Only last week Gillian's mother had forgotten to put starch in his shirt collars and he'd almost blown a gasket.

"What's wrong with you, Mary?" he'd yelled. "Pay attention to what you're doing, woman! You always seem to be somewhere else these days. I don't know what's got into you."

And then there'd been the time Gillian had left a small smear of toothpaste on the side of the washbasin. He'd exploded. "Do I have to clean up after everyone in this household?" he'd screamed. "Who did this? One of you needs to own up …" he'd added, looking accusingly at Mary. "I don't put up with liars and slovenly behaviour in my school and I most certainly won't put up with it in my own home!" And then he'd walked out of the house and hadn't returned until after tea.

Gillian hadn't thought much about it at the time, but now she was beginning to wonder if, in fact, her father had some legitimate reasons to be annoyed. Was her mother really capable of kissing another man? Did Mrs. Mathers and Mr. Hopkins do what she and Teddy had been doing on Sunday afternoon? It was hard enough to accept that her parents had done things like that together, but horrifying to imagine her mother doing it with someone else. Could—or would—someone as old as her mother—she was already forty—behave in such a manner? It seemed absurd but, at the same time, most intriguing. Gillian had difficulty deciding whether she felt angry and disappointed with her mother, or wickedly proud of her. She liked the idea that they both kept secrets from Harold. It served him right, she thought.

As the last bell sounded, Gillian tore out of the school grounds straight to the bus stop. She needed to get home and find Teddy fast so they could retrieve her satchel before anyone else knew about it.

She hovered outside Postlethwaite's for a few minutes hoping that Teddy might be there and would see her through the window, but he didn't come. Eventually, on the pretense of looking for a pan scrubber for her mother, she ventured inside.

"Hello, Gillian, haven't seen you in here for a while … was there something I could help you with?" asked Mr. Postlethwaite.

"Oh, no, nothing really. My mum wants one of those metal saucepan scrubbers, that's all. I thought I'd see if you had any," she answered.

"Oh yes. You can tell Mrs. Mathers, I always stock them."

"Is Teddy around?" she asked Mr. Postlethwaite nonchalantly.

"Nah, not today, love. He went straight home today, I think."

Gillian left the shop and decided that perhaps she'd wander over to Teddy's house. She'd never been inside his house before. Her parents wouldn't allow it because Mr. Postlethwaite was a widower and it wouldn't be proper for a young girl to visit if there was no female chaperone at the house. She'd ridden her bicycle past the house a few hundred times, though, practically wearing a rut in the road … always hoping for a glimpse of Teddy.

She walked around the corner to the street where Teddy lived, approached his front door and lightly tapped the brass doorknocker. Seconds later, Teddy appeared.

"Gillian!" he exclaimed, "what a nice surprise … what brings you over here? Come in, come in, please," he added.

The moment the door shut behind them, Teddy grabbed her, pushed her up against the wall and kissed her deeply. Tingles and a host of other indescribable sensations surged through Gillian's body. Her legs felt like blancmange.

Teddy took her hand and led her into the sitting room. She was surprised that her legs didn't buckle beneath her.

They sat together on the couch, kissed a few more times and then Gillian told him why she was there and that she urgently needed to get her satchel back.

"Stay for tea," Teddy said, "we can fetch it after."

"Oh, I couldn't," replied Gillian sadly, "my parents would never allow it. Besides, what would your dad think if I was here for tea?"

"Oh, you don't have to worry about him. He's going to Miss Frobisher's after closing to help her wallpaper her bedroom or something. He usually finds some excuse to visit her every week," explained Teddy.

Gillian laughed. "Don't you find it hard to believe that grown ups fall in love and kiss and things like that?" she asked.

"I try not to think about it," he answered. "The thought of Miss Frobisher naked is enough to turn a chap off for life!" he chuckled. "Cheer up, Gill, let's just enjoy some time together. We'll sort out your satchel situation later."

It was several hours later when Gillian quietly entered her home. She heard shouting coming from upstairs.

"No wonder our daughter is running around with that useless Postlethwaite boy with you as her mother. What sort of example do you think you're setting? Did you really think you could carry on all this time without my knowing about it?"

Mary was sobbing. "Harold, I'm so, so sorry. I'll end it, I promise I will."

"Oh, it's going to end all right," agreed Harold, "I'll make sure of that!"

"What are you going to do, Harold? You can't sack Samuel for this. Please don't do anything to hurt him," Mary pleaded.

"Of course I can't sack him, you fool. He's a damned good teacher. How could I explain it to everyone without letting on that I know my wife has turned me into a pathetic cuckold? They'd laugh at me even more than they do already. But, woman of mine, mark my words, it will end and that's a promise!"

Her parents' bedroom door slammed shut and a red-faced Harold came marching down the stairs. He brushed past Gillian without noticing her and headed straight to the drinks cabinet. Gillian's mother didn't follow. Gillian decided it was probably best if she quietly went upstairs herself and had an early night. It didn't seem that her unexplained absence was a priority at this moment.

Nor was it the next morning; neither adult was speaking to the other and only Gillian's mother made any effort to acknowledge her daughter's presence. Gillian kept her head down and went off to school without any fuss.

'Cuckold' ... what's that, she wondered. It was certainly not a term she'd encountered before and hearing it in the context of her parents rowing meant she needed to find out precisely what it meant. She'd ask Teddy when she saw him later.

After school Teddy and Gillian took a walk through the churchyard. They often went there because it was quiet and out of the way and a very unlikely place for Gillian's parents to suddenly pop up on a weekday afternoon. Besides, Teddy liked to keep an eye on his mother's grave and make sure she always had fresh flowers. Teddy's mother had died thirty seven minutes after the exhausted midwife had wrestled Teddy from his mother's womb into the world. Dr. Parsons had arrived forty nine minutes after Teddy's debut, but he was too late to save Teddy's mother.

"What's a cuckold?" asked Gillian without preamble.

"A what! Did you say what's a 'cock hold'? Are you sure you want me to answer that, Gillian, or perhaps you'd like me to show you?"

"No, not a 'cock hold' you fool," replied Gillian, blushing like a scarlet beacon, "I said, what's a *cuckold*?"

"Well, I suppose you could say he's the one not getting his cock held, if you know what I mean," Teddy replied and then proceeded to orbit around her with his arms out like a child pretending to be an aeroplane, shrieking with laughter. Clearly, he thought his answer was the wittiest ever.

"Never mind," she sighed, "boys are so childish. I should've known better than to ask you something serious."

Teddy decelerated as soon as he realized Gillian was clearly not amused.

"I'm sorry, pet, I shouldn't be laughing." He fought to

stand still and look serious but was having difficulty recovering from the dizziness his spinning had brought on. "You surprised me is all," he managed, swaying in front of her like a friendly drunk, "I'm sure you have a very good reason for asking me ... some English Lit homework is it? You're reading one of those naughty books again, aren't you?"

"No," whispered Gillian, "Daddy and Mummy were arguing last night and Daddy said he didn't want everyone to know he's a cuckold. I just wanted to know what he meant by that."

Teddy put his arm around her shoulder and drew her close. "I'm sorry," he said softly, all traces of mirth completely wiped from his face, "I shouldn't have made fun of you. A cuckold, dear Gillian, is a man whose wife is having it off with another man."

Tension in the Mathers' household remained thick as pea soup over the next few weeks. Mary and Gillian walked around on eggshells. Harold rarely spoke and Mary attempted to break the endless silences with trivial remarks and innocuous small talk that inevitably fell flat and seemed completely out of place. Gillian went about her business without fuss and neither parent seemed to have the inclination nor the energy to ask her where she was going, or where she had been when she returned. Although she felt rather sad for her mother during this period, she was thoroughly enjoying the freedom that being ignored provided. She and Teddy even went to the pictures together one Saturday afternoon without anyone questioning her. It wasn't the same as going out on a Friday night, but it was still a thrill for Gillian to be seen holding hands with Teddy at the cinema even if the audience was only a bunch of screeching brats wielding dripping ice lollies.

Their affection for one another was deepening and their

physical explorations were becoming more adventuresome. Teddy knew that Gillian was not ready to 'go all the way', but he had managed to break down several barriers with his patience and kindness. Gillian was a special girl; he knew that. He no longer cared if his mates teased him; in fact he rather suspected that, deep down, they were a tad jealous.

On the first Friday in March, Mrs. Mathers told her daughter it was very important that she be home for tea on time that evening. Mr. Mathers had something important he wanted to discuss and it would be prudent not to ruffle his feathers unnecessarily by being tardy.

Needless to say, Gillian was anxious all day wondering what on earth her father could possibly want to talk about. It sounded very serious and her mother had not provided any hints. Had they found out about her and Teddy sneaking off together? Was her last school report not good enough? Had someone told them they'd seen her and Teddy at the pictures? Had she done something wrong at home … all she could remember was not making her bed last Tuesday because she was running a little late.

By the end of the day, Gillian was a nervous wreck. She ran into Teddy on her way home from the bus stop and told him she couldn't stop, she had to get home immediately.

"We're having some kind of a family meeting," she told him. "I don't know what it's about, but I think I may be in trouble. What if they stop me seeing you?"

"Come by the shop tomorrow so that I know you're all right. They can't stop us. I won't allow it. I love you, Gillian. Remember that and they won't be able to hurt you."

"I love you too," replied Gillian softly and, hanging her head, walked slowly away as if towards the gallows.

As soon as she walked through the front door of her house she could smell cottage pie and treacle tart—her absolute favourites—and felt an instant relief. Mary wouldn't have gone to all that trouble if she was about to get a talking to … unless, thought Gillian, this is the last meal of a condemned daughter.

"You can't just wake up one morning and decide to move to Canada!" Gillian exclaimed, shock turning her voice into an abrasive high-pitched shriek.

"For your information, young lady, I've been planning this for quite some time. I applied for the teaching position in the country school months ago and accepted the job just after the New Year."

Gillian swivelled her head away from her father and stared directly at her mother across the table. But Mary's eyes refused to meet hers as she resolutely herded peas around her plate with her fork.

"Mum, did you know about this?" Gillian demanded accusingly, but Mary remained statue-still. "You can't possibly want to go to Canada ... some uncivilized colony inhabited by lumberjacks and Red Indians. No one even asked me if I wanted to go!" Gillian screamed desperately.

"Frankly, my dear," began Harold in his most self-satisfied and smug of all head-masterly tones, "your opinion on this matter is of no consequence. We leave in one month's time."

End of discussion.

Gillian pushed her chair away from the table and ran upstairs to her bedroom. Not even the delicious promise of warm treacle tart with whipped cream could keep her at the table a second longer. Mary gave up on the peas she'd been chasing and gazed despairingly at her husband. He was munching away happily, enjoying every succulent morsel of his cottage pie as if he'd simply announced that he was planning to return his library books in the morning, not shatter the lives of the two women in his life by plonking them down somewhere in the Canadian wilderness for the rest of their lives!

Even Mary had only known about Harold's plans for a few days. It had been a dreadful shock when he'd laid it all out before her *fait accompli*. She knew when he'd said he'd put an end to her relationship with Samuel that it hadn't been an idle threat, but she had never imagined he'd go to such an extreme. She and Sam were already dreading their final farewells.

"Stay," he'd implored when she'd spoken to him the previous day, "stay here with me. I love you Mary, we can carry on our lives here together, or move somewhere else where no one knows us."

Like teenagers, they'd had to meet secretly behind Marks & Spencer's on High Street although, now that their lives were being ripped asunder, it seemed like a somewhat futile precaution. Still, the less grist they fed the gossip mill, the better. Samuel still had to exist there.

"I can't", she'd sobbed, "Harold would take Gillian from me and I'd have to bear the shame of being both an adulteress and a negligent mother for the rest of my life. What would Gillian think of me then? Whether I stay here or follow my husband, I'm being punished either way, but duty calls. I love you too, Sam, you know I do, but I can't possibly abandon my daughter."

"Newtless! Your mother's bloody newtless," Teddy yelled over and over again after Gillian delivered her dreadful news the next day. "Why can't she stand up to that pompous old twit and let him go to bloody Canada or the Congo for all I care and you can stay here. Gillian, I can't bear to think of being without you. Is it because of that awful tea at your house ... is that what all this is about? Is this his way of breaking us up for good?"

"Not entirely," replied Gillian, although she wasn't completely certain herself. Young people of Teddy and Gillian's tender ages do tend to assume that whatever calamity or drama occurs in life, they must reside at the centre of it.

"... and your mother could roll around with Mr. Hopkins as much as she liked if your stupid old man was out of the picture," continued Teddy without taking a breath.

"You know about my mother and Mr. Hopkins?" asked Gillian, horrified. She'd never mentioned Mr. Hopkins by name to Teddy. She'd been too ashamed to share that bit of information with him, believing instead that if her mother's lover remained nameless the whole messy business would be easier to ignore.

"Of course I know about Mary and Sam ... the whole damn village knows about Mary and Sam. They've been sneaking around forever. Everyone knows it. Hate to say it Gillian, but I think you were probably the last to find out."

Teddy paused, let out a huge sigh and looked into Gillian's sad brown eyes. He stroked her long auburn hair and the expression on his face softened as his anger gently receded. "I'm sorry, Gillian, come 'ere, give us a hug. We don't want to waste our last days talking about the likes of them."

Chapter 2 - O Canada

On Thursday morning, April 16, 1959, Harold Mathers got up, put on his charcoal grey suit, white shirt and a navy tie and prepared to begin his new job at Cobden District Public School. Cobden was a small community north of Ottawa in the Canadian province of Ontario. Harold's new position was no longer that of a headmaster, he was back in the classroom but, he thought, it was a small price to pay to get his wife back in line and finally escape the mocking or sympathetic looks of his colleagues and neighbours. Harold was quite sure everyone was aware of his wife's indiscretions and that they took great pleasure in laughing at him behind his back. He was probably right—at least at the beginning—but, if Harold had possessed a better understanding of human nature and attention spans, he would have realized that the novelty of Mary and Sam's affair as a topic of conversation had long worn off only to be replaced by new and equally salacious gossip unwittingly offered up by some other poor soul in the local community.

"Good bye, Mary," he called cheerfully, "wish me luck!"

As he was leaving the house he picked up a small stack of envelopes ready to be posted and noticed one blue air letter addressed in his daughter's handwriting.

"Mary!" he barked, "get rid of this, will you? I won't have Gillian writing all sorts of nonsense to that dreadful boy. Do you understand me?"

"Yes, Harold", Mary answered meekly and took the offending letter from him. She was tired, lonely and sad and couldn't muster the strength to challenge her husband any more. He'd won. He'd ruined her life. She had no friends, no job and no Samuel. She still had her daughter, of course, but Gillian was barely communicating with her and actively resented everything and everyone who had anything to do with the move to Canada … including Mary.

She stuffed the envelope in the large pocket of her apron and decided to deal with it later. Meantime, she had to get Gillian up and ready. They had a meeting with Gillian's new school principal. Unfortunately, she would be attending the same school that her father was teaching at, but there was no other option.

After Mary and Gillian shared an agonizingly silent breakfast, Mary went upstairs to dress for the meeting. When she removed her apron, she remembered the letter. She held it in her hand for a few moments wondering what she should do with it but, hearing Gillian's approaching footsteps coming up the stairs, she decided to tuck it out of sight and quickly tucked it underneath a bundle notes and cards and other memorabilia from Sam that she had managed to smuggle into Canada in her old suitcase.

~ ~ ~

Dear Teddy,

Dad took my first letter to you this morning to post on his way to work. I know it's far too soon to write another one, but I can't help myself. I pretend that I'm talking to you all the time and, as usual, you don't get a word in edgewise! But I won't post any more until I hear back from you.

Mum dragged me to my new school today to meet the principal (headmaster). He was OK, I suppose. He tried to be nice about everything and said he understood what a big change this was for me. The worst part is that it's the same school Dad's teaching at! The school is pretty ugly and modern looking, nothing like Kendal High. Boys and girls are mixed together here but at least we don't have to wear uniforms.

They're putting me in form 10—'grade' 10 they call it I'll probably be the oldest one In the class because Mr. Wright thought it would be better for me to settle in over the next few months and start fresh in September. Teddy, it's going to be horrible. I don't know how I'll get through all this without you. If only you were here … imagine it, we could go to the same school if you lived in Canada!

I keep re-living our last night together. It was so beautiful to be in your arms, kissing you and lying beside you—I could have stayed there forever. Perhaps we should have gone all the way. Part of me wishes we had, but I'll keep my promise to you … you will be my first. There won't be anyone else for me. Somehow I'll get back to England and we'll be together forever. For now, all we have are our letters. I can't wait to hear from you. I will keep every letter you ever write. I'm trying to be brave like you told me to be, but I can't stop crying. I hate being here. I hate being away from you. Pleeeeeeeeese write soon.

Love always, Gillian xx

~ ~ ~

April 25

Dearest Teddy,

This is the fifth letter I've written and I still haven't heard from you. I hate not knowing how you are and what you're doing. I wish I were sitting beside you on a riverbank watching you fish like we used to. Those were the best days of my life. Why did Dad have to spoil it all for everyone! He bounces around here all grins and smiles as though this Godforsaken place was Heaven on Earth. He's so pleased with himself. And Mum, well, she hardly talks at all. I think she's really bored here. She went to some neighbour's for a ladies' coffee morning but she said she didn't know who or what they were all talking about and felt like an outsider.

School is like that for me. All the girls ever talk about is boys, boys, boys ... and all the boys ever do is stand around making stupid remarks. At least the schoolwork is easy and the teachers don't seem to care if you don't get your homework finished. There's no dining room for lunch (but, best of all, NO school milk to gag my way through each day!) I usually come home for lunch; it's better than taking some pathetic sandwiches to school and sitting by myself in the corner of the schoolyard. I prefer to come home and check the post. Each day I think ... this will be the day! If I hear a bird sing, I reckon it's a good omen and there will be a letter from you. But so far nothing. Soon I'll stop hearing birds sing.

It's the weekend and I have nothing to do. Sometimes at night I dream that I am standing outside your shop and, just as you are about to turn and see me, the shop disappears. Then I wake up and feel so empty and so alone for the rest of the day.

Dad said he might buy a wireless and a record player this week. I'm trying to be really nice to him so that he won't change his mind. I haven't had a chance to play the record you gave me on our last night together. I sing it in my head, over and over again. I pretend that when the words: 'whenever I want you, all I have to do is dream' float through my head, it's a sign that you are thinking of me too. Sometimes it would mean you were thinking about me when it's the middle of the night in England, so I hope I'm not disturbing your sleep!!

I'll put this letter with the others waiting to be posted; I keep them in an old shoebox in my wardrobe. One day I'll be packing up a parcel of them and you won't have time to do anything else but read.

Love always, forever, no matter what … your Gilly

~ ~ ~

May 13th,

My dearest Teddy,

I don't understand. What's going on? Why haven't I heard from you? It's driving me crazy. I miss you so much and I'm worried that something's happened to you. I have 15 letters now bundled up and ready to send to you. Father says you haven't written because you don't know how. He's so mean sometimes. Mum says boys aren't always very good at writing letters because they're too busy playing sports or going out with their pals. But I know you Teddy; you wouldn't abandon me like this.

I'm going out of my mind … I talk to you in my head all day and I dream about you all night. Surely, you can feel my love for you even though there is an ocean between us.

Just a short one today, I'm out of words and full of despair.

I love you so much.
Gillian xxx

~ ~ ~

May 18th,
Dearest love,

I came home the other day and saw an airmail en-velope on the kitchen table. I was SO excited, my heart nearly jumped out of my chest ... but then I saw it was a letter from Granny. But, the thing is, it took two weeks to get here so I'm thinking that if my first letter took two weeks to get to you, and you took a couple of days to reply and then it took another fortnight for your letter to get here, I should be hearing from you any day now. Oh, I hope so. I don't know how much longer I can stand this silence.

I'm so lonely and school is awful. All the boys make fun of the way I talk and call me 'stuck up'. The girls hate me because I get top marks in most subjects and I'm not interested in all their silly gossip. Some of them have television sets so they race home after school to watch their favourite programmes. Dad says we don't need a set, but it might help me pass the time if we had one. For hours on end, I just sit in my room missing you. When will this end?

Love always, Gillian

~ ~ ~

Springtime in Cobden!

Oh, Teddy, remember how we used to walk down Repton Lane and you'd pick flowers from the hedge-rows for me? I would clutch them until they wilted in my grip. I remember I dried and pressed some of them, but

I don't know what happened to them. Perhaps they'll tumble out of one of my favourite books one day and it will be a lovely surprise.

I don't think Canada has wildflowers. There are no lanes with hedgerows, just dusty roads with trees on either side. And, worst of all, there are these awful black-flies that nibble your neck and behind your ears leaving trails of blood and itchy swellings behind. Mum got bitten near her eye the other day and it all puffed up until she couldn't open it. They are so horrible that there is no point going outside. Everyone laughs at us and calls us 'fresh meat'.

School term will be over in a couple of weeks. I'm supposed to be swotting for exams, but I can't be bothered. I'm trying to persuade my parents to let me come to England in the summer to visit Granny (and you, of course!!), but I don't think they'll let me. Granny even said she'd pay half my fare, but Father says I'm too young to be travelling without a chaperone.

I don't know what I'll do all summer if I can't come. Dad says we should all go 'exploring'. He might buy a car and we could drive around the countryside. Can you imagine anything worse!

I know you'll write to me soon. Meantime, I'll try and be patient. I love you so much … I send you kisses and hugs and all my love, Gillian

~ ~ ~

Dearest Teddy,

I have a new friend; her name is Suzanne. She's just moved in next door and knows no one in Cobden, but she seems really nice. Even though she's about a year younger than me, we'll be in the same grade in

September. Anyway, we're all going to Ottawa for the day tomorrow—me, Suzanne and our mothers—to buy material to make summer dresses. I really like Home Economics (that's Domestic Science, to you!) … not the cooking, just the sewing. Mum bought a secondhand Singer so I've been practicing with it and I've made a couple of skirts already. I think it'll be fun to go to Ottawa and see the city. Mum says that Suzanne and I can go off on our own for a few hours if we want.

Of course, it would be so much more fun if I could be there with you instead … wouldn't that be a marvellous adventure! We've never been anywhere new together, have we? When I come back to England (and I will), we must go up to London one day together. I've always wanted to see the changing of the guards.

Well, I must go. I'm just going to pop over to Suzanne's to see what she's going to wear tomorrow. It's going to be a great day!

Love always, Gillian

~ ~ ~

Dearest love,

I'm so sorry … it's been days since I've written. We had the best time in Ottawa! Suzanne and I even got to ride on one of the last streetcars in the city. It was such fun. It was a lovely warm and sunny day so we had ice cream and walked around the gardens near the Houses of Parliament. Then we walked over to Sparks Street and went into all the department stores and tried on all kinds of clothes. I actually bought my first pair of trousers at Murphy-Gamble! I think you'd approve; they'd make it much easier for me to climb over gates and stiles! After that we met Mum and Mrs. Walsh at Ogilvy's in the fabric department where we bought a couple of dress patterns and some lovely material. I've been sewing like crazy ever since we got back ... which is why I have neglected you, dearest love. But, I think of you always. Perhaps I'll get good enough to make you a shirt one day!

Well, must go. Suzanne's coming over to help me pin up a hem.

I love you and hope you are well.

Gillian xxx

~ ~ ~

My dear Teddy,

Do you realize that I have nearly 50 letters ready to post to you? Oh, how I wish you'd write. But ... I shall keep on believing that one day I will hear from you.

Summer hols are over and Suzanne and I are back at school. It's not so awful now that I have a friend to do things with. There's going to be a school dance next weekend and Suzanne and I have decided to go. Don't worry, I'm not looking for a new boyfriend! Suzanne has her eye on someone, I think, so that's why she's keen to go.

I wonder if we're listening to the same music these days? Ours is mostly American. Suzanne is crazy about Ronnie Hawkins (have you heard of him over there?), but I'm more of a Paul Anka fan and he's actually a Canadian.

I don't know what I'm going to wear to this dance. I hope Mum will let me set my hair and put on a little lipstick, but I think Dad would have a fit. He says that only a 'certain type of woman' wears rouge and lipstick; I wonder how he knows that!!

How's your dad, by the way? Are you working at the shop a lot? I try to picture your normal day and what I think you are doing at the time, but it's getting more difficult. I'm scared that the memories will start to fade if I stop writing. But, I'll never forget you and one day we'll see each other again and it will be just as it was.

Loving you always, Gillian

~ ~ ~

Dearest love,

Brrrrrrr … they weren't joking when they said it gets a bit cold here! It was so cold this morning that I was sure my nostrils were going to stick together forever! We have so much snow … I've never seen so much. Do you remember that time it snowed at home and you made a sledge out of a tray and we took turns sliding down the little hill behind the chemist's? Well, that was nothing compared to this! You have to put on tall boots just to step outside because the snow is so deep and Mum and I wear hideous fur hats that tie under our chins and clumsy woollen mittens so we don't instantly freeze to death. If you could only see me all bundled up, I look like an over-stuffed teddy bear. Funny … I could be your 'teddy' bear!!

Christmas is coming. I don't know what that will be like. Suzanne is going away for the holidays and so it will just be me and Mum and Dad. What about you? Wish we could meet under some mistletoe somewhere … wish I could magically pop out of your Christmas stocking on Christmas morning … wish we were decorating the tree together … so many wishes. When will they ever come true?

Love, Gillian

~ ~ ~

"Sorry, love, nothing for you today, Teddy," sighed Miss Frobisher as she had every morning for months.

She found it sad to watch as Teddy left the Post Office each day with his shoulders drooped in a way that made him look so defeated. Why hadn't that wretched girl bothered to send even a postcard to the poor lad, she wondered?

Teddy had finished school in July and was now working full time at his father's shop. Mr. Postlethwaite was getting ready to add '& Son' to the sign that hung over the front door. At first Teddy had been reluctant for that to happen. Deep down he believed that his life would soon change ... that he and Gillian would find a way to be together and they would move away and start a new life somewhere else. But she hadn't even written a single letter and, without her address, there was nothing Teddy could do. So, he resigned himself to working at the ironmonger's and eventually taking over after his father retired as had been expected of him all along.

Teddy continued to spend time with his pals and some of the girls in the village. They'd go to the pictures on Friday nights, or meet up at The Royal Oak, the local pub. It helped fill in the time, but Teddy wasn't really interested in any of the girls and usually he went home early. At home by himself, he'd sit and play the Everly Brothers song, '*All I Have To Do Is Dream*', over and over again. It was a miracle that the phonograph needle hadn't etched its way right through to 'Claudette' on the other side!

As it became more and more apparent that Gillian had completely forgotten him, Teddy decided he had to take charge of his life. The first thing he decided to do was further his education, something he'd never considered before, but he felt he needed to expand his horizons so that, one day, when he and Gillian were reunited (a belief he clung to despite everything), he'd have more to offer. In January, 1960, he left for Manchester where he had been accepted into a business programme at the Manchester Municipal College of Technology. He got in by the skin of his teeth with the help of a glowing recommendation from his headmaster who'd always seen great promise in him. Gillian would have been proud, he thought. Even Mr. Mathers would have to agree this was a worthy achievement.

"A waste of time, if you ask me, son," grumbled his father when he heard of Teddy's plans.

"I want to do more with the business one day, Dad, and I want to learn new things. I'll be back; you know I will. But, I need to get away and do something different for a while. I miss her, Dad, and there are too many memories lurking around here at the moment."

"Take a holiday then … go to Blackpool; that's what other folk do when they feel like a change of scenery. You don't need all that extra schooling to run this place. Look at me … I've been here since I were just a lad and I've done all right for myself—for us—haven't I?"

"Of course, Dad, of course you have. But things are changing and we don't want to be left behind. It's not the same as it was in 1935."

Eventually, with a little help from Miss Frobisher, Teddy set off with his father's blessing.

~ ~ ~

March 1960
Dearest Teddy,

I'm seriously worried about Mum. I think she's really depressed. Father keeps telling her to buck up and get on with her life. He tells us he's made sacrifices too and we don't hear him complaining. He keeps saying that Mum and I should be very grateful to him for bringing us to this wonderful new country. I told him he shouldn't have gone to all that trouble and he just exploded and called me all sorts of dreadful names. Teddy, it's not getting any easier being here so far away from you.

I'll bet you're probably running your father's shop by now! I'd give anything to be able to drop by and buy a bag of nails, or a piece of gutter … or whatever else you sell these days. How did this happen? Have I really lost you forever? Most of the time, I try not to let myself think such things or I'd have to stop writing and I don't know what would happen to me then. I'd probably become like Mum … just really, really sad.

Love, G

~ ~ ~

April 14, 1960

Can you believe it? It's a year since I wrote that first letter (you know, the one you've not bothered to answer!!). Where are you, dearest love? Do you still remember our last night together? Do you still play our song?

I hate to ask, but have you found a new girlfriend? Just the thought of it brings a lump to my throat. I don't know if I could stand knowing you were kissing someone else like you used to kiss me. Ignorance is bliss for now. But, I can assure you, despite Suzanne's best efforts, I have not fallen for any spotty Canadian hockey players yet. She's so happy with her new beau that she feels everyone around her should have one. She doesn't understand that I have you. She says it's time I got on with my life in Canada and that it's obvious you've got on with yours without me. I don't listen to her when she talks like that. I suppose I envy her in a way because she has someone to go out with, but I'm usually quite content in my room writing to you or sketching in my notebook. I still haven't given up the idea of writing and illustrating a children's book. It probably sounds silly to you as you go about your day giving plumbing advice to little old ladies, or oiling lawn mowers for grumpy gardeners. I always envied you, you always knew what your future would be. I thought I did once too, but it seems I was dreadfully mistaken.

It may be years before I get back to England. My parents have no plans to return … ever, not even to visit my grandmother. I'll have to wait until I am old enough to get a job and save some money. Please wait for me. Please.

Love, Gillian

~ ~ ~

Sunday, October 9th, 1960

Teddy, oh Teddy, I wish you were here. Something awful has happened. Mum took a whole bottle of pills and when Father came home from work on Friday, he found her. She was dead. When I got home an hour later, there were police and an ambulance outside our house. For a brief moment, I thought perhaps Dad had had a heart attack … I could have coped with that … but not this, not Mum.

I know she's been miserable for a long, long time. She hasn't left the house in months and I have had to do all the shopping and take care of any errands. Father made her see a doctor a few months ago. He prescribed some kind of sedative that made her sleep most of the day. I think they must be the pills she took ... she probably saved them up for this. How could she leave me like this? How could she leave me stuck with Father? He's not said one comforting thing to me. He just walks around looking lost or angry. I can hardly look at him. I don't know what to say to him.

This morning Mrs. Walsh—you know, Suzanne's mum—came by to see if we needed anything and he basically told her to get lost.

I don't know what's going to happen now. Perhaps we can come home to England, but I doubt it. I have just under a year of school left, but I don't know if I'll be able to cope here alone with him for all that time. I'm desperate and don't know what to do. I can't believe Mum would do this to me.

You must write ... I'm still waiting.

I love you. I've never stopped loving you.

G xx

~ ~ ~

November 6th, 1960

Well, it looks like we're moving. Father's cousins in Winnipeg have invited us to come and stay with them until we can sort things out. Dad says we won't be coming back to Cobden, so it's time to pack up our belongings and move on. He says he'll find work in Winnipeg and I can finish grade 12 there. I don't think I really care one way or the other. I'll miss Suzanne, but that's about all. Living here alone with Dad has been terrible. He snaps at me all the time and blames Mum for everything that has ever gone wrong in his life ... including me.

I think I mentioned in one of my earlier letters that

he told Mrs. Walsh he thought his wife had been a very selfish woman … he told her this at the funeral of all things! Who's the selfish one, I want to know! Obviously not her. If it wasn't for him, we wouldn't even be here and Mum would still be alive and happy. And so would we, Teddy.

Anyway, I'll be writing from Winnipeg next … not that it makes much difference to you, I suppose. I've been having this one-sided conversation on paper for so long now, I don't think I could stop even if you told me to.

Love, Gillian

~ ~ ~

Chapter 3 - Secrets & Love

Richard Fulford had been waiting for this day for almost forty years; he was now officially retired and he loved the sound of it. Unlike many of his colleagues, he had no doubts or concerns about how he would occupy his remaining years. At 60, he had never been married or sired any offspring, had no significant attachments to anyone or any place and thus, free and unencumbered, he looked forward to his 'golden years' with great anticipation.

It was only a few weeks earlier that he had seen the classified advertisement in *The Ottawa Citizen*, (the newspaper he had worked for since 1948). It read:

Charming Ottawa Valley home in the small community of Cobden just north of Ottawa. This early 20th century sturdy brick house has 3 bedrooms and a fully plumbed indoor bathroom, plus kitchen, dining and sitting rooms. Includes a private garden with mature trees. Asking $13,650. Viewings may be arranged by calling Amanda Giles at Royal LePage ...

Richard had dialed Miss Giles' office number immediately. The house sounded perfect ... it would get him out of Ottawa without taking him too far away from the city he had grown to love. The following weekend he drove up to Cobden to view it. The previous occupants had already left but, even though it was empty, he could imagine himself living there very comfortably. It was solid and it was simple. It felt right. And so, after very little negotiating, he had bought himself a house. One month later, in the midst of a late-December blizzard, he drove out of Ottawa, north on Highway 17 and finally brought his cherry red Chevrolet Bel Air to rest in its new driveway at No. 25 Champlain Street. He was home.

~ ~ ~

27 Lipton Street,
Winnipeg, Manitoba
Canada

Dearest Teddy,

So we made it! We took the train from Ottawa bringing only what we could fit into a couple of trunks. Dad sold or gave away most of our furniture.

I remember hearing the name 'Winnipeg' for the first time in a Beatrix Potter story and I imagined some lovely pastoral place where bunny rabbits in velvet waistcoats and gingham pinnies pegged out their washing. Well, obviously Miss Potter never visited Winnipeg in the winter! It's minus 22 degrees Fahrenheit today and, with the wind blowing, it takes your breath away when you step out of doors. I thought Cobden was cold, but this is probably the coldest place on the planet next to Antarctica!

How are you Teddy? I never stop thinking about you. It is painful to know that we are now another thousand or more miles further apart.

Aunt Jo and Uncle Ian seem very nice and are doing their best to make us feel at home, but Dad hardly speaks these days. We spent two days on a train together and he barely said a word. Even though this isn't really our home, it's better than living alone with him. I don't know what his plans are, or when he'll get a job, but Aunt Jo says not to worry for now. I don't know what I am going to do either. I don't see much point in going back to school and I'm old enough to get a job myself now if I want to.

I love you, Teddy, always will ... Gillian

~ ~ ~

December 25, 1960
Happy Christmas, my love!

~ ~ ~

Jan 15
Dear Teddy ... you'll never guess what's happened! Aunt Jo has a friend who owns a tailoring shop where they do alternations and things like that and I'm going to start work there next week! I'm so excited! This is the beginning of my journey back to you, my love. Now that I have a job, I can start saving up to come home to you. I'll be earning 68 cents an hour. Dad says that's quite good for someone my age. He's not bothering to look for a teaching job. If you can believe it, he's working at the Great Western Garment Company in the shipping department! I don't know how he stands it, but I suppose it's better than nothing. He says we have to start contributing to the household. I hope that doesn't mean me as well, I want to save up everything I can for my

return to England.
    Love, lots, G xx

~ ~ ~

In the spring of 1962, Gillian left Winnipeg and headed west to Vancouver. She had become close friends with Janet, a co-worker at A-1 Alterations, and together they decided they would find an apartment of their own, get jobs and enjoy their first taste of freedom in a new city. As it turned out, Janet soon abandoned tailoring and enrolled in a beauty school to learn hairdressing. Gillian, meantime, got a job at Eaton's Department Store on Hastings Street, hemming skirts and trousers, and taking in or letting out waistbands. On weekends she and Janet would go to the cinema together or walk down to the sea. Janet brought home the occasional boyfriend, but Gillian paid little attention to young men and continued to write several times a week to her beloved Teddy. It was a habit she couldn't break no matter how often her friends told her she was wasting her time and quite possibly her life.

Meantime, Richard Fulford had made himself very comfortable at No. 25 Champlain Street in Cobden. His needs were simple and he furnished his home with the bare necessities and settled into the quiet and contemplative life he had always aspired to. He figured he'd earned it. He'd worked for most of his life as a newspaperman, digging up stories and poking his nose into places where he may or may not have been welcome. His last twelve years had been spent as a reporter with *The Ottawa Citizen* where he had witnessed—or been peripherally involved with—a number of significant Canadian moments: 1948 was the year Barbara Ann Scott, 'Canada's Sweetheart', won a gold medal in figure skating at the Winter Olympics in St. Mortiz, Switzerland and Richard had been part of the press delegation sent to welcome her home. Also, during his years at *The Citizen*, Louis St. Laurent became Prime Minister and was the first to occupy 24 Sussex Drive which has been the official residence of Canada's prime ministers ever since. In 1959, Richard had a brief encounter with Queen Elizabeth II when she came to Ottawa to unveil the Ottawa Memorial … brief indeed, a small jerky bow and a softly mumbled 'Ma'am' was all he'd managed as she strolled past the receiving line of which Richard was one of many. Never one for small talk, he certainly wasn't going to waste Her Majesty's precious time with comments on the weather and other nonsense, although he did notice that one or two of his colleagues managed to hold her attention for more than a mere second and, secretly, he rather envied them.

But, of course, for every high-profile story, there were considerably more less glamourous stories penned by Richard during his tenure: human stories—tragedies, injustices and prejudices. These were the ones that really left their mark on him. He understood what a huge responsibility it was to be genuinely present during moments in the lives of fellow human beings when they were at their most raw, most vulnerable and not necessarily at their most admirable. He wasn't cavalier about any of it and was often troubled by self-recriminations late at night. Had he maintained their dignity? Had he heard all sides and given a fair account? And, worst of all, had he shone an unwelcome light upon secrets he should never have disturbed? His editor would have told him it was simply the nature of the business, but it was that last question that bothered him most of all. He knew plenty about secrets and had spent most of his life asking probing questions of others as a means of deflecting any such interrogations from himself. He knew that his co-workers and colleagues thought he lived a peculiar and lonely life. He had never married, not even brought a girl-friend to any of the office events. He never entertained in his home and usually declined all and any invitations extended by others. He never thought of himself as a tragic figure, but he was an insular man, originally out of necessity but, later in life, he had to admit to himself, it was out of preference. But, as we all know, 'nature abhors a vacuum' and, in the case of folk we know nothing about, we're quick to fill in the gaps with unflattering versions of who we think they are. Richard had no doubt that the people he worked with had long since made up their minds about him, his lifestyle and his character based purely on the fact that they knew absolutely nothing about him!

He moved to Cobden intending to work on that aspect of his personality and become more affable and approach-able. As a new arrival in a small community, he knew it was especially important not to appear standoffish or aloof. He made concerted efforts to be on nodding terms with his new neighbours from the first moment he met them. Mrs. Walsh was the first person he got to know by name. She'd made a point of dropping by shortly after his arrival to introduce herself and, he suspected, to sneak a peek inside the house to see how an aging bachelor lived.

Her husband died not long after Richard moved onto the street and Suzanne, her daughter, had married a young local lad and the couple had moved to Toronto leaving Doris on her own. Richard was happy to help her out once in a while if she needed anything—like pushing her car out of a snow drift one winter, or getting her garden hose hooked up properly in the spring. She was a bit of a chatterbox, but Richard was a professional listener and rarely in a hurry these days. Life without deadlines meant he was quite content to sit in her over-heated sitting room sipping strong tea occasionally.

But, most of the time, Richard was left in peace ... just as he'd hoped. He wanted to write a book. At first, he simply wanted to tell his own story.

Richard Fulford was born on January 15th, 1900. The nuns who'd taken care of his teenaged mother soon found a home for him with a couple who owned a French-Canadian bakery just outside Montreal. They were simple, hard-working Catholic folk who loved their adopted son and provided him with a good home and sound upbringing.

In 1918, when the passing of Canada's Military Service Act required all males between the ages of 20 to 45 to sign up to be available for military service if needed, Richard, only 18-years-old at the time, decided to migrate south of the Canada-US border to avoid the whole business. He had no intention of going to war. His parents were sad to see him go, but made no attempts to stop him. He worked his way down the east coast of the United States, supporting himself with odd jobs, eventually making his way across to Chicago. There he worked for almost a year as a delivery boy and occasional stringer for *The Chicago Tribune*.

After the threat of conscription was over, he returned to Canada in 1921 and spent two years working in his parents' bakery but he knew it wasn't where he wanted to spend the rest of his life. Nor was he comfortable with Catholicism, despite his parents' efforts to engage him. For years, he'd suffered in silence, fully aware that he wasn't like other lads of his age. This was confirmed when, at the age of 24, while studying English and History at the University of Toronto, he met Julian. Julian was only two years older than Richard and was tutoring English students to earn a little cash while completing his Master's degree. He was the son of a wealthy Toronto businessman and, in 1927, was forced to marry the daughter of a similarly endowed family in order to secure a significant business merger between the companies owned by the two families. Richard was devastated by his lover's betrothal but didn't blame Julian for any of it even though it forced their secret into the deep and dark archives of dead-end memories. They never loved again; Julian remained loyal to his wife and family. Richard remained loyal to his solitude.

After graduation, Richard needed to get as far away from Toronto and Julian as he could and he moved to Winnipeg where he secured a position with *The Manitoba Free Press* (later known as *The Winnipeg Free Press*). He started out as a humble copy editor but occasionally presented his own work on subjects that interested him, mostly human-interest stories. Once in a while his by-line appeared in the paper.

After five years, he was assigned to the business desk where he remained for the next two decades until he finally decided he could no longer take the frigid Winnipeg winters and felt he needed to be closer to his aging parents. He moved back to Ontario. He was hired by *The Ottawa Citizen* and happily made his home in the capital, just a pleasant train journey away from his parents in Quebec. It was good to be where news was actually happening instead of writing about it second or third hand the next day and half a country away. He'd often said, 'news is flatter in the Prairies'.

Throughout his life he engaged in casual, covert affairs enshrouded in guilt and constrained by the ever-present fear of being caught (which is rarely as exciting as people imagine it to be), but he never 'fell in love' again, it was too risky on so many levels. Life as a gay man in Ottawa was only marginally better than it had been in the middle of the Prairies; Ottawa supported a more cosmopolitan crowd. However, he preferred Montreal or Toronto for his brief dalliances where the theatres, concert halls, fine restaurants and galleries were suitably anonymous places to meet and be met. His parents had long given up the idea of grandchildren. They'd accepted that they couldn't have kids of their own and that apparently God had chosen not to compensate them with grandkids either.

Now, well into his sixties and his parents long gone, he'd had plenty of time to reflect on his life. He knew enough about human nature to recognize that—beyond the names, dates and places—his story was not unique and that his job as a writer would be to present the universal nature of his tale in a way that anyone could identify with it on some level or another. And then, one afternoon late in the autumn of 1966, he made a discovery that would finally give him the kick-start he needed.

It all happened because he'd decided that as the soon-to-be author of the next 'great Canadian novel', he should have a proper place to work in and, thus motivated, he decided to convert his unused and neglected attic into a writer's retreat. He could have commandeered either of the two extra bedrooms, but he felt they were too ordinary and, besides, they were chockfull of boxes of books, old photographs from his newspaper assignments and other buried treasure he couldn't bear to toss out or cull. The attic would be perfect with its unobstructed view of the garden at the back of the property and the afternoon sun streaming in. It didn't take much to prepare it ... he threw out a few boxes abandoned by the previous owners, laid down a couple of scatter rugs, hauled a sturdy writing desk and chair upstairs and even allowed himself the added comfort of a small electric heater and a tea kettle beside him during the winter—providing he remembered not to plug them both in at the same time or the fuse would blow.

Although he had emptied out and cleaned up the place pretty thoroughly, there was one item he had chosen to hang on to. It was an old suitcase; a well-scuffed brown leather valise with metal corners that were beginning to come apart. He'd set it aside until the rest of the room was finished. Opening it would be his reward for a job well done, he thought. He also had a nagging sense (reporter's intuition, perhaps?) that he was about to discover something important inside. Of course, it might just contain a heap of moth-eaten old clothes that were supposed to have gone to a jumble sale; or a collection of tacky souvenirs from someone else's exotic holiday destination ... but perhaps, as Richard soon discovered, it would contain an essential building block for his soon-to-be-written story:

Darling, I miss you. I wish we could be together more often.

Darling, a single rose for my love, but you know you are worthy of thousands.

Darling, sometimes I worry about your safety. I'd hate for our love to destroy you.

Darling, Morecambe was magic. You were magic. A night I'll never forget.

Darling, meet me at our usual place after school. I can't wait to hold you.

Darling, do you think anyone knows? Mr. Hargraves took me aside between classes yesterday and warned me to be careful. He said Headmaster isn't a fool. What do you think he meant by that? Meet me during our break. We should talk.

Darling, he called me into the office today. He wants

to know what my plans are for the future. Do you think he suspects?

Darling, I caught a glimpse of you today on the school grounds. You are so beautiful.

… there were dozens and dozens of small handwritten notes just like these lying amongst the dried and crumbling remains of once-treasured pressed wildflowers and roses. Most of the notes were scrawled on lined paper obviously torn out of a notebook. Others were carefully written on tiny floral greeting cards. Here's a secret, thought Richard … a secret and a love story. Funny how often the two seem to go together. At first, he assumed it was a romantic exchange between two love-struck adolescents but, when he dug deeper, he came upon these:

Darling, I truly believe your husband knows exactly what's going on between us. He looks away if we pass in the corridors between classes and yet I feel his eyes burning into me after I walk by. Are you all right? He hasn't hurt you, has he?

Darling, meet me in the usual place after the bell. We have to accept that people are talking. Even some of my pupils are snickering behind my back; I can feel it. What are we going to do? I cannot lose you.

Darling, I'm devastated by our last conversation. I thought you'd want to come away with me. I thought you'd be happy to leave Harold. Don't you love me? Please talk to me soon. I love you.

Oh God, Mary, I can't believe it. Ever since you told me

Harold was taking you away to Canada, my heart may as well have stopped beating. I can't eat. I can't sleep. I can't teach and I can barely conceal my utter contempt for your smug husband. Are we really going to let him win?

Well, darling, I suppose that really was the end. I hope you never forget our last kiss since you've made sure there won't be any more. I hope you never live to regret your decision as much as I do already. 'Duty calls' as you so tersely reminded me. Duty trumps love apparently. Enjoy your new life. I will never forget you ... I wish I could. Forever yours, Sam.

And thus began Richard Fulford's first and only work of semi-fiction, *Secrets & Love*. He borrowed from the dialogue between these two lovers, Mary and Sam, as he developed a heart-felt vehicle for his own very personal tale of hidden love. Of course he had no way of knowing how their story evolved but, working as a fiction writer, not a journalist, he enjoyed the fact that their fate was entirely in his hands.

Although Richard had no intention of ever revealing his personal secret—partly because of how he knew society would judge him and partly because it was against the law—he still wanted to be able to tell his story, and sharing the pages with other secret loves would provide the perfect cover. The feelings would be the same—the joy, the pain, the grief—it didn't matter what the gender or gender preference was, Richard knew love felt the same everywhere and that secrets did one of two things: either they held a couple together, or they split them asunder, there were no half measures.

He read each and every tender note he discovered in the suitcase with interest and slowly began to build his story around them.

What he didn't know, however, was that the old suitcase never gave up its biggest secret, a slim airmail envelope that had slipped underneath the torn lining at the bottom of the case.

Secrets & Love was published in 1969, shortly after Prime Minister Pierre Trudeau's famous statement that there was 'no place for the State in the bedrooms of the nation'. Reassuring as that might have sounded to many a closeted gay person, or adulterous spouse, Richard chose to publish under the pseudonym, Robert Friar, and, out of respect for those whose stories he was custodian of, he changed the names of all the people and places that might have given away the true identities of his characters.

Secrets & Love told the stories of ordinary people going about their seemingly ordinary lives while clutching desperately to the hidden inner compartments that housed their personal guilt, shame and longing. There was a couple whose wife was cheating on her husband; an aspiring young male writer who suffered silently because of an all-consuming love for his male tutor; a young boy who never got over his first teenage crush; and several couples whose disappointments and losses became undeservingly cloaked in guilt and secrecy. Finally, there was a woman who lived out her entire adult life alone enduring the unflattering labels whispered behind her back—'old maid', 'witch', 'bluestocking', 'dyke', and so forth. Her secret shame did not involve illicit affairs or peculiar sexual preferences; it was the lack thereof that condemned her. Skillfully, Richard brought all his characters together, each one slowly revealing him or herself one layer at a time. On the surface, their stories may have appeared very different, but in truth they were more alike than not. We meet these people throughout our lives over and over and over again whether we recognize them or not. They are our neighbours, our co-workers, our parents, our children, our shopkeepers ... anyone with a heart has the potential to fall victim to a misfired arrow. For Richard, *Secrets & Love* was the best therapy money couldn't buy. The simple act of writing gave his own tragic story a place in the real world that it had previously been denied.

Richard's first and only novel was a reasonable success ... perhaps not the great Canadian novel he'd aspired to, but it did well nonetheless. Gillian discovered it in a bookshop in Vancouver. Reading the short bio on the back flap of the book cover, she remarked to her friend, Janet, what a coincidence it was that the author, Robert Friar, happened to live in Cobden. She wondered if he had lived there when she and her family had been there ... perhaps they had run into one another at the corner shop? Gillian understood secret and damaged love but, consumed by her own, she never suspected that the story of her own mother's affair with Sam Hopkins was the catalyst for Robert Friar's book.

~ ~ ~

April 1969
Dearest Teddy,

It's been ten years since I wrote my first letter to you. I now realize what a child I was then. But, I still love you; I still dream about you, I still imagine us being together some day. I don't know when. My life is changing, Teddy, and I have to go along with it. You see, I've met a man; in fact, we met last summer. He's not a lumberjack! But, he does work for a forest products company. His name is Bruce. I know this will be hard for you to hear, but perhaps you are already married yourself, so you'll understand. Bruce and I are going to be married this coming June. I'm really happy, Teddy. I only hope you are happy too. Don't worry, I'll never stop writing.

Love always, your Gillian

~ ~ ~

Gillian Mathers and Bruce Evans were married in Vancouver on June 14th, 1969. Gillian's father, Harold, along with Aunt Jo and Uncle Ian attended. Janet was there with her husband and Suzanne sent her regrets. Bruce's family clearly outnumbered Gillian's; he had four brothers, two sisters, both parents, aunts, uncles, cousins galore and even a grandmother and a great uncle. Following the ceremony, Bruce paid for a small reception at the Tea Room in the elegant Hotel Vancouver downtown. Jo and Ian gave the newlyweds a honeymoon in Victoria on Vancouver Island. They'd never had children of their own so they were pleased to be able to do this for Gillian. It was all very exciting for Gillian. She'd never been on a ferry before, or enjoyed a proper afternoon tea in a posh hotel (even though she was English!) and, best of all, she had never sat by the sea and felt so content in her entire life. As the waves washed up on a pebbly beach on the outskirts of the city, Bruce wrapped his protective arms around her and Gillian watched herself basking in the glow of their new life together. It all felt unusually comfortable.

"Do you ever feel like you're not really living your life, you're just watching or visiting someone else's?" Gillian asked one evening as they sat by the sea sipping wine from a bottle.

"I'm not sure what you mean, my love," Bruce replied honestly.

"Well, I mean do you fear that at any moment it could

all be taken away because someone mis-assigned you and this wasn't the life you were supposed to get. I'm so very happy with you here and now, Bruce … but it can't be real, can it? Eventually moments like these will just be memories and even we will begin to doubt them."

"Gillian, I don't know what you're talking about. We're about to spend the rest of our lives together. I'd say that's about as real as it gets."

"Bruce, you know I like to write, don't you? I write almost every day so that I can set things down on paper and trap them there. I'm always scared that things will disappear or get lost if I don't. Someday someone will read my words and know that I was here and who I was. It's important to me. Can you understand it?"

"Whatever makes you happy, my darling. Write poems, write theses, write shopping lists, I don't care. I'll always know you and I'll certainly never forget that you were here."

Bruce, a rather literal and pragmatic man, responded as best he could. He didn't really know what she was fretting about, but he didn't think there was much harm in her writing notes and journals if it made her feel more secure.

Her relationship with Bruce was not, and never would be, a titillating or particularly passionate one—no unruly butterflies in her tummy and he didn't cause her heart to summersault like Teddy had. But she so desperately wanted to belong somewhere and to someone and Bruce was a good man; he loved her and she believed she could offer him enough of herself and her heart to keep him happy. Deep down, she always knew that this wasn't the life that had been intended for her. Here, she was little more than a guest. Her real life belonged elsewhere, but Bruce didn't need to know that.

~ ~ ~

Dear Teddy,

I'm so excited ... Bruce and I are expecting! I know I said I was planning to visit England next year, but I don't think I'll be able to manage it now. I hope you will not be disappointed. I am so thrilled be a mother at last. I thought it would happen faster but I've had to be very patient these past three years. Oh, I won't have to go to work again! I won't miss it one little bit. Well, I suppose a baby will be work, but it will be different work. I won't to have sit bent over a sewing machine for 8 hours at a stretch trying to make impossibly small clothes fit unreasonably plump and vain women! Anyway, that's my news for now ... I'll write again very soon.

Love, Gillian, future proud Mama!

~ ~ ~

Dear Teddy,

This will be a brief one ... I don't know if I'll be able to stay awake long enough to write a proper sentence. What I'd give for a full night of sleep! But, no real complaints. Julie (named after my old school friend) is a jewel. I love her so much. Can you believe I am a mother? I hope I'll be a good one. Sometimes I don't know what I'm supposed to do but then Julie looks me straight in the eye, gives me her little smile and I realize she trusts me completely, so I must be doing all the right things. I'll write when I can. Between changing nappies, sterilizing bottles and all the other normal housework, I don't have much time for anything. But I wouldn't swap it for all the tea in China. By the way, do you know whatever happened to Julie Burgess? I haven't heard from her in years, not even a Christmas card. I'd love to tell her about her namesake. Hope you are well ...

Love, G xx

~ ~ ~

October 1974.

Dearest T,

William David Evans was born 2 days ago, weighing in at a respectable 7lbs 3oz. He is just a darling boy ... happy from the moment I first held him. His sister, Julie, is delighted with this new living 'doll' ... at least for now! 30-years-old and still having babies! Sometimes I feel so old ... I'll bet prim and proper old Miss Frobisher wasn't much older than I am now back when we knew her. Is she still running the Post Office? Did your father ever make a respectable woman out of her? There are so many things I'd like to know about you and about your life since I last saw you over 16 years ago. What I'd give for a photograph ... in my mind's eye you are forever preserved as a 16-year-old boy with unruly curls and mucky shoes. I'll bet you haven't changed that much. But I sure have ... giving birth isn't very kind to one's figure. Ah well, it's all worth it.

Love always, 'old' Gill!

P.S. When you write, don't forget you have to use our new postal code now. You will write one day, won't you?

~ ~ ~

1977 - Springtime ...

Dearest Teddy,

Moving again, but this time to our very own house. No more cranky landlords and broken toilets that never get fixed! Bruce has been promoted and we feel we're ready to be homeowners. We've found a lovely 3-bedroom house near the University. On a clear day (very rare around here), you can just about see the mountains from the top floor. It's in a quiet neighbourhood with other families like ours and a park and schools close by. Julie will be starting grade one this year and Will is itching to go to nursery school (even though I don't think he understands what it entails). Will is rather a shy and trusting child, always smiling—completely unlike his big sister whose moods can be quite unpredictable—I hope he learns to fit in with the other children. So, for the first time in nearly six years, I'll have a few hours to myself each day! Do you remember when I told you I was going to write children's books ... well, maybe this is my opportunity to do just that!

~ ~ ~

June 1977, letter No. 1000!!!

My dearest love,

It's amazing that even after all this time and all these shoeboxes full of unsent mail, I still can't let you go. I've outwritten you 1000 to zero! Sometimes when I'm with the children, I imagine what it would be like if they were 'our' children and you were their father ... coming home from the shop every evening and swinging them up in the air while they kick their feet and giggle. I'm not complaining about Bruce as a father, but he works an awful lot and sometimes he doesn't even see his children awake for a couple of days. He's become a fairly serious man, but perhaps you are now too. We've all grown up, haven't we? Inside, I still feel like that little girl who clambered over country gates and stiles to entertain you! We're lucky in many ways. We get to keep the memories of our love without ever spoiling them with the rude realities of jobs and housework, money and sex. You will always have a special place in my heart. I love you. Gill

~ ~ ~

Christmas 1977

Happy Christmas to you, my dearest. From our house to yours, love always, Gillian and family.

~ ~ ~

Dear Teddy,

Gosh, this writing lark is more fun than I ever imagined! The problem, they tell me, is getting published. But I don't care right now because I am having such a good time putting pen to paper.

The children are happy at school and, with Bruce being away so much, I have plenty of time to hone my craft.

Love, budding author, Gill!

~ ~ ~

January 1, 1980

… What a strange year it has been. When Dad died in November, it didn't upset me nearly as much as I thought it would. Instead, it brought back memories of Mum. I've always wished she'd met her wonderful grandchildren. She would have adored them and they her. I wasn't angry with Father by the time he got ill. I'm well passed that. Instead, I felt quite indifferent—does that make me a bad person, I wonder? Jo and Ian have been so good to him all these years. I don't know how they put up with him. They are going to visit here in the spring. It will be their first trip to Vancouver since Bruce and I got married and I cannot wait to show them the beautiful blossoms and gardens and the seaside and all my favourite little galleries and cafés. They are honourary grandparents to Julie and Will and I am very grateful to them for everything.

And … while on the subject of a 'strange' year, I can't help but wonder if Bruce is seeing someone else. I know that sounds like an awful and disloyal thing to say, even though it's almost as normal these days for businessmen to have mistresses as it is for them to carry briefcases. He always seems so happy when he knows he's about to go away and then he's morose and broody when he's stuck at home with his family. I read in *Chatelaine* that these are precisely the kinds of signs one should watch for. I don't entirely know what I feel about it. In many ways I suppose I've enjoyed an extramarital affair much longer than he, although I do realize that mine isn't 'real'. What would it be like, Teddy … to see one another again after all this time? What would it be like to be held by you again? Would we recognize the feel of one another? I know I shouldn't have these thoughts, but I can't help myself. Oh, I'm rambling. I'm a bit blue and lonely these days, I suppose. Too much time on my hands. Too much thinking perhaps. Sometimes I'm frightened that I'll become terminally sad like my mother—perhaps it's genetic or something—but how could I ever leave my children the way she left me? I'd better keep busy … there's bound to be some laundry I can fold or a Soap on TV I can get into!

Love to you, Gillian

~ ~ ~

In the winter of 1983, Richard Fulford, *a.k.a.* Robert Friar, contracted a virulent strain of influenza that quickly developed into pneumonia. He died in Pembroke Civic Hospital on December 11th, a few weeks short of his 84th birthday. Just before his death, he made one telephone call to a friend he hadn't seen in over 35 years but, nonetheless, a friend he knew he could count on. Julian Miller drove immediately from Toronto to Pembroke to say good-bye to his old friend. Sadly, he arrived too late. The Sister on duty expressed her condolences to the elderly and travel-weary gentleman and then handed him an envelope. The outside was addressed to Mr. Julian Miller. Inside was a copy of Richard's handwritten will, witnessed by his neighbour, Mrs. Walsh, on November 17, 1983. He had left everything … his house, its contents and his 1978 Chevy Chevette (a poor substitute for his once-loved Bel Air) to Julian. And, as Robert Friar, he left Julian all future royalties earned from his book; he also assigned Julian sole custody of their well-preserved secret.

Julian did not delay in attending to the business of wrapping up his friend's life. The house was cleaned out and put on the market. He gave the car to Mrs. Walsh since her 1961 Pontiac was more rust than metal, its final journey to the scrap yard long overdue. Julian also removed a collection of love notes he found sitting on Richard's desk up in the attic. With just a glance, he saw that they were all written in the same hand and signed 'Sam'. Julian assumed Sam had been one of Richard's lovers and, having vowed to protect his friend's secrets for the rest of his natural life, he destroyed them without ever reading them.

Chapter 4 - Family Time

Twenty-three years in the hands of an elderly gay recluse had not done 25 Champlain Street any favours … it wasn't falling apart or anything like that, but the décor was definitely past its best date. However, this certainly didn't deter Jim and Fiona Harper from putting in an offer on the property. Jim, a recent dental school graduate, was joining Dr. Lennon's practice in Cobden. His wife, Fiona, was happy to be escaping the city and was looking forward to raising their three children in a more community-focused environment. They paid $49,500 for the home and moved in on February 16th, 1984. Their three girls—Emily, aged 9, Bethany, aged 7 and Melanie aged 4—were thrilled with the new house. To them it seemed like a castle after living in a two-bedroom apartment in downtown Montreal for most of their short lives. Emily and Bethany agreed to share the largest of the three bedrooms and Melanie occupied the one closest to her parents' room.

Fiona wasted no time in preparing the bedrooms for her girls. She spent her days stripping stubborn wallpaper, patching holes, priming and painting. After she was satisfied with her efforts in those two rooms, she moved on to the room she shared with Jim. She opted for a dusty rose colour scheme—very popular in the early '80s—with forest green accents and a new comforter with embroidered pink rose-buds and green ivy sprawling all over it. She sewed frilly rose and green valances to hang above Venetian blinds like puffy eyebrows and arranged their gilt-framed wedding pictures on the wall.

Downstairs, renovations were a little more challenging and more costly. The kitchen stove was temperamental and the refrigerator was always more full of frost than fodder. They were probably the original kitchen appliances purchased some time in the 1960s. Once Jim had a few pay cheques under his belt, they would have to be replaced.

Typical of homes of that era, it was a very chilly and draughty place during the cold winters. The Harper family endured the discomfort for several years before taking the plunge to replace all the windows with double-glazing. Come summer time, Jim would climb up their rickety ladder to attach externally mounted screens. It was a dreaded chore and one that usually involved a lot of swearing. The first year was the worst because there didn't appear to be any kind of system for matching the right window to the right screen. After that, Jim, a meticulous man who left very little in his life to chance, made sure that each screen and window was marked with a special code so that the job would be less of a guessing game in the future. As a man who depended on order and organization in both his professional and personal lives, he couldn't understand how anyone could function without proper systems in place. Fiona understood this about her husband and did her level best to stick to the predictable routines that kept Jim happy. He got up at precisely the same time every morning, ate the same granola breakfast every morning with his one cup of coffee—never two. He wore the same clothes to work each day because he had cloned everything in his wardrobe multiple times. He would probably have worn the same clothes on weekends too, but his wife drew the line there.

"You can't be doing chores around the house, or watching the girls at their swim meets in a shirt and tie," she explained.

Jim expected his wife to have his lunch packed and ready by 7:45 each workday morning—a ham and cheese sandwich on brown bread (no mustard), two chocolate Digestive biscuits, an apple and a thermos of Earl Grey tea. Any attempts by Fiona to add something new to his lunch menu were not well received. Again, she waited until the weekends to throw a tuna sandwich at him or, heaven forbid, suggest he fix his own lunch.

Sometimes Fiona felt like little more than his domestic assistant ... the equivalent of his dutiful dental assistant at work who so predictably and obediently handed him the right tools at the right moments throughout his working day. He trained the people around him well, although even he had to admit 'training' his children was not as easy. He couldn't stand the comings and goings of their friends at unpredictable and non-scheduled times of the day. Doors would slam, petty squabbles would erupt and girlie giggles would bounce off the walls. There was a never-ending queue of unwashed cups and sticky plates sprawling on the kitchen counters en route to the sink.

"Why can't they open and close doors like human beings instead of all this banging and slamming?" he'd ask. "Why must they leave their shoes scattered around the front door? I built shelves for them and I'm sick of tripping over things," he'd moan.

"They're children," Fiona would remind him over and over again, "they're not your employees or military cadets in training, they're just kids doing what kids do."

By the time the children turned 12, 10 and 7, respectively, Fiona decided they needed a separate space to play and entertain their friends in. Even she was tired of toys and books strewn all over the living room floor and dining room table and she couldn't stand Jim's complaints any longer. So, once the children were all back at school in September of 1987, Fiona tackled the attic. She planned to convert it into a warm and comfy place for her children and their friends to gather.

She began by dismantling an old desk that had belonged to the previous owner; a bit of loose change, a couple of paperclips and a small card—the kind that usually accompanies a floral delivery—fell to the floor. The card read:

"Darling, a single rose for my love, but you know you are worthy of thousands."

How sweet, she thought, remembering a time when notes like that had been part of her life with Jim. But that was years and several children ago. Romance had since got lost in the kafuffle somewhere along the way. She tossed the card, along with the other rubbish, into a garbage bag. Next she found some heavy boxes that turned out to be full of old editions of *The Ottawa Citizen*. With great effort, she heaved them down the stairs and out to the garage; why would anyone hang on to old newspapers all this time, she wondered? Finally, she unearthed what looked like an antique suitcase. She took a quick look inside and it appeared to be empty. It was a little beaten up on the outside and the lining within was torn but, other than that, she thought it might be worth something to a collector. Rather than throw it out with the rest of the garbage, she placed it back in the corner beneath the eaves where she'd found it and told herself she'd deal with it another time.

~ ~ ~

September 1987,

Dearest Teddy,

I'm so glad the summer is over and the children are back at school. Julie has been driving me crazy! She's happy one moment and miserable the next and, of course, it's all got to do with this boyfriend of hers. She's barely 15 and thinks she's 'in love'. Nothing Bruce and I do or say is right … in her eyes. She just keeps yelling, 'you don't understand, you'll never understand what true love is.' So dramatic!

I know we fell in love when we were her age, but that was different. I know it was, otherwise I wouldn't still be writing to you. We have endured. But this thing she has with Scott, I'm sure it's just a phase. She may not know it yet, but I know he's not right for her. He simply doesn't share her passion and ambition.

Julie loves Madonna! I think she looks like a prostitute, but apparently that's yet another thing I 'don't understand'.

Will is a whole different kettle of fish … no interest in girls whatsoever … yet! He's an easy-going lad who is content to spend time at home with his friends, toss a baseball back and forth or ride his bike. In the winter, he practically lives on skis. Boys are so much easier, although I can't stand the clothes he wears! In our day, torn jeans and scuffed shoes meant you were a bit of a ne'er-do-well, but these days, it's the uniform of the 'cool' crowd. I offer to buy him new clothes, but he assures me he'd never wear them so I needn't waste my money.

In a world that seems to be changing all around us, one thing I know for sure is that my love for you remains constant … or perhaps I'm just clinging desperately to a life raft that I cannot possibly give up even though it may have already sunk. Is it too late for us?

Always, Gill

~ ~ ~

September 1991,

… I just watched Will drive away. I feel so alone. I know the kids will come back now and again, but seeing my baby head off to university to start his new life as a young independent man scares me. Peace and quiet for a couple of days is all very fine, but to know I won't hear him slamming the front door at two in the morning, or playing his rap music day and night, makes me very sad. I remember after Julie left, I'd sit in her room for hours staring at the patches on her wall where once her favourite Dire Straits and Madonna posters had hung. Why do I spend so much of my life looking at all the things that are missing?

Will's room is different, even though he's supposedly left, there are still crusty old socks and tattered sports magazines scattered around. It still feels—and definitely smells—like him!

I miss them. They've been my 'job' for over 20 years. So, no more excuses for not working on my books. I started writing the first one over ten years ago, now I'll be able to really concentrate on it. I should be excited … guess I'll have to work on that too.

I love you, Teddy. Wish you were here to talk to.

G

~ ~ ~

March 1992,
Dearest Teddy,

It's been more than a month since Bruce walked out of the house for good, but I'm still in shock. I never thought Bruce and I would be one of 'those' couples. At first, when he said he was leaving me, I thought it was just a cruel joke … another in a long line of stupid remarks that get tossed back and forth when we argue. But, this time, he really meant it. He's moved in with Cheryl, 'she understands him' … apparently I don't! He said some very cruel things, Teddy. He even said he was sick of living with someone who keeps writing letters to an 'imaginary friend'. How dare he talk about us like that! He's not suffered because of my writing. I've never neglected him. I've taken care of this family for the best part of 25 years and now he leaves me with nothing. If I'd known this is how it would turn out, I would have come home to you years ago. But I didn't. I remained loyal to that man. What a fool I've been.

Oh, Teddy, why did we leave things for so long? Is it too late now? Why did you never write back? I am tormented thinking about how life could have been so different if we had found a way to be together. But then I wouldn't have Julie and Will and I couldn't imagine my life without them.

I'm sorry this is such a miserable letter. I'm so lost at the moment and there is no one else for me to talk to. I can't burden the children with my grief. They are coping with their own and I must appear strong for them. Bruce is a coward … he's left me to clean up his mess.

I'll write again soon when I'm a little less maudlin and riddled with self-pity.

I've never stopped loving you, Teddy, and there will always be a place in my heart for you, no matter what.

Gillian

~ ~ ~

Meanwhile, time passed predictably at 25 Champlain Street. With the well-honed routines of the household marking the passage of time, most days ran like clockwork. The Harper girls enjoyed many happy times in their converted attic playroom. Melanie had a gigantic doll's house to play with. Bethany often practiced her recorder up there—that alone made the effort of converting the space worthwhile! Emily, once she grew older, snuck the occasional boyfriend up to the attic to 'help with math homework', or listen to the music of bands with strange sounding names—Radio Head, Pearl Jam and Stone Temple Pilots—to name a few. Birthday parties and sleepovers took place up in the attic and even Fiona occasionally climbed the steep staircase to spend time up there when the house was empty … it was a peaceful place to sit and read or write letters. She enjoyed the view of the back garden. She never did get around to investigating the old suitcase. In fact, she completely forgot about it. Life was hectic enough with three growing girls, a husband, a house and a garden to tend to.

Jim couldn't really understand what kept Fiona busy all day. He'd drag himself home after work as if all the woes of the world were his alone and he'd wait expectantly for the members of his household to welcome him, tend to his needs and applaud his self-sacrifice. And yet, they rarely did. It seemed to Jim that no one fully understood what it took to keep his work and his household functioning smoothly. The worst part, of course, was the fact that, in spite of his diligence, his practice was floundering. A palpable tension hung menacingly around him and his wife and it was pretty obvious that Fiona blamed Jim's lack of business acumen for the state of their finances.

"How many times have I told you it's important to get

involved in the community? Everyone in town knows Dr. Lennon but, even after all the years we've lived here, hardly anyone stops you on the street to say 'hello'".

"I'm just not that kind of guy," Jim would reply, "I don't join clubs and I'm lousy at small talk ... you know that about me."

Fiona had always assumed that Dr. Lennon's retirement would make Jim's practice busier, but it didn't. Many of Dr. Lennon's patients were elderly and not expected to require dental services much longer. Not only that, but by the 1990s, everyone wanted to see a 'specialist' of some sort or another—there was something wrong with you if you weren't taking your children to an orthodontist to be rigged out in metal braces, or to a special pediatric dentist with colourful treatment rooms and staff dressed as cartoon characters. Fiona would smile to herself when she tried to imagine her Jim swapping his pristine white lab coat for one with balloons or Care Bears all over it!

Most of the newer families in Cobden took their business to Ottawa so the patient list belonging to Drs. Lennon & Harper was shrinking not growing. Clearly Jim wasn't much of a 'salesman' and his 'networking' skills were non-existent; but, that was Jim. He liked his work and he liked the patients he had and, most of all, he liked to come home at the end of his day to an orderly house with his wife and children exactly where he'd left them. As long as things appeared to be 'normal', perhaps Jim could continue to believe that they were. But, with Emily now at university and two other daughters likely to follow in her footsteps, Jim had to admit—first to himself and then, reluctantly, to Fiona—they would have to make some changes. When a former university friend offered him a partnership in his thriving Montreal dental clinic, Jim seized the opportunity. He didn't really have a choice. He called the family together to explain what was about to happen. Fiona wept.

"I feel like we've failed," she sobbed, "this is our home, Jim, it breaks my heart to leave it."

"For God's sake, Fiona, I've just been offered a position in a successful Montreal practice! How is that 'failure'? It's a promotion, an opportunity … if you're too blind to see that …"

"Well, I'm not going!" Bethany suddenly blurted out. "I can't go. I'm not leaving Billy," she explained.

"Oh come off it, Beth. You two are just kids. There'll be many more boyfriends in your life," Fiona said.

But Bethany wasn't listening. She'd placed her hands over her ears and was marching defiantly up the stairs to her room.

Fiona jumped at the sound of Bethany slamming her bedroom door with the super power only a disgruntled adolescent can wield. "She'll come around …"

"Well, she's not got any choice in the matter," Jim stated matter-of-factly.

And so, in 1994, almost ten years to the day since they had moved in to 25 Champlain Street, Jim and Fiona sold up and returned from whence they'd come. But they were very different people. A disappointment exposed does that to a couple.

~ ~ ~

September 1994
Dearest Teddy,

Can you believe it … Harper Collins has just published my second book and wants even more! The first one, *Mr. P Goes To Work*, was such a success that I wasn't sure if I could write a second one that would be as appealing but, apparently, *Mr. P Goes Fishing* is equally loved by my young fans! So, what do you think Mr. P; what should you get up to next? What about 'Mr. P Posts A Letter'???? Perhaps a letter to Canada, eh?

In the fishing book I told the story of the day you caught the duck, remember that? Oh, we laughed so hard. Poor duck!

When the kids were young we took them on holiday to Vancouver Island and stopped to do some fishing in Tofino. Bruce caught a humungous salmon and the children were so impressed. You'd love it here, Teddy; you could actually catch something! Ah well, you can't blame me for dreaming, can you? I do a lot of it these days; it's so quiet here now.

Love always, Gillian

~ ~ ~

Dear Teddy,

Well, I've finally met him … this year's boy-wonder, according to Julie at any rate. His name's 'Fly' of all things! Really, what were his parents thinking? I asked if it was a nickname or short for something, but apparently it's not. He's an earthy-smelling hippie kind of bloke. Quite pleasant, but not exactly a fireball of energy and prospects! He and Julie are going to backpack around New Zealand this winter (summer over there, of course). Funny how those without jobs or obvious means are the ones who get to do all the travelling and enjoy all the adventures while I still haven't made it back to England even once over the past 35 years. Now, I've lost my nerve. I don't know if I could do it on my own. I've not travelled abroad since Bruce and I had our holiday in Bermuda back in 1982. That was a treat. Jo and Ian took care of the children and Bruce and I had 11 fabulous sun-soaked days to ourselves. I think he still loved me back then. I know I loved him.

And I love you too … is that so bad? I wouldn't need to go anywhere exotic with you … I'd be happy just to be beside you for the rest of eternity. Gill

~ ~ ~

April 1995
My dear Teddy,

Well, it seems Julie and Fly are parting ways. I thought that would bring Julie home pretty quickly, but she's decided to stay. Somehow she's managed to get a job with a travel agency in Nelson on the South Island. She sounds very excited about it so I hope it works out for her. Strange to think she is so far away.

Will's still enjoying his studies at the University of Toronto and usually comes home once or twice a year for a dutiful visit. How did my children end up so far away from home? It's different from when we were young-sters, isn't it? They think nothing of travelling around the country, or even the world these days.

Love, Gillian

~ ~ ~

June
Dear Teddy,

I'm so excited … I'm off to Toronto tomorrow to at-tend Will's graduation. It's so long since I've flown any-where, but I think it will be good for me to break out of my shell for a change. Apparently Bruce is unable to go. Cheryl doesn't want to travel with their new baby and Bruce wouldn't dare abandon her for a few days!

God, poor Bruce. Imagine being a new father again at 57! Well, that's what you get when you marry a younger model, I guess.

I've got to get myself packed. I hope I'm taking all the right things. I don't want to embarrass my poor son with my west coast casualness. Toronto's a more city-like city than Vancouver and it's been ages since I've needed to dress for a part. Well … I'd better not procrastinate any longer. I'll let you know how it goes. G xx

~ ~ ~

Dear Teddy,

I was so proud … so proud of my handsome young son as he walked onto the stage and received his degree. In a way, I wish Bruce had been there too. This was something we helped bring about together and we should have had the chance to enjoy the fruits of our labour (mostly mine!) together.

You'll never guess what we did on Monday after the events were all over. We drove up to Cobden. I wanted Will to see where I'd first lived when I came to Canada so long ago—children have such a difficult time believing that anything ever happened in their parents' lives before they were born! It was quite an emotional moment for me as we cruised slowly past No. 25 Champlain Street. It looked very much like it had when we were there except that the trees in the garden had grown considerably and the gingerbread detailing on the front porch was now a shade of soft green instead of cream. Were it not for the unfamiliar car in the drive and the name 'Shepard' carved into a piece of wood hanging above the front door, I could almost imagine my mother rushing out to greet us. Her hair would be disheveled and her apron less than spotless, but she would be smiling. Or, at least, that's how I like to think it would have been even though she rarely smiled after we moved here. Funny to think she'd planted the currant bushes that are still growing along the side of the house, and there was the washing line that Dad had finally put up for her after weeks and weeks of nagging him.

Wish I could take a similar journey back in time to see you. I wonder if I would even recognize you. I think that if I heard you laugh, I'd know immediately it was you. Such fond memories. I miss you.

Love, your Gillian

~ ~ ~

"Do we have to?" moaned Will. He really wasn't that keen on getting out of the car to visit some old woman that his mother had once known well before he even existed.

"Yes, Will. I want Mrs. Walsh to meet you and, besides, it's a long time since I've seen her and I want to know how she is. Suzanne and I were really good friends when I lived here. I'd like to hear what she's up to these days. We won't stay long, I promise."

"That's what you always say," he mumbled.

Gillian got out of the car and walked up the front path to Mrs. Walsh's front door. It was a faded shade of the royal blue Gillian remembered. She rapped the brass doorknocker like she had done so many times before and then she waited. In the past, Suzanne would have come running to the door in an instant, but time had slowed things down considerably in this house since then. She could hear movement within so she knew Mr. or Mrs. Walsh was coming.

"Hello, Mrs. Walsh … remember me?" she said as an elderly woman cautiously opened the front door a few inches. "It's Gillian, Gillian Ev … I mean Mathers. We used to live next door."

"Gillian! Oh, my gosh … what a surprise. I didn't recognize you, child. You can't be too careful these days, can you? You can't just open the door to anybody anymore. What are you doing here? It's been years, my dear," exclaimed Mrs. Walsh as she ushered Gillian inside. Then she looked up and saw the handsome young man behind her … "and who is this good-looking youngster?" she asked.

"Mrs. Walsh, this is Will. He's my son. In fact, he just graduated from university. That's why I'm visiting out here. We drove up from Toronto because I thought it would be nice to show him where his mother had lived when we first came to Canada."

Mrs. Walsh steered them both into the small sitting room at the front of the house and they all sat down. For a few moments there was silence as both women studied one another assessing the inevitable passage of time etched into one another's faces as if trying to read how much pain, or how much joy, had visited the other over the years.

"And Mr. Walsh? How is he?" Gillian asked.

"Oh, he died years ago, my dear. I've been on my own for a good long while now. But, I'm used to it. Suzanne lives in Fredericton. I try to go out there once a year to see her. She's got a couple of grown up kids. She'll be so surprised when I tell her you've been to visit. It's a shame you didn't keep in touch. But, after all that business, I'll imagine you and your father wanted to make a clean break of it. How is your father, by the way?"

"He died about 15 years ago, I'm afraid."

"Oh, that's very sad, my dear. What a sad life he had. Did he ever re-marry?"

"No," replied Gillian. Her father had become such a reclusive and needy person, she couldn't have imagined him ever marrying again. "He lived out his life with his cousins in Winnipeg," she continued. "By that time, I'd moved to Vancouver. I was married and had two children. My eldest, Julie, is working in New Zealand at the moment."

"Young people these days," remarked Mrs. Walsh, "they're always on the move. Not me, I just stay here and watch everybody else around me come and go."

When she rose to step out to the kitchen and make tea for all of them, Will gave his mother 'the look'—he'd given her that same look ever since he was a boy whenever they were visiting somewhere he couldn't wait to escape from.

"Soon", his mother mouthed silently.

"There's a strange couple in your house these days. They've just moved in but the wife doesn't seem that friendly," said Mrs. Walsh when she returned to the sitting room with her old tea tray. "Oh, we've had some interesting people living there since you folk left. Richard Fulford, the writer, lived there for many years before he died. Such a nice man he was. It's hard to believe he was a homosexual. They say he died of AIDS, you know.

"After him, the Harpers moved in. It was nice to have a young family around again. I think they were here about ten years. He was a dentist and she was a lovely lady. We didn't socialize much, but I enjoyed watching their three bonny girls grow up. It reminded me of the days when you and Suzanne were coming and going all the time.

"And now, this Shepard woman and her husband. She's never invited me over. She'll stand on the front step forever gabbing away until my old legs are 'bout ready to give out, but never invites me in. Ah well, to each their own, I say. More tea?"

Forty minutes later, Gillian, and a much relieved Will, were back on the road.

"I don't know what the big deal was, Mum. You didn't

even live there that long," commented Will.

"I know, but it was an important house in many ways. Sad in many ways, but unforgettable. It still has a very strong hold on me. It sounds crazy, but I feel as though there's a piece of me still trapped in that house ... something more than just memories and grief. Ah well, I guess I'll never know for sure."

~ ~ ~

Dearest Teddy,

So strange to be back in Mrs. Walsh's living room again. Nothing much had changed and yet, as we all know, so much has. I wish I could have gone into our old house. I was never particularly happy there but it was the place where I wrote my first letter to you all those years ago. I think if Mrs. Walsh hadn't told me that the new owner wasn't very hospitable, I'd have been tempted to ring the doorbell and see if she'd invite me in for a quick tour.

This trip down memory lane has me wondering who lives in our old house in the village. Do you ever walk by and think about me? I'll bet you've not forgotten Mrs. Mathers' famous sponge cake! I've never stopped thinking about you, Teddy. You are always with me. I love you still.

Your Gillian

~ ~ ~

Dear Teddy,

Silly me ... I had assumed that once Will had completed his degree, he'd be eager to return to Vancouver, but he's started working for a firm in Mississauga (just west of Toronto) and is unlikely to move back here in the near future. He's got himself a good job ... entry-level environmental planner. It's what he wanted and, in this day and age, he's darned lucky to get work in his field of study. But, selfishly, I'm disappointed.

I guess I'll just have to keep busy. *Mr. P Goes To The Seaside* will be coming out in a few months and I'll be setting out on another reading tour. It's quite fun reading the stories out loud to fidgety children squirming on gymnasium floors. If it's a good story, they eventually become still and that's very satisfying.

This is the first one I've had to write on my new computer. My agent said that typewritten manuscripts are no longer appreciated and so I've had to learn to 'word process' ... which is little more than glorified typing anyway, so I don't know what all the fuss is about! I quite enjoy it actually. It's nice to be able to make mistakes and not have to white them out and wait for that wretched stuff to dry before typing over them. Maybe one day I'll be writing my letters to you on my computer too ... 'though I doubt it very much. There's not much warmth or humour in perfect typefaces and regiments of perfectly aligned exclamation marks!!!

~ ~ ~

Dear Teddy,

Are you getting all this Y2K nonsense in England too? It's amazing what's going on over here. People are hoarding water, canned food, batteries, generators ... and terrified that their computers and microwave ovens will cease to work in just a few hours !

So, how are you spending this momentous New Year's Eve? I'm at home alone hoping that my TV won't crash before the countdown at Time's Square is complete. It's exciting to be on the brink of a whole new century, isn't it? Wish I were celebrating with you. At least now I can say I've loved you in two centuries. What the heck, if the world comes to an end in a few hours perhaps that'll be our big chance to be together for eternity. There'd probably be a bit of a bottleneck to get into Heaven but I'm sure we'd find one another up there eventually … wouldn't we?

Feeling sentimental … I'll drink a toast to you my dearest and oldest friend. Love always, Gillian

P.S. Just realized … you're already in the 21st Century, eight hours ahead of us. What's it like so far?

~ ~ ~

Chapter 5- Letting Go

November 29th, 1994, was a date Norman and Muriel Shepard would never forget. It was a particularly cold and blustery evening; a harsh reminder that winter in the Ottawa Valley was getting serious. Eric, their son, announced that he was going out that night.

"I don't want a ride," he answered when his mother offered to drive him over to his friend's house. "I'm taking the bike. We're going across. Don't know when I'll be back," he added.

Still too young to drink legally in Ontario, Eric and his friends often went across to Quebec for a night of drinking and partying. Muriel didn't condone this behaviour but, like she said to her friends on many an occasion, "what can we do to stop them? They're not babies anymore."

Tonight, however, Norman decided to give it a try. It was a miserable night to be out on a motorbike. There was talk of freezing rain later that evening once the temperatures started dropping. He wasn't going to allow Eric to ride his motorbike on a potential skating rink.

"Not tonight, son. You're not going out on that lethal machine tonight," Norm told him.

Eric just shrugged and looked at his dad like it was some kind of joke. "Of course I'm going out," he sneered, "how you gonna stop me?"

Norm suddenly lunged forward and, taking his son completely by surprise, managed to grab Eric's keys from his right hand. That was probably not such a good idea in retrospect. It freed up Eric's fist to land a mighty punch on his father's face. Instantly, blood streamed from Norm's nose and both he and Muriel looked up at their son in disbelief. Eric had not been raised this way. His parents had never hit him and they had never seen him lash out physically like that before.

"Oh my God, look what you've done to your father," Muriel exclaimed. "What's got in to you, Eric?"

"Nothin'. I told you I was going out tonight and you're not going to stop me."

Eric reclaimed his keys. Norman had set them down on the hall table when he'd clasped his hands to his shattered nose.

"Let 'im go," Muriel said with a sigh, "it's not worth getting beaten up over this." She was busy gently mopping her husband's face with a damp cloth. "Be careful," she added over her shoulder as Eric grabbed his jacket and walked away. The front door slammed defiantly.

That was the last she and Norman saw of their son.

They were stunned when they got the call from the Ontario Provincial Police just forty-five minutes after Eric had stormed out of the house. He'd never even made it as far as the bridge that crossed over the Ottawa River. A family of four had been travelling south in a grey Ford minivan. The driver had lost control on a patch of ice and crossed the centre line of the highway. Eric had died instantly from the impact. He'd died perfectly sober and none of it was his fault. It was an accident ... nothing more, nothing less.

Norm cursed the wretched motorbike that he'd never wanted his son to have in the first place. He should have got rid of it a long time ago, well before Eric was old enough to ride. It had belonged to Norm's brother who had bought it to satisfy some random, short-lived mid-life craving but had soon concluded that it wasn't really his cup of tea ... he decided he was more of a kayaking, mountain biking kind of guy. He'd asked Norm to store it in his garage for him and he'd told his nephew, Eric, that he could ride it as soon as he got his license. Norm hadn't been happy with the arrangement but he hadn't stepped up and outright forbidden it, had he? No, so this was partly his fault, wasn't it?

Norm cursed the family in the hulking minivan. They'd all survived. One day, he thought to himself, their two precious little children will grow up and become defiant mouthy teenagers and that'll teach 'em what pain really is. Norm was not usually such an uncharitable soul, but his pain was deep and relentless and it often bubbled to the surface in unbecoming ways.

"We never saw it coming, did we Muriel? One day we had a cheeky young lad whose idea of trouble was plucking wings off flies or sneaking penny candy from the corner store. And then, before you know it, he's carrying condoms in his jeans pockets, stashing joints in his dresser and tearing around the countryside on a fucking motorbike."

Profanity was also out of character for Norm who never swore at home. In fact, he only used the f-word when he was around the guys at work—not because he liked to use it, but because it was what they all did and he wanted to fit in. It was probably the most versatile word in the English language ... useful as almost any part of speech. Using that word in front of his wife was merely an indication of how fucking awful and fucking useless he felt.

Muriel didn't flinch, in fact she didn't respond at all. She'd hardly spoken a word since news of the accident and her silence failed to give Norm the relief he'd once thought it could. There was a time when he'd have given anything if she'd just shut up for a few minutes so he could enjoy a moment's peace; but not this, he hadn't meant he'd give up Eric.

Norm cursed Eric for the huge space he'd left behind. It was a vast black hole and Norm spent most of his time keeping a lookout for the edges that might trip him and cause him to tumble right in. They would appear at the least expected moments … like when he was shaving a few days after the accident and thought back to the day he'd first noticed a little peach fuzz on his son's chin; now he'd never get to see him with a full beard. Or when he'd put out the garbage last night and remembered how many times he'd yelled at Eric to get off his fat ass and help with the chores. The black hole was behind him, it was beside him and, he feared, it was likely to remain in front of him for the rest of his life. He'd always have to watch his step.

Norman didn't return to his job at the fibreboard plant until after Christmas. He didn't really want to go back at all but he couldn't stay at home any longer with Muriel who spent her days drifting about the house like lost lint. She didn't speak, her face remained expressionless and even her footsteps had become silent. There was a time he knew exactly where she was at all times because she never used to do anything quietly, or without a running commentary even if there was no one else in the room with her. But now she was completely silent and he'd stumble upon her in unexpected places without warning.

She didn't go into Eric's room, but sometimes she'd stand in his bathroom and flip the top of his toothpaste open and closed over and over again. On several occasions, Norm had found her sitting cross-legged on the dirty concrete garage floor tracing the oil stain left by Eric's bike with her finger.

He couldn't bear it any longer. He decided they would have to move. It was time to sneak out from beneath the sadness, guilt and anger that were holding them hostage in their home and their lives. After a couple of weeks discreetly looking at real estate, Norman found them a lovely old house in Cobden. It would make his commute to work a bit longer, but he decided it would be worth it if the change could help jolt Muriel out of her current state. When Norm told Muriel they were going to move, she didn't seem to care one way or another, but at least she didn't offer any resistance to the idea and that was a great relief to him.

On moving day, Muriel sat quietly watching her friends and neighbours pack up the house, carefully loading things that Eric would never need again into boxes and stacking them by the front door. Muriel discovered that things that had once held meaning lost their hold on her when stuffed in boxes out of sight and, with each load, what had once been Eric's room soon became nothing more than a powerless empty space. People wandered in and out of the house carrying things, offering food and cups of tea, often stopping to ask her how she was doing. "Fine" she muttered indifferently as if it had absolutely nothing to do with her. In fact, she couldn't really remember when she'd last felt she was a participant in anything, least of all her own life.

They moved into 25 Champlain Street in the spring of 1995. Muriel went about doing what she assumed was expected of her, putting one foot in front of the other, setting the breakfast table each morning, hanging out the washing on Wednesdays, brushing her teeth before bed and, slowly but surely, unpacking the boxes and putting her house to rights. She actually quite enjoyed opening up boxes … hoping to find something unexpected inside even though, moments later, she'd be disappointed when nothing magical emerged. And so she'd move on to the next, reliving the cycle of anticipation and disappointment over and over again. Norm had told her she could buy a few new things for the house so, when all the boxes they'd brought with them were unpacked, she started to bring in new ones. Again and again, she experienced an anticipatory thrill as she plunged her X-Acto knife into the packing tape, lifted the cardboard flaps and peered inside. It was an extraordinary rush and, for that brief and fleeting moment, she could celebrate something shiny and new that had not been tainted by the death of her son.

Norm set off to work early every morning and, each evening, he'd return to a wife he was finally beginning to recognize again. She seemed very content sorting out their possessions and setting up their comfortable new home. She never complained. She no longer wrapped herself in silence, or sat on the sofa crying. Norm was both pleased and relieved; he'd made the right choice. The only thing he couldn't quite understand was why, despite all Muriel's hard work, she never seemed to run out of boxes to unpack.

As time went by the mountain of boxes failed to shrink—in fact, Norm began to suspect it was actually growing—and he began to notice an increasing number of unfamiliar objects around the place. Of course, he'd told Muriel she could buy a few new odds and ends for the new house thinking that would give her a bit of a lift, but it seemed there was now something new almost every day.

"Muriel, where did these come from?" he asked one evening as he cleared a pile of neatly folded multi-coloured chenille throws from his chair.

"Oh those?" she said, looking up from the magazine she was reading, "aren't they beautiful? They were such a deal. Six hand woven genuine chenille blankets for only $49.99, plus shipping of course."

"Plus shipping? Shipping from where? And what are

we going to do with six of these things?" he asked.

"I saw them on TV. It was a special offer," Muriel replied proudly, "lucky I was watching at that moment because the offer was only good for 29 minutes! Don't worry; I'll find a use for them. They're so soft and beautiful. Anyone would cherish them."

Muriel was beaming up at her husband. When had he last seen her smile like that, he thought? Ah well, it's just a few blankets. If they make her happy, where's the harm?

But, over the next few months, those few blankets became 'a few lampshades', 'a few soap dishes', 'a few crock pots' and so on. Unbeknownst to Norm, Muriel shopped from the moment he left for work until he returned. Sometimes, she even crept out of bed in the middle of the night while he was sleeping in order to get her shopping fix.

"I'm a collector," she'd insist if challenged.

"But, what are you collecting?" he'd ask. "You told me you wanted to collect figurines … so why are you buying all these hanging crystals?"

"Figurines? That was last month, Norm. These crystals are amazing. Some of them are even beneficial to your health," she'd answered triumphantly. "I've done my research, Norm. These are really special. Here …" she said, offering what looked to Norm like a chunk of broken glass, "this'll help you with your indigestion. Put it in your pocket for a couple of days and you'll see what I mean. I haven't had heartburn in ages."

"How much?" he demanded, "what did this piece of smashed up Coke bottle cost you?"

"Well, this one was a special one," Muriel began, "still, I got it for a good price. It's normally $119.00 for a piece like this. But I got it for only $69.00 and it came with a *free* velvet-lined box to keep it in. You wanna see?"

No, Norman didn't want to see. He didn't want to see

any velvet box, or his wife grinning up at him expectantly, or what the hell was happening to his marriage. He really preferred not to look at any of it even though you'd think he'd have learned his lesson about the consequences of avoidance after what happened to Eric. He put the 'magic' crystal back on the kitchen table and, without another word, walked out of the room.

Muriel's habit was ramping up. She simply couldn't help herself; the addiction demanded she feed it. Besides, a bargain was a bargain … even if she had absolutely no use for the items she was indiscriminately accumulating. She pored over the ads on the back of trashy magazines and sat glued to those awful television commercials that aired in the middle of the night on cable. If she saw or heard about a super-duper anything, she had to have it. K-Tel must have loved her. She had practically every useless gadget they'd ever produced—most of them still in their original packaging since she had no real interest in crushing ice or dicing vegetables at great speed. Her '*as seen on TV*' collection included classics like the smoke-swallowing ashtray, a record rack that flipped through LPs with the touch of a finger and, of course, enough lint gathering brushes and sticky rollers to clean all the dark suits on Bay Street several times over. She was addicted to the Shopping Channel and, credit card in hand, had spent more on those 'three easy payments' than any item could ever be worth. Muriel was feeding the black hole left by Eric's untimely death even though all the factories and sweatshops in Taiwan and China combined couldn't mass-produce enough of anything to satisfy it.

Norm continued to go to work and come home at the end of each day. But the accumulation of stuff was insidious; sort of like the mildew that crawls up the grout between the bathroom tiles, you don't really notice it until, one day, it is all you can see. Slowly, but surely, he was being entombed in stuff.

After just a few years, their home had become a warehouse of grief and futility, necktie organizers and 'miracle' cleansers. Norm wouldn't have survived without his work and his buddies at the plant. He could go to work for his 12-hour shift—plus overtime if there was any going—and forget everything for a while. Only at the end of the day, when he returned home and found another heap of useless gadgets and trinkets taking over his living room, was he forced to remember that this was now his life.

He knew he was slowly suffocating under the weight of the stuff. It was killing him … emotionally, spiritually and, he had to admit, financially. He detested the piles of junk lining every hallway and room in his home. He hated that his hard-earned money was being disposed of so recklessly. He despised the ever-present sadness in their home represented by the endless boxes of plastic re-sealable food containers and knitted toilet roll covers. He resented Muriel's emotional gluttony. And, he loathed himself for not being able to stand up and put an end to it all.

Muriel had deliberately chosen not to participate in her new community since the day they'd moved in. In fact, she rarely left the house except to pick up groceries. Her anonymity and isolation made her secret easier to maintain. No one—other than her husband—entered 25 Champlain Street during their occupancy. Neighbours occasionally appeared on her doorstep—sometimes collecting for a charity, or simply trying to be friendly (particularly Mrs. Walsh from next door)—but no one ever got past her. Deliverymen, eager to earn extra tips, would offer to carry particularly large or heavy items inside for her, but they never got further than the front porch. Even repairmen were unwelcome. If the plumbing needed fixing or a telephone jack replacing, Norm had to do it.

By 2008, the impact of the 'Great Recession' south of the border was being felt in Canada and, sadly for the Shepards, the lumber industry was one of its first casualties. At Christmas, after thirty years with the same company, Norm, along with many of his cohorts, was abruptly laid off. For some reason, Muriel believed it was now more important than ever to increase her 'inventory'. She assured her husband that she was focusing exclusively on quality items that would be easy to resell over the Internet and at local auctions.

"These are investments," she argued over and over again.

She'd suddenly started buying Victorian tea services, silver teaspoons, jewellery, old picture frames and vintage clothing. The credit cards were maxed out. The account that once held their savings had long since been closed. Norm couldn't have been under more stress and yet his attempts to convey the seriousness of their situation to Muriel fell on deaf ears … in part, it was his own fault because he never told her the complete truth. He didn't tell her he was behind on their mortgage, hadn't paid the electric bill in over four months and was barely making a dent in the interest on their credit card statements. Nor did he tell her about the collection agencies breathing down his neck.

But, all that was about to end. It happened one Saturday in June, 2009. Norm got up that morning, tripped on a new shipment of purses as he made his way to the kitchen to brew a pot of coffee in one of their 17 coffee makers, and suddenly realized just how sick of his life he really was. He was sick of the smell of shipping cartons. He was sick of dodging boxes and containers whenever he moved about his house. He was sick of hearing his wife telling him about her plans for selling her 'inventory' (as she called it) and how one day he'd be thanking her for her investment savvy and expertise as a discerning collector. He'd heard it a hundred times before. It meant nothing and, on this particular morning, he forced himself to admit that nothing would ever change unless he, the man of the house, pulled himself together and took charge. He would start that very day.

Ignoring his wife's desperate protestations and, for the first time in years, tuning out her sobs and pleas, Norm began reclaiming his house. He wasted no time sorting or even looking at the items concealed in their heavy damp boxes, he simply took whatever he had the strength to lift and dumped it on their front lawn. He began in the cupboard below the stairs and slowly worked his way upstairs. He worked non-stop for all the hours the day provided.

He was so fixed upon his task that he had no idea where his wife was, or even if she was upset anymore. He may have passed her several times in the hallway, or on the stairs, but he was blind to all but his mission. In fact, Muriel spent the day perched on the side of their bed. She never left the room. Once he'd got going, she'd put away her tears and arguments and wordlessly surrendered. All day, she listened to the sounds of things being shoved, pulled, tugged and tossed with Norm cursing and huffing and puffing as he struggled to undo all that she had done. By the end of the day, she had finally come to realize that there was not an un-opened box in the entire world that could ever contain what she was really seeking.

The last item Norm took out of his house was an old, mildewed leather suitcase that he'd found in the attic. It was, quite literally, falling apart and its journey to join the awaiting heap on the front lawn was almost too much for it. When the suitcase landed it popped open and a thin blue envelope fluttered unnoticed to the ground.

At 5 o'clock that same afternoon, a large truck with the

words 'Al's Auctions' painted on the side, pulled up outside 25 Champlain Street and everything that had been resting on the lawn went into it. The driver handed Norm a bundle of banknotes and drove away. Norm stuffed the sixty-five hundred dollars in his jeans pocket and, for the first time in over ten years, walked back in to a house where he could kick off his boots at the front door and hang his jacket in a closet without fear of being knocked out by an unstable stack of boxes and junk. He could run his fingers across the surface of a dining table he'd not seen in years. He could sit in his armchair without squashing some 'valuable' ornament or 'innovative' new tool. He suspected Al had grossly underpaid him and the cash would put barely a dent in his debts, but he didn't care. It was all gone and that was all that mattered.

The following morning, Mr. Campbell-Blair was out walking his dog when he noticed what looked like a blue envelope trapped amongst some leaves and litter by the side of the street. Curious, he stopped to pick it up and saw it was an airmail letter.

"Gosh", he muttered to his four-legged companion, "I haven't seen one of these in donkeys' years!"

The carefully printed return address on the back read '25 Champlain Street', which happened to be right across the street from where he was standing. So, on his return loop, he decided to place the envelope in the mailbox at 25 Champlain Street and let the people who lived there take care of it. They obviously checked their mail infrequently, he thought, as he forced it in among an assortment of other letters, bills and newsprint flyers.

After the almighty household purge, Muriel was left floundering in a sea of emotions, including guilt, despair and shame. But, the feeling that surprised her the most was relief and, because of it, she was finally free to grieve the death of her son … and grieve she did. Dark days stretched into dark weeks and Norm, now unemployed, stayed out of her way as much as he could.

Muriel was never the one to collect the mail, she was too afraid that if she lingered out front near the mailbox, Mrs. Walsh might suddenly appear and want to gossip. So, whenever Norm noticed the box was full, he'd grab whatever had accumulated inside and stuff it, sight unseen, into a compartment in his roll top desk. He never bothered to look at it anymore. He knew there was no point. It was just bills, more bills and batches of increasingly offensive and unpleasant demands and threats from various collection agencies.

But, by September, Norm's head-in-the-sand strategy was not working and, finally out of options, he and Muriel were forced out of their home with little more than the clothes on their backs. Muriel did not go quietly, but Norm didn't care. He took her in hand and dragged her and their meagre belongings down the street to the bus stop on the corner, passing all the curious neighbours who'd poked their heads out to see what all the screaming and hollering was about.

"They were such quiet people all the years they lived here, kept to themselves," remarked Mrs. Walsh to Mr. Peterson who lived across the street.

"Hrrmph", grunted Mr. Peterson in response; he really couldn't care less.

Norm and Muriel boarded a Greyhound bus to Ottawa and moved into a basement apartment in a low-rise building on Catherine Street where Norm had made arrangements with the landlord to work as the on-site manager and general dog's body in exchange for rent. Muriel stopped screaming when Norm stopped listening.

25 Champlain Street now belonged to the bank.

~ ~ ~

October 2008
Dearest Teddy,

Oh, what a dismal day it is outside. I look out from my window and it's as if the mountains have been wrapped in cotton wool. I remember days like this on the Fells, don't you? Those misty mornings when everything seemed so soft. Even sounds seemed softer for some reason.

How are you, my dearest? You have no idea how many times I ask myself that question hoping that somehow, some way, you will hear me. I don't like being alone, Teddy. Sometimes it scares me. It's difficult to keep track of things. I try to apply a routine to my days, but I'm not very disciplined I suppose. I'm still doing a bit of writing … this will be my fifteenth and final Mr. P adventure: *Mr. P Goes To Canada*. Wish it were true!

Love always, Gillian

~ ~ ~

All the Mr. P books were early-reader books with wonderful illustrations (not Gillian's as it turned out because her publishers preferred to employ their own illustrators). The tales were simple and, by today's standards, refreshingly innocent and unsophisticated. They were about ordinary people doing good things. Mr. P was portrayed as a friendly egg-shaped chap with a crop of curly red hair on his head. He wore egg-shaped spectacles and a dark navy carpenter's apron over a white shirt and lime green trousers. He wore his apron at all times—maybe even over his pajamas at night, but nobody knows that for sure. Sometimes its enormous pockets were filled with hammers and plumbing parts and sometimes with fishing gear and fishing hooks—it all depended on what he was about to do that particular day. When he embarked upon his trip to Canada in Gillian's final book, his pockets contained his passport, a book of crossword puzzles, an inflatable neck pillow for the long flight and two sticks of barley sugar to prevent his ears from popping during take-off and landing.

Gillian's first book, written back in 1979, opened with:

Every morning at precisely 7:20, Mr. Postlethwaite (known by the village children as 'Mr. P' because his name is almost impossible to pronounce if you have a loose tooth) hops out of bed to start his day.

It became the opening passage in every book thereafter. Her young fans memorized that first sentence, always adding an exaggerated lisp and plenty of flying spittle when they said 'Mr. Postlethwaite', and then dissolving into heaps of happy giggles. It was all good fun.

The first in the series, *Mr. P Goes To Work*, described a typical week in the life of a hardware shop owner:

On Monday, Mr. P mended Silly Gilly's bicycle chain.
On Tuesday, Mr. P sold Mr. Buildit a bag of screws for the shelves he was building for Mrs. Buildit.
On Wednesday, Mr. P oiled Bobby Blade's push mower.
On Thursday, Mr. P helped Miss Bloom choose some marigold seeds for her garden.
On Friday, Mr. P sold Mr. Buildit a can of white paint for the shelves he had finally finished putting up for Mrs.

Buildit.

On Saturday morning, Mr. P sold some birdseed for Mrs. Wren's budgie.

On Saturday afternoon, Mr. P counted up all his money and went home.

On Sunday, Mr. P went to Church in the morning and fishing in the afternoon.

The fourteen books that followed included many other stories taken from Gillian's memories of Teddy. She wove an amusing tale around the day that Teddy caught his fish-hook in the feathers of an angry duck. She mentioned Teddy's favourite meat paste and Marmite sandwiches in her story about his day at the seaside. She imagined the letter he might have written to a long lost friend in *Mr. P Posts A Letter*.

By the time Gillian wrote *Mr. P Goes To Canada*, it seemed like the moment to retire the good old egg in his iconic work apron had finally arrived. Children—and the parents who created them—expected so much more these days. If a storybook character wasn't 'merchandised'—that is, emblazoned on T-shirts, pencil cases and lunch boxes, or had its very own television cartoon show—it was unlikely to survive. Gillian's books had many loyal followers but, like her, they were part of an aging minority. Mr. P had run his course. Besides if, as Gillian hoped, Mr. P really did make it to Canada, what else was there left for him to do?

~ ~ ~

Dear Teddy,
Happy 2009!
Oh, how time drags by these days. Half the time

I don't even know what day it is. I have to tell you a funny story … last weekend I went to buy some fruit at my usual little shop. It's only a ten-minute walk and it was a particularly lovely day on Sunday, so I took a scenic detour. The strangest thing happened, I got completely lost! Lost in my own neighbourhood where I've been walking for years! I must have walked for hours because the sun was beginning to go down behind the mountains and I was getting chilly. I can laugh at it now, but at the time it was quite frightening. Eventually, I had to stop and ask a passer-by for directions. As it turned out, I was only a block away from home! What an old fuddy-duddy I'm becoming. I left the oven on overnight last week and came downstairs to an unusually warm kitchen before I realized what I'd done. Do you think I'm losing my marbles, Teddy?

~ ~ ~

July 2009,
Dear Teddy,
Will's home for a short visit. It's so nice to see him. He's been running around the house doing all sorts of little jobs for me. I think he thinks I'm not keeping up with things very well. He keeps saying things like: 'when was the last time this was cleaned?' Or, 'how long has this been leaking?' Honestly, I don't know. I don't seem to notice things like that. It's hard enough just getting up in the morning and remembering to eat breakfast these days! That's another thing Will's been harping on about. He thinks I'm not looking after myself properly. He actually *told* me to wash my hair the other day! What a nerve. I wish Julie were here.

She's staying out there, you know, or did I tell you

that already? She's got a new man. His name's Roger and he's some kind of sheep farmer, of course! Lots of family money, so that's always good. I suppose they might get married one day … neither of them are in their twenties anymore, so they'd better get cracking if they want to give me any grandchildren. The saddest part is that New Zealand is so far away. I ring her occasionally, but I always get the hours mixed up and catch her in the middle of the night. She's not the best conversationalist at that time of day.

~ ~ ~

"Look Mum, you're going to have to make up your mind. If you want to come to the wedding, I need to book your flight. It's only a month away," said Will for the umpteenth time. "We need to make plans."

He and Gillian had had this conversation almost daily since Julie announced her wedding date a few weeks earlier. Will was at his wits' end. One day she'd say 'yes' and the next she'd have a panic attack and beg him not to make her go.

"Why can't she get married here?" Gillian demanded. "Brides usually get married at their parents' home; it's tradition."

"Well, not this time, Mum. I've told you this before. Julie and Roger are getting married in New Zealand and there's nothing any of us can do about that! Now, for the last time, are you coming or not?"

~ ~ ~

September 2009
Dear Teddy,

Can you believe it, it's Julie's wedding day and, guess what, the 'mother of the bride' is not in attendance! Bruce went over and so did Will, but I don't think they wanted me to come. Will refused to even book a ticket for me and I can't do things like that myself anymore. I can't remember what Julie's husband's name is, but Will says he's very nice. Will's got a new job starting in January, right here in Vancouver. He's going to stay with me. He says it's just for a while, but I think Julie and he have put their heads together and decided I need someone to keep an eye on me. I guess Will drew the short straw! Ever since my fall in the spring—did I tell you about that? I'd left the bath running and dashed in to turn the tap off but water was already spilling over the rim and I slipped on the floor. It was such a silly mistake. The worst of it was that I sat there on the floor up to my waist in water for several hours with the water still running. It made an awful mess.

I phoned Will and told him it was raining in the kitchen and I couldn't stop laughing. He got angry and then called a plumber. And then a plastering guy came over and made an even worse mess, dust everywhere! I wrote my name on all the furniture with my finger. I even had a game of naughts and crosses with myself on the dining table top!

~ ~ ~

2010
Oh, Teddy, I woke in such a panic this morning. I couldn't remember the way to your shop. I told Will we had to go to the ironmonger's as soon as possible. He took me to some enormous do-it-yourself shop and kept screaming at me to tell him what I needed. I need you,

Teddy. But I told him I needed a hammer instead. He says it's the fifth hammer I've bought in as many weeks. I don't remember. I don't remember buying a hammer before. What would I need a hammer for? It's ridiculous. Sometimes I think Will is losing his mind! I have to be gentle with him, though. He's just a boy. He's my boy. I have a daughter too, but she's away at the moment. She must be at school. I haven't seen her for days.

This is the third night I've made Bruce's supper and he's not shown up. Where is he? Will says he doesn't live here anymore. That's absurd. He's my husband. Where else would he be living? I've decided that I'm not going to cook for him anymore, I'm that angry. I'll just keep putting the same plate of food out each night and he can eat it when he bothers to show up. It'll serve him right!

~ ~ ~

December 2010
Julie's here. It's Christmas. I've told her that I think Will's trying to kill me. He puts pills in my food so I try not to eat it. I have to sneak food from my own refrigerator. I have a stash of potatoes and a tin of custard powder under my bed for emergencies. I'm a prisoner here. Julie may be in on it too, so I have to be careful about what I say. She says she's going back soon … to her *husband*. What husband! She's just a schoolgirl. I hate it when my children lie to me. I brought them up to be better than that.

~ ~ ~

2011
Dear Teddy,

The young man that lives in my house forced me to go to that doctor again. The doctor in his spiffy white coat asked me such stupid questions! I know they're trying to get secrets out of me, but I keep telling them I don't know any secrets. Well, that's not entirely true. I remember about Mr. Hopkins and my mum, but they're not going to get me to spill the beans on that. The doctor told me to remember some words and say them back to him later. Why doesn't he just write them down on his notepad instead of asking me to remember things for him? I told him that. He just smiled at me. Stupid, stupid man.

~ ~ ~

Dear Teddy,

Back to the doctor again today. The man that lives in my house talked to him as if I wasn't even in the room. They said I needed to be *placed*. What does that mean? I kept asking over and over again what they were talking about. I screamed. I cried. I hit the man who tried to comfort me and then they gave me a needle and I think I went to sleep. It was a lovely sleep. I saw you, Teddy. I saw you. You looked so young and I am so old. How did that happen?

~ ~ ~

(Sometime early in 2012)

Dear t ... I dont know where i am. Im lost. How do you spel your namemy name is Gillian.

~ ~ ~

109

teddy … pls come and get me. i live in Canada.

~ ~ ~

In February 2012, Gillian wrote her last letter to Teddy Postlethwaite. Along with the thousands of other letters penned by her over the years, it was stuffed into her travel trunk which, along with her favourite armchair and her old Singer sewing machine, was the only other personal item in her room. In amongst her written letters, the trunk also contained a huge stack of blank aerogrammes. An aerogramme was a sheet of blue air mail paper that, once folded with its pre-cut flaps licked and stuck down, became a lightweight ready-to-post envelope edged in dark blue and red stripes. There was space for the addressee's information on the front and a return address on the back. By the time Gillian was settling in at The Serengeti Nursing Home, aerogrammes were no longer in use and most people wouldn't have known what they were. Judging by the ten cent prepaid postage on Gillian's stash, she must have been holding on to them for close to forty years.

Moving Gillian into a 'home' had been a very difficult decision for Will to make, especially since he had little or no support from Julie who was so far away she couldn't possibly understand how bad things had become at home since her last visit. Will could no longer leave his mother unattended and had had to hire a day nurse, but it still meant he was completely tied to her during the evenings, nights and weekends. His entire life revolved around work and mother-sitting and he knew he couldn't keep it up forever. Besides, his mother was quite nasty to him most of the time and it was become wearisome.

One evening, as he was getting her ready for bed, she accused him of trying to steal her letters to Teddy. Up until then, Will knew very little about his mother's obsession with her 'imaginary friend' (Bruce's term for whomever Gillian had been writing to for as long as he'd known her). Earlier that day, Will had lifted the lid of Gillian's travel trunk thinking it might be a suitable place to store all the clothing his mother no longer wore until he had a chance to donate it to the Sally Ann. He was completely unprepared for what he saw when he peered inside. There had to be a couple of thousand sealed letters inside … each of them addressed to a Mr. Teddy Postlethwaite.

"What the hell is this, Mum?" he'd called. "Who the hell is this Mr. Postlethwaite?"

"He's my boyfriend," she'd answered matter-of-factly, "and don't use that kind of language with me. I'll send you to your room."

"But these letters, Mum, why are they all here? You wrote *all* of these?"

"I did! And you can't have them … I'm watching you, young man. I won't have you stealing my letters to Teddy. I'll be taking them down to the post office one day very soon," she'd insisted.

"And, precisely when is that likely to be? Looks like you've been sitting on these for decades."

"I'll post them as soon as I hear back from him," she'd said.

"How long, Mum? How long have you been waiting to hear from him?"

"I don't know … it's been well over a month … he should've received my letter by now. It can take up to two weeks to get over there you know … that's how long it took for Granny's letter to get here."

And then she'd walked away and shut herself in the bathroom for a couple of hours. She often did this but, since Will had rigged the tap handles with childproof covers and removed the lock, he didn't worry about it. He was content to leave her in peace. Still, it was quite staggering to imagine her writing to this 'boyfriend' all this time and believing there was still a chance he might actually reply.

Will couldn't help but conclude that the mysterious Mr. Postlethwaite (ah, of course … the same name as the chap in the Mr. P stories!) probably figured far more prominently and significantly in his mother's life than his own father ever had, even if it was only in her mind. He wondered how much Bruce knew about this silent pen pal. Will was almost tempted to open up the letters one by one and start reading them but decided against it fearing that the contents could potentially ruin his version of his mother's life story and he didn't want to deal with that—at least, not for now.

It was only a couple of months after that incident that Will received a call from The Serengeti Nursing Home to let him know a place for his mother had 'become available'—meaning some old coot had kicked the bucket and they had an empty bed to fill. They advised him to snap it up immediately or Gillian's name would have to go to the bottom of the waiting list and another opportunity might not come up for months or even years.

Will's thoughts returned to a conversation he'd had with his father the day after Julie's wedding. It was the first and only time he and his father had discussed Gillian's decline and it hadn't gone well. He'd quickly realized that neither his father, nor his newlywed sister, was going to reach out and help him.

He and Bruce had been staying in a rudimentary shack on the beach at a place called Takaka on Tasman Bay. All the other wedding guests had already left and only the two of them remained. It took a trip to the other side of the world for Will and Bruce to sit down and have a proper chat.

"So, why'd you do it, Dad? Why did you leave us? Were you really that unhappy?"

"Oh, don't be so dramatic, Will … I never left you and Julie. Besides, you were both grown up by the time I moved out. It wasn't like I left your mother with two babies to raise by herself. The marriage had been over for years. I finally got around to packing my suitcases, that's all."

"But what about Mum? You used her. And, as soon as your children had left the nest, you decided you didn't need her anymore."

"Nothing's that simple, son," Bruce began, "and let's be completely frank here, shall we? Your mother wasn't easy to live with. She was so distant. She was completely wrapped up in you two when you were growing up—which was a good thing, I suppose—but between you, Julie and her imaginary friend, she didn't have time for me. I was on the road a lot and met people who were more interesting and interested in me. I liked the attention, I guess."

"Really? That's it? And what about us? Didn't you care about your own children? We hardly ever saw you when you lived with us and then, after you moved out and hooked up with Cheryl, it was like you were relieved to have that chapter of your life behind you once and for all. You left me to look after it all, Dad. You're always saying how well Julie's done and what a great life she's made for herself. What about me? You left me with no choice but to come home and take care of the messes you left behind: your ex-wife, the house, everything. It really pisses me off sometimes."

Will had never spoken to his father that way before. Something about being far away from home and their regular lives, sitting on a beach in the moonlight listening to the ocean breathing in and breathing out and, of course, enjoying some fine New Zealand wine, allowed Will to finally speak his pent-up truths.

"What could I do, Will? I think it's admirable that you're taking care of Gillian, but I have new responsibilities now. I have Cheryl and I have a new baby. It's not the same as it was when you and Julie were infants. Gillian looked after all of that but Cheryl expects me to 'participate' in everything! She dragged me to all the pre-natal classes to huff and puff with all the other happy couples. It was ridiculous! Women like your mother didn't have to attend classes to learn how to have babies. And now she expects me to take turns with her, getting up in the night if the baby needs something. I never had to do that with you guys. Next she'll want me to go to playgroups with all the other oppressed dads. I feel very cut off these days. Cheryl's friends aren't much older than you and Julie and my friends have stopped inviting us to cocktail parties and Sunday barbecues. And I can hardly invite them over to our house to sit in our Fischer-Price living room, can I?"

"If you're complaining, Dad, I'm not interested. You chose this. Did you really think you could spend the rest of your life basking in the attentions of this younger woman and give her a kid to play with like it was a new kitten? This is your child. You're stuck with this. Julie and I don't really want to hear about it. You made your choice."

"You make it sound like it was all my fault. As I've said before, living with your mother wasn't easy. There was always a wall up between us. I don't believe I was ever the love of her life. I think I was simply a reasonable alternative. I loved her, you know, and I think she loved me, but we were never passionate. I was lonely and I needed to fill up the empty spaces. I know you judge me for that. But your mother did it too … and we grew apart and became less and less interested in one another's lives. Cheryl was a breath of fresh air. She was young, vivacious, attentive, and I fell willingly. And you're right, Will, I've made my bed. But what about you, son? What about your life? Is there anyone special at the moment?"

"Are you kidding me, Dad? Like I'm going to bring some poor girl home to Mama's house where Mum'll be roaming around talking to herself or leaving taps on or sobbing in a corner. You don't get it, do you? Mum *is* my life at the moment. And it's going to get a whole lot worse before it gets any better. She's ill, Dad. She has dementia. Why can't you and Julie understand this? It's not that she's just a bit forgetful, she's sick."

"Are you really sure about that, Will? She was always a little off her rocker. I mean, her secret writing and her inane stories about Mr. P; perhaps she's just an eccentric old bat," Bruce chuckled.

Will looked at his dad and sighed. He'd had enough. There was nothing more to be said. Feeling a little wobbly from both the wine and the frustrating conversation, he stood up slowly. They had a long journey ahead of them the next day. He was suddenly very weary and it was time for bed.

"Night, Dad," he called over his shoulder.

"Night, son."

That was three years ago and Will had been on duty ever since. He was exhausted. Although he knew it was probably a waste of time, he called Julie for advice. He was tired of making all the decisions and he needed someone to back him up.

"What should I do?" he asked Julie.

He had only 24 hours to make up his mind about the newly available room at The Serengeti.

"I don't know. I mean, how bad is it really? Could you hang on a bit longer?"

"I don't know, Julie … maybe, but what if it turns into

another year or more? I need a break, Julie. If you were here, it would be OK, but I'm doing this all alone."

"It's your decision then, little brother. You know what's best for you ... and hopefully for Mum too."

Will didn't miss his sister's last few words and the subtle accusation they contained, but he didn't bother responding.

"Damn her!" he yelled, after they'd hung up. "She knows nothing about what I have to do to get through each day. She has no idea how difficult it is to protect Mum from herself ... make sure she doesn't turn on the stove or stroll out to the garden and forget to return. Or, how painful it is to watch her set the table for Dad every evening and then sit there, chin in her hands until bedtime waiting for him to come home. And then, the personal care ... never did I think I'd be reminding my mother to wipe her bottom, or helping her brush her teeth! And all the time, she's yelling at me, or crying, or laughing at something that isn't even funny. Most of the time, she thinks I'm an intruder ... 'where did *you* come from', she screams, or 'how did you get into *my* house? I'll call the police!' It's hell on earth living with this mad woman. I never spend time with any of my friends ... in fact, I don't even remember who my friends are anymore! I don't go to movies or out to restaurants ... when was the last time I went on a holiday? Julie's wedding, that was it. Some holiday that turned out to be ... listening to Dad complain about Cheryl and the brat they're raising and going on and on about how well Julie has done for herself: 'at least she stepped up and took a few risks and started a new life,' he'd said. Well, yeah ... so did I, for a while. Do you really think I wanted to move back to 'Mummy's house' at the age of 36! Julie, Julie, Julie ... it's always about Julie. Well, damn it! This time it's about me and I'm not ashamed to say so! YES, Serengeti ... how soon can I drop her off?"

Gillian knew very little about the move from her Vancouver house to the Home, but she knew enough to insist that her travel trunk accompany her. "I won't leave my Teddy alone with that young man living in my house; I don't trust him!"

At The Serengeti Nursing Home, families were encouraged to make their loved-one's room feel as much like home as possible, so there were no objections to her bringing her travel trunk and a few other small furnishings. After all, it was rather exciting to have a well-known author in residence; the staff wanted to make her feel as comfortable as possible. Many of the younger nurses had grown up listening to their parents reading the Mr. P books to them; perhaps they could convince Ms. Evans to autograph a few copies.

Time meant nothing to Gillian anymore. When she arose each day she had no idea whether it was a day she was supposed to meet Teddy at the ice cream shop, or whether she was supposed to be preparing for a school exam.

"Where's my satchel?" she'd scream accusingly at the nurses and other residents. "Why don't you leave it by the front door where I put it so I don't have to go looking all over the house for it? I have a Maths test today and I need to revise. Why don't you all just leave my stuff alone! Now I'm going to be late."

For Gillian, every day began as a mystery and, by day's end, most mysteries remained unsolved. All Gillian knew for certain was that her boyfriend would come soon.

When she'd first moved into the facility, she'd cried for Teddy day and night. The staff assumed she wanted a teddy bear and so they all chipped in to buy her the biggest, fluffiest, most gorgeous honey-brown teddy bear they could find. Like a spoiled child whose Christmas wishes had not been met, she looked at it briefly and then cast it aside.

"I don't want *that*. I'm not a baby!" she snapped and went back to crying for Teddy.

But, despite her irascible temper and unpredictable moods, Gillian was well looked after. She received three square meals a day, medical treatment when needed and professional care by friendly, kind and patient nurses who wore brightly coloured uniforms with smiley faces or frolicking bunny rabbits on them. What a happy haven it was!

Will visited his mother every week without fail. And, every week without fail, Gillian would denounce him. It was very painful for Will and there were times when he resented his sister, Julie, for not being nearby to share not only the responsibilities, but also the pain of rejection. He'd lost his mother by increments over the past few years and yet it never got any easier to see her familiar physical form in front of him and know that she didn't have a clue who he was.

"I know who you are!" she'd scream and, for a very short-lived moment, Will would think, 'she knows me, she's getting better' … but, of course, she'd follow with: "you're the chap who brings the school milk, aren't you? You needn't bother. I never drink the ghastly stuff anyway!"

Other times she'd think he was one of the orderlies, a film star, or even a bank robber … but never just Will. As far as Will could tell, his mother was completely unaware that she had, or had ever had, any children, or an ex-husband … the only person that seemed to exist in her life was her wretched Teddy!

"There's not much point in my coming all that way if she's not even going to know who I am," Julie repeated for the umpteenth time when last they spoke.

"That's not the point, Julie. I could use some help. Mum's well looked after now, but I still have this falling-apart house to fix up and sell so that I can pay the bills and make sure she can have proper care until the end. She could go on like this for years. It's a lot of pressure on me and you contribute nothing!"

Apparently whatever family money Roger was purported to have access to, there was none about to come Will's way.

"It's a difficult time for us, Will. Since Roger hurt his back he's hardly worked and, with the two girls and another on the way to take care of, there isn't a penny to spare. Perhaps you should ask Dad to help."

Will had, in fact, done just that a few months before but Bruce had said it really wasn't his problem. "Sell the house, son, that's the best thing to do, it'll give you some cash."

"Yeah," thought Will despondently, "and leave me homeless to boot."

Chapter 6 - Found It!

Georgiana Harris let herself out through the back door and strolled unnoticed across the parking lot to her car for the last time. She couldn't face leaving via the front door and having to walk through the main lobby and endure any more tearful farewells. Her departure marked the end of an era. Georgina's family had owned and run Kaufmann's Dairy & Cheese Factory for four generations. When her great-grandparents arrived in Canada they started a dairy farm near Kemptville, Ontario. Then, a generation later, her grandparents added the cheese factory. The next generation sold off the farm but kept the dairy and factory. And now, here was Georgina, sixty-something years old with no heirs or relatives to pass the business on to, and with no other option but to sell it. She felt a mixture of relief, guilt and grief. After all, she had practically grown up in the factory. Apart from the few years she'd been away at college, she had always lived on-site and so, by selling the business and property, she had also sold her home.

But here was her chance, finally, to break out on her own. She'd always loved the Ottawa Valley and still had a few cousins farming in the area, so that was where her house hunting began. It didn't take her long to find a charming old brick home in the small town of Cobden. The real estate agent explained that it was a foreclosure and the bank was keen to unload it. Georgina was delighted when her offer on 25 Champlain Street was accepted by the Court.

Georgina Harris had lived a fairly sheltered life. Her world revolved around milk and cheddar. She had worked in the dairy as a child and spent her entire adult working life at the factory. Her parents worried that she rarely went out with young men and kept herself to herself most of the time. Some of the locals called her unpleasant names assuming that she must be a lesbian, or a man-hater, or something that was equally offensive in their parochial minds. But, after her parents died and she was forced to take over the reins of the business, her fairness, hard work and generosity soon earned her the respect and affection of her employees. It seemed that Georgina Harris had finally found her stride. She accepted her lot in life and rarely yearned for the more traditional domestic set-up she and her parents had assumed would someday be hers. Secretly, she considered her employees to be her 'family' and she lived vicariously through all their domestic woes and triumphs. She was also an avid reader of romance novels and a loyal follower of several television soap operas. Her own romantic experience was limited to one or two high school and college boyfriends and a brief, but painful, romance with one of the Kaufmann's Cheese Factory salesmen. The end of that relationship had been tragic and Georgina vowed never ever to let her heart be torn asunder again. She much preferred the romantic shenanigans of other people, real or fictional.

On Friday, January 15, 2010, Georgina moved into her new house. She was so excited to finally, at the age of 61, be 'leaving home'. The house was probably a little large for her needs, but she decided she could always resurrect the original back staircase if she decided to convert it into two residences. She thought it might be fun to be a landlady, particularly if she was able to find tenants with interesting and dramatic lives to amuse her.

Georgina didn't have a vast collection of possessions to bring to her new home but the previous owners had obviously departed in haste and had left behind a few functional pieces of furniture, including a roll top desk, two bed frames, a kitchen table and several bookshelves. Besides, to start with, Georgina planned to live only on the first and second floors. The attic would serve as storage for the time being.

Several days after her arrival, Mrs. Walsh, from next door, came by with a warm apple pie to welcome her to the street. Georgina was delighted to meet someone who knew all the neighbourhood gossip and Mrs. Walsh was equally happy to finally find someone who wanted to hear it.

"Well, there's quite a history to this house," she began after Georgina had poured them both a dry sherry. Georgina had insisted that her new life be toasted with a proper drink rather than a cup of tea and Mrs. Walsh had been happy to comply.

"We've had all sorts living here, my dear. There was a family from England living here years and years ago. That was back when Mr. Walsh and I first moved next door. Then the mother upped and killed herself, you know. It was very sad, leaving her husband and her daughter behind like that. The husband took his daughter and moved west shortly after.

"After they left, we had that author … Fulford was his name. He was a quiet sort, kept to himself, you know. But he was a gentleman nonetheless. After Mr. Walsh died, he'd come over and help me with things around the house. Turned out he was a homosexual of all things, but I didn't know that until after he died of course."

"Can I top up your glass?" Georgina interjected. She

was keen to keep the narrative going.

"… and then there was the Harper family. They were nice people. They had three girls and he joined old Dr. Lennon's dental practice here in town. They stayed about ten years, I think; it was nice to have children running around the yard again. Their middle girl—Bethany, I think her name was—she was a bit of a handful, 'specially once she got involved with young Billy Taylor. I'd see her and Billy parked in the back lane here right behind my house … steaming up the windows they were, and then, innocent as can be, she'd walk back into her house and her parents probably never new a thing about it. Like I always say, where there's love there's bound to be secrets. Bethany came back here a year or so after her family left, but Billy had already moved on. Young love rarely lasts."

"Sometimes it does," Georgina said, thinking about Luke and Laura on *General Hospital*, but Mrs. Walsh didn't appear to have heard her. She kept on talking.

"After that, the Shepards moved in. I never took to Mrs. Shepard. She kept pretty much to herself, never even invited me in if I dropped by to say 'hello'. I often wondered if she was running some kind of shady business out of the house. There were deliverymen coming and going practically every day to drop off various boxes and parcels. And then there was the foreclosure on their house. If she was running some kind of business, I guess it wasn't doing too well, or perhaps the law caught up with them. They were here one day and gone the next. I remember poor Mr. Shepard dragging his wife kicking and screaming down the street when they left … everyone could hear her calling him all sorts of names. What a spectacle! I can't say I was sad to see them go. But I didn't like seeing the house empty; it was like living beside a skeleton. So I'm glad you're here Mrs. Harris … oh, listen to me jabbering away. I'm sure you're not interested in all this past history."

"Oh, but I most certainly am, Mrs. Walsh and it's *Miss* Harris, actually. Never married. But please, call me Georgina."

"OK, Georgina. That's a nice name. Never married, eh? None of my business, I suppose, but what's a woman of your age doing moving up here all alone? Are you one of those homosexuals too? Don't mind if you are. I'm not that stuck in my ways, you know … just curious why you'd want to come to a new town all by yourself."

"Well," began Georgina, "First of all, no I'm *not* a lesbian. I've worked all my life and now I am retired and I'm looking for a peaceful, friendly place to spend the rest of my years. Besides, I know this area fairly well. I have cousins who farm around here and I've always been a country girl. I suppose I could have bought a little condo in the city, but this house called to me as soon as I saw it."

"It's a bit big for just one person, don't you think?"

"Maybe," Georgina answered, "but if I find I'm rattling around in it, I'll get a roommate or a big dog!"

"Well," said Mrs. Walsh, slowly hoisting herself up and out of her chair, "I should be on my way. I'm sure you have plenty more interesting things to do than sit around listening to the tales of an old lady. I'm glad you're here, Georgina. I think we will be good friends. If you need anything, you know where I am; I'm home most of the time."

Georgina liked the elderly lady and, after seeing her safely home, she allowed herself another glass of sherry and settled in to watch *The Young And The Restless*. "This is going to be perfect," she thought out loud.

Over the next couple of years Georgina became a valuable member of her new community. She volunteered at the local library several times a week, delivered Meals-on-

Wheels to a number of elderly people in town and partici-
pated in a book club. The book club was a bit of an ordeal
because many of the bright, young, university-educated
women involved liked to read rather esoteric novels with
explicit sex and hidden meanings so obtuse that Georgina
rarely understood them. It was only when it was her turn to
choose the book that she really got involved in the discussion even if some of the women dismissed her selections as
'fluff', or 'too predictable'.

Georgina had read *The Bridges of Madison County* a
dozen times and never tired of it.

"It's a ridiculous story," exclaimed Hermione Potter at
one of their monthly meetings. "There's no way that little
country housewife would have primped and preened to im-
press a complete stranger. She didn't have it in her! And
then to go back to her husband like nothing had happened?
It's not believable on any level."

"How would you know?" challenged Georgina. "Have
you never indulged in a fantasy … be it with a real person or
an imaginary one? Francesca had an opportunity presented
to her and she took it. He showed her what her life might
have been like and she treasured that glimpse. That's why it
was all so sad."

"It wasn't sad at all," Hermione persisted, "it was pathetic. She was pathetic. She had a family and a duty to remain loyal to them. This Kincaid guy wasn't the real thing
and I don't think an unsophisticated woman would fall for
him in that way and then cling to those memories forever
like she did."

"I disagree," said Georgina. "I think there are many
people in this world whose happiness is sustained in part
by reliving short-lived moments and stretching them into
eternity."

Georgina felt sorry for Hermiones of the world who

lived their lives so literally. She concluded that Hermione was probably very unhappy with her life; why else would she resent possibilities and fanciful escapes so vehemently? On the other hand, Georgina recognized that her own preoccupation with fantasy and escape was likely due to a dearth of real life experiences in her own life; but, it had served her well thus far and she wasn't about to abandon the 'Lukes and Lauras' and the 'Francescas and Roberts' who inhabited her imagination and made her uneventful and ordinary life more interesting.

More than a year went by before Georgina got around to investigating the contents of the roll top desk the previous owners had left behind. It was a particularly cold and unpleasant wintry day outside, so Georgina saw it as a good opportunity to hunker down and tackle some of the jobs that she'd been postponing for so long.

The desk had remained in the second bedroom upstairs ever since she'd moved in. Occasionally she dusted it, but she rarely opened the top or any of the drawers because she knew she'd then have to deal with the old papers, broken pencils, bent paperclips and dirty-looking loose change that the Shepards had abandoned. Cleaning it out seemed like a rather uninspiring task but today she told herself she'd get it done. Besides, she liked the idea of filling it up later with her own things.

Armed with a garbage bag, she quickly sorted through the contents of the shallow drawer below the writing surface. It contained the usual scraps of paper, old receipts, candy wrappers, dried up pens and thumbtacks that most people accumulate over time. She scooped up the lot and dumped them into the bag. Next, she carefully raised the roll top, making a mental note to wax it one day soon as it didn't move very smoothly. She pulled out the miniature drawers above the working surface at the back of the desk and quickly tipped their contents into the bag. Again, there was nothing worth keeping.

Finally, she opened the little door to a cubbyhole in the centre of the back of the desk. It was stuffed with envelopes of various shapes and sizes. Most of them looked like unopened bills. Several—including envelopes from Sears, Mastercard, Mike's Motors and the Government of Canada—were stamped 'final notice', or 'urgent' on the outside. There were also handfuls of unopened Christmas cards going back as far as 2002, a glossy flyer promoting a sale on lawnmowers at Canadian Tire and a black and white pamphlet introducing a local political candidate.

And then, just as she was about to consign the whole lot to the garbage, she saw a thin, blue, airmail letter in amongst all the others. It caught her attention because she hadn't seen one of those folded aerogramme forms in years, maybe decades. She dropped everything else and took a proper look at the blue envelope. It was addressed to a Mr. Postlethwaite somewhere in England and the return address on the reverse side was '25 Champlain Street'. The age of the letter, and the mysterious fact that it had never been sent, were most intriguing. She knew it couldn't have belonged to the Shepherds. Mrs. Walsh said they'd moved in some time in the 1990s and this letter was considerably older than that.

Georgina tucked it in her pocket and finished cleaning out the desk. Later that evening, she poured herself a sherry and sat down to examine the letter properly. Needless to say, she was very tempted to open it. The potential contents of this missive were limited only by her imagination: perhaps it was a sad letter announcing the death of a dear relative, or a letter planning an upcoming trip to visit the recipient in England, or maybe it could even contain the final words of a dying lover far from home. Whatever it was, the intended recipient never heard about his deceased relative, never showed up at the airport to greet his friend and never discovered the fate of his true love.

As custodian of this intriguing secret, should she open it, or not? What if she stuck on a few extra stamps and simply posted it? Would that be the right and moral thing to do? What if it contained some information that radically altered, or even ruined, the life of this Mr. Postlethwaite?

While contemplating her dilemma, she casually toyed with one of the loose flaps on the envelope. It would be so easy, she mused, to slit it open, read it and then, if it seemed appropriate, tape it up and send it on its way. On the other hand, the message within might contain something she'd be better off not knowing—someone confessing to a particularly sordid murder, or someone engaged in some sort of blackmail perhaps—besides, it clearly wasn't intended for her.

Suddenly, imagining herself as Theresa Osborne from Nicholas Sparks', *Message In A Bottle*, she decided her moral obligation was to do whatever she could to ensure it arrived safely at its intended destination—better late than never. Of course, in Nicholas Sparks' book, Theresa reads the message but, thought Georgina, this is different because it's sealed.

She could hardly sleep that night. It was all so exciting! She loved a mystery and she desperately hoped that her part in this one was only just beginning. First thing the following morning, she walked to the post office and, after purchasing sufficient postage, dropped the flimsy blue aerogramme in the mailbox. On its way ... finally.

Chapter 7 - New Friends

It had been a record-setting Christmas season for Postleth-waite's Home & Garden Supplies. Ever since Teddy had in-troduced interior decorating products and up-market garden tools and accessories for the urban gardener (who didn't re-ally like to get his or her hands dirty), his shops had become big players during the gift-giving seasons. In the old days, few people thought to pick up presents for their loved ones at an ironmonger's, but things had changed since his father's day. As of Christmas, 2011, there were thirteen Postleth-waite's Home & Garden stores dotted around the north of England. The original shop, on High Street in Hawesdale, still remained but it was not particularly profitable. Teddy hung on to it more out of sentiment than anything else. Be-sides, he still liked to escape from the city now and again and hunker down in the flat above the shop. He'd done it all up years ago imagining that one day he'd be sharing it with Gillian; absurd to think like that after all this time.

More than fifty years had passed since Teddy last saw Gillian. She'd never written to him and yet he'd never stopped thinking about her. He still remembered her beau-tiful hazel eyes and long auburn hair. He remembered the smell of Pears soap on her skin. He remembered her shyness and, at the same time, her determination and stubbornness.

She had promised they would be together and that no parents, no ocean, no passage of time could, or would, keep them apart. They had both pledged their endless love to one another on that last night. He'd believed her then and, sadly, he still wanted to believe her even now.

"Silly old man, that's what I've become," he mumbled to himself one Friday evening as he sat wedged in traffic in his car. He'd had a busy week and the drive to Hawesdale from Leeds had been at a tedious crawl. Coming home to the flat was just like stepping into an old pair of shoes and he couldn't wait to get there.

'Silly old man' he might be, but he was also a wealthy, successful and extraordinarily good businessman. The only trouble was he had no one to share the fruits of his labours with. On the other hand, perhaps the fruits of his labours would not have become so abundant had he been distracted by a normal family life with a wife and children and all the obligations that accompany them. Instead, Teddy had poured his entire heart and soul into his work. He'd achieved things his father had never even conceived of. No more handwritten ledger books, IOUs from unreliable customers, or free advice doled out over cups of tea. This was the age of computerized inventories, websites, point-of-sales machines and struggling to keep up with the high expectations of customers whose loyalty, in the face of so many options, had to be earned and re-earned time and time again. Teddy had got on board with it all and met every challenge head on. He loved it.

But, for the next few days, he would let it all be. He'd got through the Christmas season and was going to enjoy a few days walking in the Fells, perhaps casting a fishing line or two and, as always happened when he returned to the village, thinking about Gill. It was a self-indulgence he secretly relished and it amused him to know that this sort of romantic daydreaming was something his colleagues and employees would never, in a million years, attribute to him. They saw him as the well-dressed corporate figurehead who lived the good life. They admired and respected him, but few would consider him a sentimental soul, or imagine him trudging about the Fells on a rainy day in his favourite muddy boots.

The next morning, Teddy arose after a wonderful, deep sleep—he could always count on a good night's sleep at the flat—and headed across the road to buy his morning cappuccino. Oh yes, things had definitely changed in the sleepy little village of Hawesdale. It was now a bit of a tourist Mecca, catering to weekenders and other holidaymakers from Leeds, London and elsewhere.

Audrey Frobisher's post office had all but disappeared. Nowadays postal transactions were handled in a small cubicle at the back of an arts and crafts shop that sold local pottery, a few postcards and other useless items of interest only to tourists. As in many popular small communities, the residents complained about the out-of-towners and how they treated the locals as if they were actors on a film set instead of real people going about their daily business. But, those very same residents were also the shopkeeperw, B & B hosts and café owners whose livelihoods depended on those 'dreadful' outsiders.

Teddy recalled a conversation he'd overheard in the pub the previous evening. It was the same conversation he'd heard many times before and would undoubtedly hear many times again until there was no one left to initiate it:

"I remember back in the day when going to the pub was like dropping in on friends," one old-timer remarked to another, "now I look around and most of the people in here don't even know my name."

"And all this fancy food," added another with disdain.

"I remember when a good ol' hot pot or bangers 'n mash was all we needed. What's this raw fish they're serving these days? *Sooshy*, they call it. Give me cod 'n chips in a proper newspaper any day. At least you know it's cooked proper."

"Good morning, Mr. Postlethwaite," called young Tim, the postman, as Teddy stepped out onto the street. Of course, he wasn't really 'young' Tim anymore. The lad must be well into his forties, thought Teddy with a smile.

"Are you staying for a while?" Tim asked.

"Just a few days, Tim," Teddy replied.

"Well, I'll be dropping by your place later. There's a letter for you."

"Here?" asked Teddy with surprise. Hawesdale had not been his home for decades. All his post, personal and otherwise, went to his flat in Leeds.

"Yep. I'll be by with it later on today."

"Thanks, Tim."

Teddy went on with his day. He savoured his cup of coffee and read the newspaper at leisure without interruption. He heard the occasional mobile screaming for someone's attention at another table, but not his. He'd left his in the flat as he always did when he was taking a break in Hawesdale.

Later that morning, despite the damp and drizzly weather, he walked down Repton Lane as he had many, many times before. Of course, it too had changed. A cluster of modern bungalows at the end had taken over a couple of former farmers' fields. Still, it wasn't long before Teddy was up in the unspoiled Fells, climbing over the same old stiles and gates that he and Gillian had clambered over so many years before. Up here, one could almost believe the world had not altered since 1959. Bittersweet, as they say. Often there was little to separate Teddy's pleasant memories of the past from an all-consuming sadness. Why had she never written? He never understood it. Equally, why had he never just hopped on a plane and gone over there to find her? The answer had to be fear. Perhaps hanging on to the dream was preferable to having it torn apart by a reality he might not want to accept. She could be dead for all he knew. She could be married to that great big lumberjack he'd teased her about so many years ago. Perhaps the worst thing of all would be to discover she'd never really loved him and that as soon as they had parted, she'd forgotten him. Yes, he thought, that would be the worst—worse even than her death.

He walked and walked that day and, as he did so, he allowed his mind to go to the best and the worst of the memories left behind by his beloved Gillian.

He kicked himself for being so timid back then. Gillian always had a plan. He smiled as he remembered the day she'd announced she would become a writer one day. And what had he replied? Nothing … he had been content to stay put and do nothing more than was required of him, or so he thought. Why didn't he speak up that day and tell the truth? Why didn't he put a voice to his own dreams and trust her enough to hear them without ridiculing him? Here he was, all alone now … walking in the rain on weekends but driving a Mercedes during the week and she'd never get to know these things about him. Perhaps she would have loved him enough to stay in touch had she known there was going to be more to him in the future.

Next he thought back to their first trip to the cinema together. He couldn't recall the name of the film, but he remembered how proud and happy he was to be sitting holding her hand in the dark. It was a matinee and the audience had been full of squealing children holding sticky ice lollies, but he was holding her hand and that was all that had mattered at the time.

They'd put on so many miles together in such a short

time … walking the Fells and strolling around the village, dodging people who might tell Mr. Mathers they'd been seen together. It was fun … good clean fun. And the kisses … so many kisses and stolen embraces. He remembered the feel of her small breasts beneath his clumsy hands and that lovely curve in her back where he rested his arm to draw her closer in to him. Of course, he'd done much more with many more since those days, but nothing and no one came close to matching the magic of the moments he'd shared with Gillian.

She'd ruined him forever. How could he be glad of it and yet so angry about it at the same time? All she'd had to do was write him a letter … one letter, that's all.

The light was beginning to fade and it was late afternoon by the time Teddy strolled back to the village. He walked into the shop and greeted Bradley Hamilton who was busy counting the day's takings from the cash register. Bradley had managed Postlethwaite's Ironmonger's for close to twenty years. He employed his son and his daughter-in-law and his wife took care of the accounting. Bradley and his family were so well-liked in the community that many of the more recently landed locals referred to the shop as 'Bradley's' despite the Postlethwaite's sign that still hung over the door. Teddy didn't mind. He liked the Hamilton family and he liked the time warp this little shop seemed trapped in. It was still a place where customers could come in and discuss their projects, receive a little common sense advice and, at the same time, purchase most of the tools and supplies they needed for everyday home and garden projects. Bradley himself had always been a dependable manager. He was roughly the same age as Teddy, a tall slender man with a good head of grey hair remaining. He wore tortoiseshell NHS glasses, had imperfect British teeth and was always affable.

"Miserable day to be out walking," he remarked as Teddy came inside.

"Oh, it was fine. I'm used to it. How was your day, Bradley?"

"Busy enough, I reckon."

Bradley rarely discussed business with Teddy unless they had arranged a meeting specifically for that purpose. He knew that when Teddy came to Hawesdale, it was to get away from work and to recharge his batteries. He respected Teddy's privacy. He'd never ventured up to the flat above even though he'd always held a key for it and Teddy had never invited him to.

"By the way, young Tim dropped this off for you," said Bradley, holding up a flimsy blue envelope. Teddy took it from him. Instantly he thought he recognized the handwriting on the front of the envelope, but realized that was impossible. Then, he turned it over carefully and saw the Canadian return address and knew he hadn't been mistaken after all.

"You OK Teddy? You suddenly look a little peaky. Perhaps you caught a chill out there. Shall I make you a nice hot brew?"

Indeed, the rosy cheeks Teddy had earned from his day's ramblings had suddenly lost their bloom. Not trusting his own voice, Teddy had to ignore Bradley's offer of a cup of tea. Instead, while struggling to maintain his composure, he commanded his wobbly legs to walk to the back of the shop, climb the stairs and deliver him safely to the sanctuary of his flat.

~ ~ ~

'Exile'
25 Champlain Street,
Cobden, Ontario,
Canada

April 14th, 1959,

My dear Teddy,
I can't believe I'm here. It's just so awful knowing
how far apart we are. The aeroplane flight was dreadful … I'll write every day but I need to be sure you've
received this …Teddy, I need your letters more than anything right now … no, I need your kisses more.
Missing you, love always, Gillian xx
P.S. Haven't met any lumberjacks yet! (And I hope
I never do.)

~ ~ ~

Cromwell Court
10 Bowman Lane
Leeds, UK

January 15, 2012

Dearest, darling Gillian,
Where do I begin? Well, first and foremost, you cannot imagine the mixed emotions I experienced when I
received your letter. I've waited most of my life for this
and, while it brings me great joy to know my patience
has finally been rewarded, it also brings me deep sadness to know that we have lost so many precious decades.
It was pure chance that I happened to be in the vil-

lage when your letter arrived. As you can see from my return address at the top of the page, I now live in a flat in Leeds. Big change for a country boy, wouldn't you agree?

But, of course, for both of us, there have been many changes. Your letter is so old, I don't even know if you still live at the address provided, but I hope that whoever does live there will know of your current whereabouts and forward this letter to you. I can't help but wonder where it has been all this time … I'm sure it would have a story to tell.

And, I suppose, if I am honest, considering how many years have gone by since you wrote, I can't even be certain that you will want to hear from me now. I only hope that you have kept and treasured the memories of us as I have over the years and that this opportunity to re-connect is will be as joyful for you as it is to me.

I do not know where to start with my questions … there is so much I need and want to know. Perhaps I'll just come out and ask you directly—rip off the sticking plaster, so to speak—are you married? I'm not. Never have been … never even come close, to tell the truth.

When I visit Hawesdale, I stay in the flat above the shop. I moved in after Dad and Audrey got married (remember Miss Frobisher from the post office?) and I did it up especially for us. I always thought you'd come back to me. I've not done much to it in the ensuing years because I like it just the way it is. It's familiar to me and it is the one place I feel truly at home. All that's lacking is a woman's touch … your touch.

I'm sorry to hear you're not keen on your 'new' house. Of course, it was a long time ago that you wrote that … perhaps you have grown to like it since? I should certainly hope so.

How are your parents? I was always quite fond of your mother but, as you know, less so of your father. I try not to blame him for taking you away from me, but it's not always easy. I waited and waited to hear from you and almost convinced myself that either your father had convinced you of the error of your ways, or you'd simply embraced your new life and completely forgotten me. And now this!

I will send this off now and hope I don't have to wait another fifty years to hear from you again. I sincerely hope you will want to stay in touch. Perhaps we can make up for some of our lost time. Tell me about your life.

I never stopped loving you even though there were so many times when I wished I could. (I'm sorry if that is not something you want to hear.)

Yours with love,

Teddy

~ ~ ~

When Georgina saw the envelope with its airmail sticker and British stamps lying in her mailbox she knew immediately that it had to have something to do with Mr. Teddy Postlethwaite. Even though she didn't know the man, she prayed she wasn't about to receive bad news ... she didn't want to discover he was dead, or dying, or in prison, or angry. She genuinely hoped that by deciding to forward the letter, she had done something good.

Immediately, she went back inside with the letter, brewed herself a cup of fresh coffee and sat down at her kitchen table to read the contents. She was not disappointed. This was better than her wildest dreams and imagination could ever have conjured up ... better than the start of any romantic tale she had ever read. This was the stuff of television soap operas without the bother of having to bring anyone back from the dead! This was a real life love story and, in her own small way, she was part of it. She rubbed her hands together with an air of deep satisfaction and wondered what her next move should be.

Step one, she realized, was to discover as much as she could about this Gillian Mathers girl.

Step two was less clear. Should she write to Teddy and share with him whatever she was able to dig up about Gillian Mathers? Or—and she liked this option more—could she pretend to be Gillian and spare him any potential disappointment? What harm could it do? There were thousands of miles of ocean between them and, if corresponding with 'Gillian' made Teddy happy after all this time, Georgina's participation would surely be regarded as altruistic in spite of any deceit.

"Like I told you before," Mrs. Walsh began after pouring them both a strong cup of tea and opening a packet of Peek Freans, "they weren't here very long. After Mrs. Mathers did what she did, Gillian and her father moved away. Too much tragedy in the house, I suppose. You can't blame them."

Doris Walsh was a kind woman. She'd survived her own share of troubles and looked upon the world through a veil of tempered benevolence and resignation. Well into her eighties, she was determined to live out her life in her own home. Many times over the years, Suzanne had urged her to move in with her, but Doris knew she never would. She liked her street. She knew most of her neighbours and, for the first time in years, she felt she was making a new friend in Georgina. She recognized Georgina as a kindred lonely soul whose interest in the lives of others enriched her own.

Hanging on to every word Doris uttered, Georgina sat forward on the overly stuffed sofa in Doris' front room and prayed that the giant cushions wouldn't swallow her up completely. In fact, she was completely safe because Georgina was quite a robust woman. She had short wiry grey hair that sprouted upright most of the time giving her a slightly eccentric appearance. She generally wore poorly fitting casual clothes that confirmed a lack of preoccupation with her personal appearance. Her most attractive features were her piercing blue eyes, her perfect skin and her inviting smile that could draw out conversation from even the most taciturn of subjects.

Today her cheeks were quite flushed—in part because Doris kept her house cloyingly warm and in part because she was so excited about her 'project'. She had considered bringing a tape recorder or a notepad with her, but then decided it might put Mrs. Walsh off, or arouse suspicion.

"Gillian and my Suzanne were great friends, you know."

"Oh, that's interesting," said Georgina encouragingly.

"You'll have to meet my daughter. She usually comes once a year. Next time, we'll have to have you over."

"I'd like that," replied Georgina, "perhaps she'd be able tell me more about Gillian."

"Oh, I don't think she's been in touch with Gill since she and Mr. Mathers moved away. I saw Gill a number of years ago, you know. She dropped by unexpectedly; you could have knocked me over with a feather when she came to the door! She had her son with her. She said they were in the neighbourhood and she wanted to show her boy the old house. It was nice of her to come and see me."

"Did she tell you where she's living now?"

"Not as I recall. She probably did, but it was a long time ago. My memory's not what it once was."

"Did she mention a husband?" asked Georgina.

"Again, I don't recall, but she said she had a daughter as well, so I imagine she must have had a husband somewhere. I sure hope so."

There was a brief pause and then Doris asked Georgina why she was so interested in the Mathers, especially since they'd only lived on the street briefly and that was a long time ago.

"Are you a writer, or something, dear? Mr. Fulford was a writer, of course. He was interested in the Mathers too, but more interested in Mrs. Mathers than her daughter. He said there was a love story to be told about that woman. I didn't really believe him. She didn't look the type. Are you working on a novel too, dear?"

"In a manner of speaking," Georgina replied softly.

"That Mrs. Mathers was such a sad soul," Doris continued, "and then when she took those pills, well … that just left Mr. Mathers and the girl to fend for themselves. I never really took to him. He was a teacher here in Cobden, but a rather cold and disagreeable man. I can't imagine Gillian's life with him was all that pleasant, poor kid."

After her third cup of tea, Georgina left Mrs. Walsh's knowing a little bit more about Gillian Mathers and her family. She was curious to know what Richard Fulford's angle had been … had he too stumbled upon some letter or keepsake implicating someone in the Mathers family in some kind of tragic love story? This was getting better and better, thought Georgina.

The following day she stopped by Mrs. Parr's house on her Meals-on-Wheels rounds. As she was dishing up a portion of hot shepherd's pie and peas, she asked Mrs. Parr if she'd known the Mathers.

"Oh, yes," she replied. "Harold and I taught at the same school. Not for long, of course. He left after about eighteen months, right after Mrs. Mathers passed. That was a sad thing."

"Do you know where they moved to?" asked Georgina.

"I think he said he had family in Winnipeg or somewhere west."

"Did you know Gillian?"

"Not well. She was in my art class for a while. She could have been quite good at art, I think. But she was a sad child. I think she had difficulties adjusting to life in Canada. They'd come here from England, you see. It was a big upheaval for a young teenaged girl. I don't imagine her father was particularly sympathetic. He seemed rather stern and unapproachable, but maybe that's just the British way of dealing with things."

"Well, thank you Mrs. Parr. Is there anything else you need help with while I'm here?"

"No, I'm all set, thank you, dear. I'll see you next time."

"Yes," replied Georgina, "see you on Thursday. Enjoy your lunch."

~ ~ ~

Dear Teddy,

How lovely to receive your letter and what a surprise! Indeed, it has been a very, very long time. It is quite extraordinary to think my letter only just found its way to you! As you said, one can only begin to imagine where it has been all this time and how different our lives might have been had it not been delayed.

As you can see, I still live in Cobden and, yes, I have grown quite fond of the place. It took a bit of getting used to, but I happily call it home now.

How nice that you still get to spend time in Hawesdale (*Georgina had already Googled it*). It has certainly changed since I was last there. I suppose living in Leeds is necessary for your work? (*What kind of work, she wondered*).

Of course I remember Miss Frobisher ... or rather, Mrs. Postlethwaite. How is your father these days? My father is no longer with me (*Georgina felt that was a true statement although she didn't really know for sure whether Gillian's father was dead or alive*) and, as you may have heard, my mother died shortly after we arrived here in Canada. She wasn't happy here.

I have recently retired. (*Georgina decided that if she mixed the parts of Gillian's life that she knew for certain with parts of her own life, she could probably weave a credible tale*). I spent my working life in a dairy and cheese factory.

In answer to your question, no, I am not married. (*True*).

After all this time, it is so wonderful to hear from you. Yes, I too hope we can stay in touch.

Kindest regards,
Gillian Mathers

~ ~ ~

Dearest Gillian,

'Kindest regards, Gillian Mathers'? I certainly hope we move beyond such formality soon, but I understand your reticence; it feels a bit like meeting someone for the first time even though we certainly aren't strangers to one another.

I cannot, for the life of me, imagine you working in a dairy ... my Gilly—the gal who could barely scramble over a gate without blushing—mucking cowsheds and hooking up milking machines? I seem to recall you don't even like milk! I'll bet Harold was a little disappointed in your career choice. He had big plans for his privately schooled daughter and I doubt diary maid was amongst them.

By the way, weren't you going to go off and become a writer some day? You always had dreams, didn't you? I hope you achieved some of them. I, who never dared to dream out loud, exceeded my personal expectations by leaps and bounds … I think even your curmudgeonly old father would be impressed!

Sadly, my father died some years ago, but I still remain close to Audrey. Remember what a prim and proper lady we thought she was? Well, I've grown very fond of her over the years and she made my old man very happy. I was grateful to her for that; she gave him a new lease on life. I'll tell her you said 'hello'. She always liked you. After you left, I would drop by the post office at least twice a day to see if there was a letter from you. Each time she shook her head I think it broke her heart almost as much as mine. She was a woman in love, so she understood the heartbreak your silence caused me. That's why I went off to college. Dad thought it was a waste of time, but I really needed to get out of Hawesdale and escape from the memories.

Yes, I live in Leeds because of my work. Leeds is where the head office of Postlethwaite's Home & Garden Supplies is situated. We have 13 shops now, including one in Kendal, your old stomping ground, and two in Manchester. We're still very much a northern outfit but one day I hope we'll crack the southern markets. I've kept the original shop in Hawesdale because it is a good reminder of our humble beginnings and, to be completely honest, letting it go would be like letting yet another piece of 'us' go.

I'm sorry to hear about your mother. That must have been very difficult for you. Poor woman, perhaps she never got over Mr. Hopkins.

Well, my love, my warm bed beckons. (Probably too soon to say I wish you were waiting there too?)

Sweet dreams,

Love always and with *the kindest of regards* (!)

Teddy xx

~ ~ ~

"Susan, do we have any books in the library by a Richard Fulford? I've looked everywhere and can't find anything," Georgina asked one of her library co-workers.

"He was a journalist, wasn't he?"

"Oh, maybe. I just thought that perhaps he'd written a book too. Did you know he used to live in my house?"

"Yes, I vaguely remember him. You might find something about him in the newspaper archives, or even on line," suggested Susan.

Since receiving Teddy's second letter, Georgina was determined to get to the bottom of the mystery surrounding Mary Mathers' apparent suicide, this Mr. Hopkins person that Teddy mentioned, and Richard Fulford's interest in Mrs. Mathers. Perhaps all three were in some way connected. If so, this adventure was getting better and better by the day. In fact, it was beginning to take over Georgina's life and there were some days when she almost believed that she was Gillian, not Georgina. She even toyed with the idea of changing her name to Gillian. She liked what she imagined Gillian's life could have been.

Georgina's research led her to discover that Richard

Fulford had died in Cobden in 1983 after a serious bout of pneumonia. He'd had a successful career as a journalist, retiring from *The Ottawa Citizen* in 1960. His only novel, written under the pseudonym, Robert Friar, was published in 1969. *Secrets & Love*, while not particularly well received by critics—'Limp and fluffy' wrote *The Ottawa Citizen*'s own book reviewer—became a moderate success amongst romance novel fans.

Immediately, Georgina found a copy and immersed herself in it. It was her kind of book. Perhaps she'd suggest it to the book club someday, particularly since there was a local connection.

The story took place on some grand estate where an anonymous and unidentified host had invited an odd collection of what appeared, at first glance, to be randomly selected guests to a week's retreat. The guests were to spend their days horseback riding, enjoying the on-site spa, hiking in the woods and so forth. Each evening, when they gathered around the dining table for the evening meal, there would be a folded piece of paper at one or two of the place settings. Written inside each one was a very personal question—the kind of question only someone who intimately knew that person would know to ask.

One couple was asked why she, the wife, had cheated on her husband. Another guest was asked about his male lover … and so on and so forth so that each evening elicited a new sordid secret about one or two of the characters. The narrative was rife with mystery because the host (whose seat remained empty at the head of the dining table every evening) was not revealed until the very end of the story. He turned out to be some wealthy old man who'd been hurt by all of these people in one way or another over the years and had waited almost his whole life to get his revenge by forcing them confront and expose their secrets and pain.

At the conclusion of the narrative, she decided that Robert Friar's adulterous couple might have been loosely based on Mr. or Mrs. Mathers but, without knowing where or how he had done his research, even Georgina accepted that her theory was more wishful thinking than fact. As for the other storylines—the Romeo and Juliet couple, the gay student and the unwed spinster—she put the novel aside and never gave them any further thought; after all, it was just a story.

~ ~ ~

April 4th, 2012,

Dear Teddy,

Thank you for your last letter. I'm sorry I have taken so long to reply, but I have been very busy with my Meals-on-Wheels and volunteer library duties. I like to keep busy.

For your information, I was not a 'dairy maid' and I don't know if my father was disappointed in me or not.

Finally we are getting some warmer weather here. England always looked lovely at this time of the year. I am reminded of wildflowers and green pastures … all very Wordsworthian (*hardly surprising since Georgina had been reading Wordsworth and Beatrix Potter like a fiend!*).

I'm pleased to hear you have a friend in your stepmother. I feel awful knowing that you used to check the post office so regularly and always walked away empty-handed. Of course I never forgot you. You were always in my thoughts.

You must tell me where in Kendal your shop is so I can picture it in my mind (*thank goodness for Google maps, thought Georgina*). You have certainly made a great success of yourself, Teddy. It sounds like you're running a small empire over there. How exciting ... I always wanted to expand my business, I mean, the dairy where I worked, but of course I wasn't in a position to do so. Perhaps you and I would have made good business partners as well as great friends. (*It took so much self-control for Georgina not to tell this apparently successful businessman about her own career successes, but she was pretty sure they were not the sort of accomplishments Gillian would have been pursuing. 'Dairy maid', indeed!*).

I look forward to writing to you again soon,

Take care of yourself,

Gillian

~ ~ ~

My dear Gillian,

I don't think I have the patience for this anymore. Letters take forever to swim across the ocean and back. Why don't we join the rest of the 21st Century and e-mail instead? You do have Broadband in the backwoods of Canada, I assume? (Just teasing!). My e-mail is: tp@postlethwaites.org.uk

Wish you were here so I could pick wildflowers for you again. Or, maybe now that we're all grown up, I should send you some real flowers.

Tell me more about your life in Canada. You told me you weren't married and, I confess, I was relieved to hear it. But, I hope your life hasn't been lonely.

Darling, I must go. I have a busy day ahead of me. I admire your volunteering work. I always knew you had a big heart.

Love to you, Gillian. Send me your e-mail address as soon as possible. I can't wait to be able to communicate more regularly.

Teddy

P.S. Please accept my apologies for the unfortunate use of the term 'dairy maid'. I did not mean to offend.

~ ~ ~

The following Wednesday, two dozen red roses were delivered to 25 Champlain Street. The card attached read: '*As promised, Teddy*'. Georgina was on cloud nine! She arranged the bouquet in a cut glass vase and placed the magnificent bouquet on her living room windowsill for all and any passers-by to admire. Plain old Georgina Harris had a lover ... of sorts ... and she wanted the world to know it.

"Sorry I'm a bit late today, Mrs. Parr. I received twenty-four beautiful red roses this morning and it took me a while to arrange them properly."

"How lovely, my dear. May I ask who your admirer is?" enquired Mrs. Parr right on cue.

"Oh, he's a very old friend. We've just reconnected after many, many years, but we never stopped loving one another. I'm his one true love and he is mine," answered Georgina, grinning from ear to ear.

"Well, you're very fortunate, my dear. At your age a little romantic attention is very flattering, isn't it?"

Georgina chose to disregard Mrs. Parr's patronizing comment and went back to the task at hand.

"Your favourite today, Mrs. Parr. Batter-fried sole and chips. There's coleslaw too and tinned peaches for dessert."

"Good morning Ms. Harris," called the mailman one morning. Georgina was just on her way out. "Do you want me to do something about these letters you've been getting?

Addressed to a 'Gillian Mathers' … she doesn't live here so I could have them returned to sender if you like."

"Oh, no, that's quite fine, thank you. She's a friend. She's living abroad for a while and I said she could have her mail sent here to me. I'm just holding it for her until she returns," explained Georgina.

"All right, then. Just thought I'd check. Have a good day."

"You too. Thanks for checking."

~ ~ ~

```
TO: tp@postlethwaites.org.uk
FROM: champlain25@hotmail.com
SUBJECT: Hello!
Dear Teddy,
Yes, I think e-mail is a great idea!
I'll write properly soon.
Gillian
```

~ ~ ~

```
TO: champlain25@hotmail.com
FROM: tp@postlethwaites.org.uk
SUBJECT: Hello!
Gillian, this is great! How was your
day? I've just spent 7 hours I'll never
get back stuck in a tedious boardroom
meeting. People really like the sound of
their own voices, don't they? The Chair
was useless and eventually I simply tuned
out and thought about you. Remember when
I bought you that huge Knickerbocker Glo-
ry? You ate considerably more than your
```

share! I was so impressed.

Darling, I feel so much closer knowing that I can write to you any time and my words will find their way to your Inbox without delay. Imagine if we'd been able to do this 50 years ago … things might have turned out very differently.

You're probably thinking about lunch right about now if I've got the time difference correct. I'm about to devour a huge steak 'n kidney pie from Marks & Sparks. I'm not a bad cook really, but I'm a lazy one. I'll cook for you one day. Maybe we'll have dinner in the flat above the shop like I'd always intended.

Love to you, T xx

~ ~ ~

Over the next few months Georgina and Teddy e-mailed daily like a couple of teenagers. Slowly Georgina told Teddy the story of her life in Canada. She relied on as many of her own real experiences as she could so that she wouldn't have to worry about getting her facts mixed up. She tailored the truth only when absolutely necessary. She explained to Teddy that she'd started working at the cheese factory on weekends while she was still attending school. She'd worked in the little shop at the entrance selling dairy products and occasionally giving factory tours to tourists, scout troops and school groups. After her mother died, she said the owner's wife, Mrs. Harris, took her under her wing. "We became so close, she was like a second mother to me. She had no children of her own," she wrote. "I stayed on at the factory after I graduated from high school because I couldn't bear to leave my father on his own."

As time went on, Georgina explained that she became more and more involved in the business of the factory, particularly as Mr. and Mrs. Harris cut back their own hours to enjoy more time to themselves. "I became their right hand gal," she said proudly. "By the time I retired I was basically running the entire operation." She told Teddy how difficult it had been to walk away from the factory after so many years but, after the owners passed on and the business was sold, she felt her time had come. "I miss everybody who worked there," she said. Indeed, Georgina had made a point of knowing as much as she could about her staff. If someone had a baby, she'd want to see all the baby pictures; if someone died, she'd give everyone the afternoon off to attend the funeral. When her personal assistant broke her leg in a skiing mishap, Georgina took care of all her grocery shopping for six weeks. After all, said Georgina, she had no family of her own to make demands on her at home, so she had all the time in the world to help others.

~ ~ ~

TO: champlain25@hotmail.com
FROM: tp@postlethwaites.org.uk
SUBJECT: Hello!
... I always loved that about you, Gillian. Even back when I knew you, you wanted to make everyone around you happy ... even at your own expense on occasion. You were so sweet. I remember thinking: this girl couldn't tell a lie if her life depended on it. I'm glad you never lost that.

~ ~ ~

Georgina told Teddy that her favourite subjects at school had been home economics and chemistry. She'd played on the school basketball team and competed in school track meets, although she was never an outstanding athlete. She almost told Teddy that English and art had been her worst subjects—because they had been—but then she remembered Mrs. Parr saying that Gillian was a promising art student and that Teddy had mentioned she'd dreamed of being a writer someday.

When Georgina wasn't writing careful e-mails to Teddy, she was researching all things British. She'd added *Coronation Street* to her list of must-watch TV dramas. She'd read all James Herriot's books to learn about life in rural northern England. She forced herself to sit through dreadful British comedies—*Keeping Up Appearances* and *Last of the Summer Wine*—hoping to better understand and appreciate the nuances of British humour. She listened to the old British pop music that would have been current at the time she and Teddy were supposedly together and she even struggled to cook a few of the British staples she was sure Gillian would have been raised on.

~ ~ ~

TO: tp@postlethwaites.org.uk
FROM: champlain25@hotmail.com
SUBJECT: Domesticity!
I made a Swiss roll the other day and took it over to Mrs. Parr's as a special treat. Of course it wasn't as good as my mother's, but I think she enjoyed it.

~ ~ ~

```
TO: champlain25@hotmail.com
FROM: tp@postlethwaites.org.uk
SUBJECT: Domesticity!
```

Oh yes, Gillian, I remember your mother's famous 'sponge'. It was always a favourite of yours, she'd said. Frankly, I found it rather dry and flavourless. British cuisine (now, there's an oxymoron for you) has always tended towards the timid and the stodgy. But, we've expanded our horizons and appetites considerably since conquering our fear of foreign travel. Even I go to Spain once a year. I play a little golf, swim and drink sangria. I'll take you one day. Have you ever been to Europe?

~ ~ ~

Georgina admitted that she had never left the continent 'since coming to Canada'. She'd gone to Niagara Falls once on a school trip and they'd crossed over to the American side, but that was about as exotic as her explorations had been. She told him instead about the trips 'Mr. and Mrs. Harris' had taken her on. One summer they'd travelled up to Manitou Island and stayed in cabins by the lake. "We were almost eaten alive," she told Teddy, "mosquitoes as big as buzzards." On that same holiday, Mr. Harris (Georgina's father) had taught her how to fish. She learned to put squirming worms on the hook by herself and to contain her hysteria when a freshly landed fish continued to flap about on the floor of the dingy well after it was supposed to be dead.

~ ~ ~

TO: champlain25@hotmail.com
FROM: tp@postlethwaites.org.uk
SUBJECT: Fishing?

Is this really Gillian writing to me, or some imposter? Fishing … baiting your own hook? What happened to that squeamish little girl I knew? Don't worry, it's not a criticism. I'm delighted to know that I can look forward to reeling in a trout or two with you one day (I've given up fishing for ducks, you'll be pleased to hear!!).

~ ~ ~

'*Imposter*'? Little did he know, thought Georgina.

One evening, after Georgina had enjoyed a couple of glasses of wine and was feeling particularly mellow, she shared with Teddy a slightly edited and modified version of the story of her love affair with one of the sales representatives who'd worked at the factory. She'd never told anyone about this before. She was 28 at the time, he was 42. Bernie Cooper was an attractive middle-aged man with a charming smile and irresistible nature. One day in the winter of 1970, her 'boss'—as she referred to her father, Mr. Harris, in her communications with Teddy—suggested she accompany Bernie on one of his sales runs and introduce herself to one or two of their regular clients.

"The only way you can prepare yourself to take over the helm of this business in the future is if you know how every department works and why each and every one of our employees is an essential part of the team," her father had said. (In the version Georgina's shared with to Teddy, however, she simply said that Mr. Harris thought she, 'Gillian' would make a good sales assistant for Mr. Cooper).

And so Georgina and Bernie had hopped into the company van and set out for Ottawa. It was only about an hour's drive and Georgina was happy to spend some time with Bernie. She had always liked him and he always paid a little extra attention to her when he saw her. Often it was just a wink, or a small compliment about her appearance; sometimes he'd give her a flower stolen from one of the pots outside the office or a souvenir he'd filched from a hotel bar or dining room on one of his road trips.

"This is great, Bernie. It's so nice to get out of the office now and again. You must love your job," she'd said.

"I'm certainly loving it today, Miss Harris," he'd answered and gently patted her left knee with his free hand.

They made a few stops before arriving in Ottawa and, at each grocery shop or corner store where Kaufmann's cheese was sold, he made a point of introducing her as one of his bosses. She was both flattered and impressed by his professionalism.

As they were driving, she couldn't resist glancing over to her left to admire the line of his jaw and the thickness of his dark brown eyebrows. Then she'd looked at his hand as it rested on the gear shift between them and found herself wondering what it would feel like to hold that hand or to have that hand resting on the small of her back.

Georgina had minimal experience with boys and love and it was easy for her to become attracted to this older man who treated her like someone special. Unbeknownst to her, Bernie regarded her as merely a plaything and had eagerly accepted the challenge of the guys in the packing department when he'd overheard them say "it would be a cold day in hell before any guy found his way beneath the skirts of that frumpy Miss Harris."

"I'll do it," he'd volunteered. "Give me a month or two, and I'll break that little gal's cherry, just you see."

He knew that if he played his cards right he could have the sweet little thing eating out of his hand in no time. It had worked before and he knew he'd still got what it took.

The outing to Ottawa was merely the first part of the seduction. In the days that followed, Bernie made a point of always being around when Georgina finished work. Sometimes he'd just wave to her; other times he might stroll over and whisper a compliment in her ear … "that strawberry pink sweater you're wearing today looks delicious on you."

Georgina fell for it all. And then one day it was she who was hovering around at the end of the day hoping to encounter Bernie. When he pulled up in the van she walked over, opened the passenger door and stepped inside.

"Let's go for a drive, Bernie."

"Sure, sweetheart … whatever you say."

The first time they drove down to a park and sat watching ducks in a pond. The second time they drove further into the countryside and he kissed her. The third time, he kissed her more and she allowed his hands to wander over her body until they found their way up and under her sweater.

The next time she asked if they could go for a drive, he declined. Bingo! … he could see she was hooked. He could read it in her eyes. Her disappointment was almost palpable. "I'm busy tonight, honey. We'll get together another time."

Almost two weeks passed before they went out together again in the van and, as Bernie later told it: "she couldn't keep her hands off of me."

He was a tough guy around the boys but a smooth lover with Georgina and by the time she gave herself to him, she believed she was deeply in love. She told him she wanted to tell her parents about their romance, but Bernie warned her it was too soon. He told her they might not want their daughter, heiress to the Kaufmann fortune, consorting with a travelling salesman. They should wait, he'd said.

They continued to sneak around together for several months. Usually they went off in the van, but sometimes Bernie claimed his passion for her was so intense and uncontrollable he couldn't wait until the end of the day. And so, they'd made love in a storage room, they'd made love in Mr. Harris' office one day when he and his secretary were both out for lunch and they'd even made love in the rhododendron bushes behind the factory.

Every once in a while, Georgina would find a way to persuade her father to let her accompany Bernie on his sales calls. On those occasions, they'd have lunch in a nice restaurant in Ottawa, or walk by the Rideau Canal together like a real couple.

And then one day, her father called her into his office.

"Look, I'm really not much good at these kinds of things, so I hope you can take care of this for me. Bernie's wife has just given birth to twins … I'd like you to go out and buy something special for the new arrivals. Your mother will go with you if you like … Georgina … Georgie …?"

But it was too late, she was already lying passed out on the floor.

~ ~ ~

TO: tp@postlethwaites.org.uk
FROM: champlain25@hotmail.com
SUBJECT: A confession
… I know I was an idiot, Teddy, but I had no idea he was married. I was so naïve. I really thought he loved me

and, worse than that, I really believed I loved him.

He broke my heart … I don't think it's worked the same since. Oh, there were a few men here and there; I dated a botanist for a couple of years until he flitted off to South America with his butterfly net, followed by a dentist from Quebec who insisted I needed braces (I was well into my forties by then), so that was the end of him! I'd basically put that part of my life on hold until now. I feel like a young girl again, Teddy, and it's all thanks to you.

~ ~ ~

TO: champlain25@hotmail.com
FROM: tp@postlethwaites.org.uk
SUBJECT: A confession
My dearest Gillian,

Obviously, neither of us has been living under a rock for the past decades … life has hurt us both and we've both done things we wish we hadn't. But that is all part of what makes us who we are today.

How or why your letter took all this time to find me will likely remain a mystery to us both, but I am SO glad it did. Reconnecting with you has injected some romance and love into my otherwise banal existence. You have made a sentimental old man very happy :)

Love, Teddy xxx

~ ~ ~

"You were telling me about Suzanne's wedding, Doris … I'd love to hear more," Georgina remarked one afternoon as they sat together sipping bitterly strong tea in Doris' hot and stuffy living room.

"I'll do you one better than that!" exclaimed Doris, "I'll show you the pictures."

Inwardly Georgina groaned … nothing worse than wedding photos of people you don't know, but perhaps she'd learn something.

"Was Gillian there?" she enquired hopefully.

"Oh no, dear; like I told you, I don't think she and Suzanne stayed in touch after they moved. I've got a picture of her though, if you'd like to see it. The girls used to make their own clothes and put on little fashion shows. They'd borrow Mary's and my jewellery and fancy shoes and get all made up. It was very sweet."

"Yes, I'd love to see a picture."

Georgina could hardly contain herself. For so long she had wondered what the young girl Teddy had been so smitten with had looked like? Would she in any way resemble the middle-aged woman he was now corresponding with? She desperately hoped so.

Georgina could hear Doris riffling around in the bureau in her bedroom down the hall. While she was gone, Georgina stood up and gazed out of the side window at the profile of her own home. It was certainly a handsome square box of a building with its solid red bricks and delicate gingerbread detailing dripping from the porch eaves like icing on a cake. So many people with so many stories … if only walls could speak, she mused.

"Here you are!" announced Doris as she shuffled back into the room. "Now, this is a photo of Gillian, me, Suzanne and Gillian's mother, Mary. We were on a shopping trip to Ottawa. Oh, and here are the two girls modelling their 'haute couture'," she added fondly.

Both girls were wearing sleeveless gingham shifts with lace around the collars. They'd put their hair up in the heavily backcombed beehive style popular in the '60s and their eyes drooped under the weighty burden of great swaths of thick black eyeliner. Gillian was wearing a pair of over-sized plastic hoops in her earlobes and Suzanne wore a matching necklace, both probably borrowed from one of their mothers. The dresses were very short and the tall boots they wore looked totally out of place.

"The girls had begged for the high-heeled patent leather boots that were all the rage then, but they'd hardly be practical living here," commented Doris, "so, for the pictures, they put on their winter boots. Oh, they were a funny pair, bless them."

Georgina held the two square photographs in her hand. They were no longer black and white, more like grey and greyer, having faded with the passing of time. Gillian appeared to be a rather slight child, several inches shorter than her dark-haired friend, Suzanne. She was a pretty girl, however, no doubt about that. Still, Georgina wondered, how did this slightly self-conscious looking child manage to capture and hold on to Teddy's heart for all these years?

Any notions that Gillian bore any resemblance to Georgina at the same age were now completely shattered. Georgina had been a rather solid girl and 'pretty' was not an adjective that would have come close to describing her in her mid-teens. She had been an unremarkable, ruddy-faced child with the same unruly, springy hair she'd still not learned to tame. Her best features then, and now, were her piercing cobalt-blue eyes. What Georgina lacked in grace and reserve, she'd made up for by being totally non-threatening and genuinely interested in the lives of others.

Georgina was a little bit disappointed by the photographs and, all of a sudden, keen to get home and be by herself. She knew she couldn't sit and endure page after page of wedding photos with Doris' non-stop commentary throughout.

"I'm sorry, Doris, I just remembered there's something I have to do. Perhaps we can look at your album another time," she said as she trotted towards the front door and quickly let herself out.

If Doris was surprised, or hurt, she didn't let on.

As Georgina entered her own house, she realized that she still had a firm grip on the two photographs of Gillian. She considered running right back and returning them to Doris but decided, instead, there was no big hurry.

~ ~ ~

TO: champlain25@hotmail.com
FROM: tp@postlethwaites.org.uk
SUBJECT: Good morning, my love
Hi Gillian,

How's your day going … mine's over and I'm sitting sipping a fine single malt and thinking about you. What a blessing it is that we have re-found one another.

I had lunch with a colleague today. He said he and his wife were celebrating their fortieth wedding anniversary. Of course, I congratulated him … it doesn't happen that often these days. And then,

I thought, in many ways we are celebrating our own significant anniversary. How often in life do we get second chances like this?

Much as I love our daily e-mails, there may come a day when it's not enough for both of us. So, to help prepare us for that delightful eventuality, I am attaching a photograph of myself. I know this is a bit risky, but I sincerely hope you can still see your version of 'Teddy' deep inside this considerably less-youthful wrapping.

Teddy xxx

~ ~ ~

TO: champlain25@hotmail.com
FROM: tp@postlethwaites.org.uk
SUBJECT: Photo, please
Gillian, it's been two days since I sent you my photo and you haven't reciprocated. Darling, I am desperate to 'see' you … please send something! Love, Teddy

~ ~ ~

TO: tp@postlethwaites.org.uk
FROM: champlain25@hotmail.com
SUBJECT: Photo, please
Teddy, my love, I don't actually have any recent photographs of myself (*that was true*). I've dug up a couple of me with my best friend, Suzanne, taken shortly after

we moved here. You'll probably recognize my mother in one of them. I'm sorry I have nothing more recent. A number of my boxes of books and papers were mislaid during a recent renovation (*that wasn't true*) and, sadly, all my recent photographs were among them. I'll get a new picture taken soon, I promise (*also not true*). Love, Gillian.

~ ~ ~

Georgina had spent hours staring at the photo Teddy had sent. Of course, once you see what someone looks like you completely lose the mental picture you've carried around up until that moment. Was this round-faced, friendly looking man what she'd expected, or had she been imagining someone more refined and 'corporate-looking'? Teddy was fortunate for a man of his years, he still sported a full head of wavy hair and he had a smooth, youthful complexion. But it was the slightly mischievous twinkle in his eyes that had probably served him best throughout his life. In fact, she'd wager, it was that delightful twinkle that had first attracted Gillian to him all those years ago and now, years later, here it was working its magic on Georgina.

Georgina obviously couldn't provide a current photo of herself and had hastily scanned the two purloined from her neighbour hoping they would satisfy for the time being.

~ ~ ~

TO: champlain25@hotmail.com
FROM: tp@postlethwaites.org.uk
SUBJECT: Photo, please

Darling Gillian,

What a sweet young girl you were … just
as I remember you. But, let's be honest …
I've shown you mine, it's time I saw what
you look like now. I have no doubt you
are as beautiful now as you were then.
All that's changed for us is that we now
wear a few life experiences on our faces
and, in my case, a little extra padding.
It would be sad if we didn't. Go and ask
that delightful neighbour you keep talking about … I'm sure she'd take a picture
of you for me, particularly if you bribed
her by promising to tell her the story of
your long lost love!

~ ~ ~

Georgina managed to put him off for several more
weeks. First she told him her camera had been in one of
the infamous lost boxes. Then she explained she'd have to
make a trip to Ottawa if she wanted to purchase a new digi-
tal camera but, with the winter roads being what they were,
she'd rather wait until spring.

Winter had, indeed, taken a frigid hold of Cobden and
Georgina had finally given in and added proper insulation to
the attic. It was a messy job and a rather costly, but necessary, investment.

She often took long walks along the banks of the Ottawa River. On certain magical winter days, it was like walking through a gallery of fine glass sculptures. Sun-kissed
ice on heavily burdened branches would be caught mid-drip
and instantly turned into shimmering icicles. With a slight
wind, they would tinkle like glass chimes and flicker in the

light as the sun toyed with them. They were exquisite and all the more precious for their ephemeral nature. The same could be said for her 'relationship' with Teddy. It was exquisite but, one day, like a falling icicle, it would be unable to hold on. Nothing stayed the same for long; besides, Georgina couldn't keep this charade up indefinitely and she sure as hell didn't want to get caught. It would leave only a legacy of deceit and betrayal. Hurting Teddy again would be reckless and irresponsible, she thought. She knew she walked a tenuous line and, well intentioned or not, she would probably not emerge from this in a particularly flattering light whatever the eventual outcome.

In mid-December, she was returning from one of her winter promenades when she noticed a parcel sitting on her front step. She carried it inside where the warmth immediately fogged up her glasses and she had to wait patiently for it to clear before reading who it was from.

While she waited for things to come back into focus, she paused at the threshold of her cosy living room and admired the efforts she'd gone to to make it warm and festive. She'd put tiny white lights around the window frames and an assortment of beeswax candles stood on a bed of cedar bows on the deep windowsill. In the opposite corner, stood her little Christmas tree decorated with a few baubles and garlands of tinsel. Most of the ornaments had belonged to the factory. Her mother would put up a tree in the lobby each year and then on Christmas Eve, after the office was closed, she'd strip it of most of its decorations and run home to put them on the tree in the Harris home! She was nothing if not a practical woman.

This felt like Georgina's first real Christmas at 25 Champlain Street. Previously, she hadn't made the effort, but this year she seemed far more settled. She'd even invited Doris and her family, who were visiting for the holidays, to come over on Christmas Day for a glass of something. She was very keen to finally meet Suzanne. Besides, she had a rather special present to give her.

Beneath Georgina's tree were a couple of wrapped gifts. One, probably a calendar of some sort, was a gift from Mrs. Parr. They'd exchanged small gifts when Georgina had delivered her lunch last week. Three small jars wrapped in foil paper stood beside Mrs. Parr's present. Last weekend Georgina had finally gone up to Pembroke to visit her cousins on their farm. They'd invited her to come on their annual Christmas tree hunt. Sandra was Georgina's mother's sister's daughter and Malcolm was Sandra's husband. They were a lovely hardworking couple and they made Georgina feel very welcome even though the two women hadn't met since they were teenagers. It was nice to have someone to exchange familiar stories with, although there were times when Georgina had to remind herself who she was. On occasions like that, she had to concentrate on being herself and remember that she had *not* grown up in a small English village, or lost her mother as a youngster. She and Sandra were both Kaufmann's, after all. Georgina had taken them a slab of Kaufmann's best cheddar presented on a beautiful, hand-crafted cherry wood cheese board and they, in return, had given her the three small jars—probably homemade jam or pickles, she thought.

There was one other gift under the tree. It was a fairly large boxed package and the gift card on the side read 'To Suzanne'.

When Georgina had been rooting about in the attic to get it ready for the guys who were going to install the insulation, she'd discovered several unmarked cardboard boxes at the very back of one of the wedge-shaped cupboards beneath the eaves. Georgina was delighted. It was like finding buried treasure!

The first box she'd pulled out contained a bag of musty old clothing. A slip of paper inside read 'donate'. The contents smelled moldy and Georgina certainly hadn't wanted to stick her hand inside the bag … what if there was a packrat or a spider's nest inside? So she'd quickly resealed the box and set it aside.

The second of the three boxes was much more interesting. In amongst a collection of old school textbooks, she'd found a high school yearbook: *Cobden District Public School, 1960*. Now this is more like it, she'd thought.

She'd flipped through the pages not sure whether she should be studying the Grade 10 or Grade 11 classes in search of Gillian but, eventually she'd found her—Gillian Mathers, Grade 11. There was something about her black and white expressionless photo that made her look as if she'd rather be anywhere other than pasted onto that two-page spread with every other spotty bored teenager in town. Most of the children looked awkward, except for the occasional perky-looking girl who grinned at the camera—probably a popular cheerleader and future lingerie model—and one or two cocky young men who probably figured they could take on the world with nothing but their good looks and brawny bodies. High schools were all the same and hadn't really changed much over the decades, thought Georgina.

Next, she'd turned to the faculty page. The women teachers wore smart twin sets, modest knee-length skirts and low-heeled pumps. They all looked so young, they could have been children themselves, dressing up in their mothers' clothes. Except, of course, the gym teacher who, like all gym teachers, wore culottes to show off her muscular legs, white tennis shoes and a soft-collared shirt with a whistle on a string dangling from her neck. They were always the same, lady gym teachers, with their smug, almost sadistic, expressions worn to intimidate and prove just how tough and unfeminine they were. The boys' gym teacher looked like a Ken doll with a head of perfectly combed dark hair and a toothy grin. He wore the uniform of his vocation, Bermuda-length white shorts, an open-necked shirt and the necessary white tennis shoes. And, just to be sure everyone knew who he was, he'd chosen to pose with a football held over the heads of the staff in the row in front of him, poised as if he were about to throw it.

The rest of the male faculty members looked identical, standing stiffly in their dark suits, plain ties and white shirts. Third from the left in the middle row, stood Harold Mathers, Gillian's father. He was the oldest in the group by far. He had a strange look on his face, his nostrils slightly flared as if there was a bad smell in the air or throughout life in general. Georgina had to agree with Doris' assessment of the man; he certainly didn't look like a fellow one would easily warm to.

Finally, she'd pulled out the last box beneath the attic eaves and opened the top. Without knowing it, she had definitely left the best to the last. Inside was a beautiful, pristine, brand new sewing basket—not like the cheap plastic ones you see these days, but a proper wicker one. She'd lifted it out to take a better look. The basket was about fourteen inches wide, ten inches deep and probably ten inches tall. It was mostly white basketry with the occasional rows of pink and mint green raffia woven into it. The handle was white and the lid was covered in rose satin, quilted like a pincushion. Green ribbons, connected to the lid and body of the basket on either side, prevented the lid from flipping over completely when Georgina had opened it. The inside consisted of a series of satin-lined compartments and a removable notions tray perched on the top. The tray contained needles, pins, a thimble, bobbins, a rolled up fabric tape measure, tailor's chalk and, finally, a small gift card edged with delicate pink rosebuds. The card was written in rather clumsy script and read:

'To Suzanne, future fashion designer. Remember me when you're famous! Love from Gillian'.

Having finally shrugged off her heavy coat and unwound her scarf, Georgina's attention returned to the newly arrived package she was still clutching in her hand. Once her lenses had cleared, she recognized the writing immediately. It was Teddy's. The parcel was the size of a thick tile and almost as heavy. She couldn't imagine what it contained and, after tearing at the outer layer of brown paper, she saw that the contents were crudely wrapped in sparkly red tissue paper held together with a silver ribbon. There was also a rather fat green envelope in the parcel. She placed the wrapped gift on the floor beside Suzanne's sewing basket and opened the envelope. Inside there was a Christmas card ... nothing fancy, just a fat snowman on a hillside with 'Happy Christmas' written in flaky glitter across his ample white belly. As she held it, loose glitter fell slowly to the floor like disco dust motes, likely to remain trapped between the floorboards forever.

The card contained the usual sentimental, mass-produced greeting ... something about good cheer, good friends, blah, blah, blah and, beneath that, Teddy had scrawled a brief message:

Wish we were together, maybe next year? Hope you enjoy the small gifts. Please read the enclosed letter and keep an open mind and an open heart. Happy Christmas dearest Gillian, my love always, Teddy.

The letter Teddy referred to was several pages long. Georgina was eager to read it, but she was also a bit anxious. What could it contain that couldn't have been said in an e-mail, she wondered?

~ ~ ~

December 7, 2013

My dearest Gillian,

Much as I enjoy our daily exchanges across cyber-space, I feel that what I am about to write warrants a more conscientious and focused approach and delivery. Fear not, my love, there is nothing sinister in what I am about to write, but some of what I am going to tell you may give you pause.

The truth is, we're not some desperate middle-aged people seeking love on some silly Internet dating site. We are so much more than that and we owe one another the truth … not just the retelling of stories and events that put us in the best possible light. Nor can we live off our finite stash of memories indefinitely. We hardly know one another now and I want to be sure that as/if we move forward, it is this man—*me*—you want, not just the boy you once loved.

It has been (and is) so wonderful to reconnect with you, my sweet, but it's been over 50 years and a lot can (and has) happened during that time. It's not all been about rising soap powder sales and high performance lawn mowers. Aside from my work, I've not managed the rest of my life particularly well and I think you should know what you're potentially getting into. Besides, you were so candid when you told me about your affair with Bernie, I feel it would be unfair and cowardly of me not to share in kind.

When you left Hawesdale, I really believed that it would only be for a short while. I had no idea how or when you would return, but my belief was so entrenched that I was able to disregard the logistics. As I've mentioned before, I went to the post office daily expecting a letter from you. To begin with, your silence made me sad … I moped about and kept to myself as much as school and work would allow. After a while, my misery evolved into anger. I blamed everyone and everything for the pain I was feeling.

I was a teenage boy, remember, so I also had to protect my pride. I sure as hell couldn't let the lads know how depressed I was becoming so I put on my armour and started hanging around with the guys and infecting the group with my inner rage. All of us had something we believed entitled us to feel hard done by in our lives, so it wasn't difficult to trigger anger and rebellion in the others. We dressed the part … *teddy*-boy hair-dos (there's irony for you!), tight jeans, leather jackets and buckets of 'attitude'. We 'hated' everyone. We fought our parents, talked back to our teachers, stole from the shopkeepers and disrespected the girls. It's easy to do when you are part of a group.

After school was over, the group dispersed. Chad and Louis set forth for London; Danny joined his father's cabinet-making business and Stan put on his gumboots and went to work on the farm. I was alone. I couldn't stay in the village. The shop bored me, I felt like a third wheel around my dad and Audrey and, as far as I knew, you'd abandoned me.

I was bloody lucky to get into Manchester Tech. Someone must have been looking out for me. Dad was livid. He thought it was a complete waste of time and money and that I'd be back, tail between my legs, within a matter of weeks. But I proved him wrong. I think that was the intention ... to prove everyone wrong—you, your arrogant father, your mother, teachers, neighbours, everyone. Not the most positive form of motivation I suppose, but it was the kick in the rear I needed.

I did well at college. In fact, I enjoyed the work immensely. Socially, however, I remained a loner ... never quite sure where I fit in. I lived in a rooming house in the city and the rules were strict. Curfew was 11 p.m., no girls, no loud music and no booze. So, I put my nose to the proverbial grindstone and got to work.

I'd come back to Hawsedale during the holidays bursting with ideas ... ways to improve and modernize our little shop. But I was just a lad and didn't have the maturity to recognize how tactless I was being. Poor Dad, having to listen to this smart-mouthed little whippersnapper teaching his grandmother to suck eggs (whatever *that* expression is supposed to mean!).

After college, I got a series of jobs around the city, but I was not a patient lad. I guess I felt I was too good to sweep out stockrooms, or count the till takings at the close of business. I wanted to be at the top without bothering to climb the ladder one rung at a time. My arrogance was my downfall. I kept getting fired ... time and time again I'd be let go because of the way I ordered co-workers about, or challenged my employers. I feigned indifference and started spending more and more time hanging out at the pub, or lurking around the betting shops. If I lost money, I drank. If I won money, I drank.

I was penniless after a few months of this lifestyle and had to crawl back to Hawesdale. I promised to turn over a new leaf, swallow my pride, and get on with the job I'd always been expected to do. I did up the flat above the shop and moved in. Back in the village, it was easy to revert to planning a life for the two of us even though I still hadn't heard a squeak from you. But, it gave me something to focus on and I found it oddly comforting.

I coasted along for quite some time after that. I was still lonely and depressed but most of my anger was spent. I still drank too much and I used women appallingly when there was opportunity.

I went to visit some old college mates in London one year. They'd both done very well and built stable, comfortable lives for themselves. In their company, I was embarrassed by my lack of focus and achievements and decided to learn what I could from their experiences. Jack offered me an entry-level job in his shipping business. I accepted. Dad was angry, although years later Audrey confessed to me that he'd been more relieved than anything. Ouch!

London was a great place for a young man to learn a trade, learn about life and do some serious growing up. Through Jack I met a number of delightful young women, most of them daughters of successful London businessmen.

I stepped out with a girl called Tessa for close to a year. She was bright, attractive, spoiled and useful. She eventually convinced her father to hire me as a sales executive in his Bentley dealership. Finally, I got to wear a suit and tie and was expected to wine and dine clients over luncheons in posh restaurants. Obviously, I was a bit of a fish out of water to start with, but I soon caught on. It's like anything else, you just have to don the costume, assume the pose and the rest will follow. Of course, overindulgence and extravagance were important aspects of my new life … I became intimately acquainted with fine wines, single malt scotches, horse racing, fast cars and fast women. It was the kind of life that required you to keep moving faster and faster … holidays on clients' yachts off the coast of Spain, or a week at a villa in Tuscany were among the perks.

It turned out that I was good at what I did—very good in fact. I earned more money during those few years than I'd dreamt of earning in a lifetime. But it was merely a means to an end as far as I was concerned. I had no intention of living such a vacuous and ostentatious life indefinitely. You can take the lad out of the North Country, but you can't take the North Country out of the lad! And so, on September 15th, 1972, I signed the papers for the loan that would help open the first Postlethwaite's Home & Garden Supplies in Leeds. I'd already been home for a week's holiday during the summer and found a suitable location. I'd said nothing to Dad about my plans, I wanted it to be a surprise … well, it most certainly was!

Of course, I needed his signature on all the papers because it would still be his name on the business. At first, he yelled at me … called me a traitor, told me I'd 'sold out', etc. It wasn't the response I'd expected. I thought he'd be proud. Instead, I had made him feel small and inadequate. But, I was committed and determined that the transaction would proceed one way or another. Thank God for Audrey … she placated him, acted as mediator between the two of us and eventually persuaded him that this expansion would be an admirable legacy guaranteeing Postlethwaite's a place on the high streets of England for at least another generation.

And so began my humble chain of Postlethwaite shops. Dad remained behind the counter at the village shop until the day he retired. He never once visited any of the other shops. I, on the other hand, devoted every ounce of my being to the business and the expansion that took place over the next decades. There was nothing I did during or after work hours that did not relate, in some way, to bolstering the business and increasing my personal wealth. I got into bed—quite literally, on occasion—with a number of unsavoury characters if I thought our association would expedite my success. I was greedy, ruthless, driven and painfully isolated. I had nothing else to work for. My dad wasn't interested or impressed. You, my love, were gone. What few friends I'd once had I'd discarded along the way once their utility had expired. You wouldn't have liked me, Gillian, I'm ashamed to say.

On my 54th birthday, I suffered a heart attack … truthfully, perhaps I should say I 'earned' a heart attack. I was overweight, I drank in excess, I took pills to help me sleep and pills to keep me awake, I didn't exercise, except to climb on and off a golf cart once in a while, and I was miserable.

The heart attack was not as severe as I probably deserved, but it was, as they say, a 'wake-up' call and a timely birthday present. I'll not pretend that I've given up drinking, eating foie gras occasionally, and working long hours, but I have reined myself in somewhat. I've dropped a couple of stone, I exercise two or three times a week, and I walk around the golf course instead of riding in the geriatric chariot. I'm not perfect, my love, but I've got a pulse!

Dearest Gillian, having read the account of my dismal life, you are probably counting your blessings … just look what you managed to avoid! But seriously, I need to know if you can still love me knowing all this about me, or would it have been better to remain in love with the memories and 'what ifs'?

For my part, dearest one, I love you no matter who, or what, you have become. I knew the innocent, loving Gillian you once were and I cannot imagine for a moment that that pure spirit has been spoiled. Oh yes, I understand there have been hurts, disappointments and moments of questionable choices … there would be something dreadfully wrong with you if that were not the case. However, I know the essential Gillian lives on and, for the first time in years, I believe the essential Teddy has not been irrevocably lost or damaged either.

Thank you for finding me again.

I love you, Teddy

~ ~ ~

Georgina read Teddy's letter several times. What was she going to do? Here was a man who had poured his heart out to her in the name of transparency and truth and, here she was, a player whose part required her to maintain the very antithesis of those virtues.

"I hope you don't mind that the grandchildren opted not to join us this afternoon," said Doris, apologetically.

"I completely understand," replied Georgina, "it's a perfect day for cross-country skiing, I can hardly blame them. But, I'm very pleased you and Suzanne decided to come," she added.

Doris and Suzanne had arrived moments before. Doris had made the introductions and now the three women were settling into Georgina's living room.

"The room looks lovely," observed Doris, "I've not seen it this warm and welcoming in … well, years, my dear."

Georgina had taken special care to make her home

look nice for the occasion. She'd lit the fire in the hearth, turned on her Christmas lights and laid out an arrangement of nuts, homemade snickerdoodles, marzipan stuffed dates and a small selection of Kaufmann cheeses on the low coffee table.

"What can I get you?" she asked.

"Is that mulled wine I'm smelling?"

"Yes, Suzanne, can I get you a glass? And, how about you, Doris … a sherry perhaps?"

"That would be lovely, dear."

Georgina served her guests and then perched on the edge of her favourite blue velour armchair beside the fire.

"It's so lovely to meet you after all this time," she said to Suzanne, "your mother has told me so much about you."

"And you," replied Suzanne. "She tells me you are very interested in my friendship with Gillian Mathers. Why is that, if you don't mind me asking?"

"Oh, nothing really," Georgina replied as nonchalantly as she could, "I guess I simply want to know as much about this house, its history and its occupants as I possibly can. Pure curiosity, that's all."

There was a pause before Suzanne spoke again: "You have to understand we didn't really know one another for very long, or even very well for that matter. I was a year younger than she and we'd moved here after they did. As you know, they didn't stay here long. I think we became friends out of necessity and convenience. Neither of us knew anybody else here and, living next door to one another, it was only a matter of time before we started playing together."

"Did you stay in touch after they left?" Georgina asked.

"'Fraid not. She and her father—can't say I was too fond of that man—moved to Winnipeg from here and then, last I heard, Gillian was living in Vancouver. She sent me a wedding invitation, but I couldn't go. She's about as far west as you can get on this continent, and I'm just about as far east as you can get. It's a big country sometimes, isn't it? Anyway, she married and had a couple of children I think. We were very different, really. She was quite prim and proper and rather shy. I was more outgoing. When I started hanging out with some of the local boys, she rarely joined in. She said she had some boyfriend waiting for her back in England. I don't know if that was true or not. It seemed more like an excuse than anything."

Georgina hid her irritation when Doris interrupted the conversation.

"We can't stay long, dear. Someone's got to keep an eye on that turkey. But, I have something for you," she said holding out a flat, carefully wrapped Christmas gift to Georgina.

"Can I open it now?"

"Oh, it's nothing special, my dear, but go ahead."

It was a small scrapbook containing dozens of crudely glued press releases and grainy photographs of Richard Fulford.

Georgina was temporarily lost for words. What am I supposed to do with this, she thought.

"I know you're interested in all that's gone on in this house, Georgina. I thought you could add this collection to your own. I put it together over the years. He was such a lovely man and, I think, the only famous one to have lived here. I figured you'd be keen to have this," Doris explained, smiling proudly at her own thoughtfulness.

Georgina thanked her profusely and promised to treasure it. Truthfully, she couldn't be less interested in the tatty-looking book with its discoloured newsprint inserts.

"I have something for you!" she said as she walked over

to the Christmas tree and picked up two wrapped gifts.

Doris accepted hers and tore into the wrapping. It was the December issue of *Chatelaine* and a subscription to cover the next two years. Georgina knew Doris would be pleased.

"Guess I'd better live long enough so this subscription doesn't go to waste, eh?" she teased.

Georgina leaned over to give Doris a quick hug and then pivoted to place the larger gift onto Suzanne's lap.

"Oh, my goodness! What is this?" she exclaimed. "You shouldn't, I'm sure," she added, somewhat embarrassed by the scale of the present.

"Oh, I didn't," Georgina whispered softly.

Suzanne carefully removed the wrapping paper and pulled out the beautiful sewing basket. On the top, Georgina had pinned Gillian's little gift card with the pink rose buds. Suzanne read it and looked up at Georgina questioningly.

"I found it in the attic," Georgina explained. "I was cleaning out the attic because I had some workmen coming and there it was stuffed in the back. It's obviously been there since the Mathers moved out. It's amazing no one else ever found it ... I guess it was 'meant to be'. Isn't it absolutely delightful?"

"Yes, yes it is," replied Suzanne. Then she laughed, "'fashion designer', my ass! (Sorry Mum). If only she knew the truth. My life has been considerably less glamourous; besides, Gillian was always the better seamstress. She was very creative, you see. She always told me she would grow up to be a writer, or a children's book illustrator.

"Georgina, thank you for this. It's very special. I can't promise to start making my own clothes again, or mending Paul's socks, but I shall definitely cherish it."

Suzanne got to her feet and planted a light kiss on Georgina's cheek.

"We'd best be away," she said, leaning over to help rescue her mother from her seat. "It's been a lovely afternoon and a pleasure to meet you at last."

And then they were gone and Georgina was left alone beside her Christmas tree, toasting her left flank as the flames in the fireplace continued to gyrate to their own private tune.

She picked up Teddy's gift. She hastily peeled off the wrapping paper to reveal an exquisite silk scarf—Liberty's, no less. Even she, a country girl from the backwoods of Canada, knew a Liberty scarf was a special present. Of course, Teddy couldn't possibly have known that her lifestyle and day-to-day wardrobe couldn't carry off such a luxurious accessory, but perhaps she could lay it over her chair, or hang it on the wall. For now, she'd drape it over her shoulders and enjoy the feel of it against her skin.

The scarf had been wrapped around some rigid oblong object that, at first probe, Georgina had assumed was a thin hardcover book of some sort. However, upon further exploration, it turned out to be a package of something called 'Kendal Mint Cake'. Nothing 'cakey' about it whatsoever, she thought; it was as hard as a slab of granite! Teddy had written a note on the corner of the package:

Bet this brings back some memories from your childhood. Hope you've got a hammer on hand, or a 'Postlethwaite's' nearby so you can buy something to smash your way into it!! xx.

After a little bit of 'Googling', Georgina learned that Kendal Mint Cake, manufactured in the very Kendal where Gillian had attended school, was a famous sweet treat in England and abroad. Apparently it had even been taken on expeditions to Mt. Everest because it was a good source of instant sugary energy. Besides, thought Georgina, they could always use it as a small splint if one of the climbers twisted an ankle!

She immediately regretted not having sent a gift to Teddy. It wasn't that she didn't want to, or hadn't thought about it, it was simply that she couldn't think of what to send and she certainly didn't want to waste the postage on some tacky Canadian souvenir—like one of those miniature Mounties you see in the shops on Sparks Street, or a box of disgusting maple candy. Instead, she'd sent a Christmas card depicting a typical wintry Canadian scene painted by one of The Group of Seven and had enclosed a polite acknowledgement of the early parcel she had received from him and explained she would wait until Christmas Day to open it. At some point, however, she would have to respond to his letter.

~ ~ ~

TO: tp@postlethwaites.org.uk
FROM: champlain25@hotmail.com
SUBJECT: Thank you!
Hi Teddy,

I hope you're enjoying a lovely Christmas. Perhaps you are sharing it with Audrey? I had my neighbour over for afternoon drinks. Suzanne's visiting for Christmas so it was great to get together again and enjoy a catch-up. We haven't seen one another in so long.

Teddy, thank you for your lovely gifts. The scarf is exquisite. Turquoise, blue and green are my favourite colours! Yes, I remember Kendal Mint Cake. I'll keep it on hand in case I ever lose a shingle from my roof … I reckon it could do the job!

Most importantly, my dear, thank you for your candid letter. It hurts me to hear how you suffered. In many ways, I feel responsible for the sadness in your life. Had you been free of me, or thoughts of me, I'm sure you would have had an easier time of it. Nonetheless, I too remain grateful to have rediscovered you and nothing—absolutely nothing—you said in your letter changes that. You are still the Teddy I remember, but I am thoroughly enjoying getting to know the Teddy you've become. Happy Christmas, my love.

Gillian

~ ~ ~

TO: champlain25@hotmail.com
FROM: tp@postlethwaites.org.uk
SUBJECT: Thank you!
Darling Gillian,

You have no idea how relieved I am to hear that my letter and shameful confessions have not sent you running for the hills. You must not blame yourself in any way. For the longest while I blamed everyone, including you. It took many years for me to admit that my own choices—good and bad—were responsible for the life I was dealt. Blame is a toxic, life-throttling emotion. I am well rid of it.

So, let's move on to happier things:
now that I know I have not scared you
away, I can share my exciting news with
you. I am planning a holiday. A real holiday … not a schmooze-cruise with other
business types, but a proper adventure.
I'm coming to Canada! Finally, we will
see one another again. I have booked my
ticket and will be at your disposal on
April 14th of this coming year … exactly
54 years to the day since you left! So,
be prepared to be my official guide to
all things Canadian. I can't wait. What
an amazing New Year this is going to be.
Love, your Teddy

~ ~ ~

Chapter 8 - A Little Research

TO: champlain25@hotmail.com
FROM: tp@postlethwaites.org.uk
SUBJECT: Suzanne
March 16, 2013,

Gillian, I am so, so sorry to hear about your friend. Of course you must go and be with her at this time. And, of course, I understand. I shall postpone (not cancel) my travel plans for now and look forward to coming out there as soon as you return from New Brunswick. I know that Suzanne has been more of a friend to you over the past fifty years than I have and I completely understand how important it is to both of you that you spend her last days at her side. I hope you will be OK. Stay in touch when you can. I realize you won't have access to the Internet while you are there, but perhaps you can go to an Internet café once in a while and let me know how you are coping. Suzanne is fortunate to have such a loyal and selfless friend. Bless you, my love, Teddy

~ ~ ~

At Christmas, when Teddy had first mentioned his intention to travel to Canada, Georgina had panicked. It had taken her a few days to respond to him because she knew she couldn't proceed without some serious soul searching.

Her first notion had been not to reply at all, shut down her e-mail address and wash her hands of the whole thing. But she soon reconsidered when she realized she couldn't possibly let 'Gillian' abandon Teddy again. Like it or not, there would have to be a reunion ... somehow, somewhere.

Initially, she'd told Teddy how excited she was at the prospect of seeing him again after so long. But, as January quickly dissolved into February and February became March, Georgina realized she still didn't have a proper plan. To buy her a little extra time, she decided Suzanne would have to come down with a serious illness and she, 'Gillian' would be summoned to her side. Teddy would understand if she had to attend to a friend in need, she was sure of that.

Georgina knew she was beginning to overstay her welcome in this peculiar relationship and soon it would be time to take herself out of the picture before someone else did. Obviously, she couldn't maintain the pretense indefinitely. She would have to find Gillian. And so Georgina began a relentless search for Gillian Mathers. The biggest obstacle to her search was that she wasn't sure if Gillian Mathers even existed as Gillian Mathers anymore. Suzanne had confirmed that she'd married so, in all likelihood, she'd taken her husband's surname.

Georgina 'Googled' like a demon ... first Gillian Mathers, then Harold Mathers, her father ... she checked the telephone books in Winnipeg and Vancouver and called each and every Mathers listed, systematically 'eliminating them from her enquiries'—an expression she had learned from watching far too many television police dramas. No one had heard of Gillian. She even opened a Facebook account hoping that Gillian might be found through social media connections. Nothing. Gillian Mathers was flying well beneath the radar.

Georgina spent hours and hours scouring on-line newspaper archives ... she searched *The Winnipeg Free Press* and *The Vancouver Sun* looking for death notices, wedding and birth announcements as far back as she could. One 'Timothy Mathers' had died 'after a brave battle with cancer' in 1983, survived by no one with the name Harold or Gillian. Someone named Claudia Beale had married a John Mathers in Vancouver in 1972, and Roberta and Jeremy Mather (no 's' on the end) were proud to announce the birth of their twin girls on August 11, 1996. Tedious as the work was, Georgina rather enjoyed the lives she imagined these complete strangers might have lived. Had Timothy really been 'brave' in the face of cancer? Did Claudia and John's marriage endure? Where were those Mather twins now, she wondered?

And, of course, she still had to handle Teddy's e-mails. He was being very patient, but she knew her gig was nearly up. Whatever happened, she would not come out of this looking particularly good but, at the very least, if she could pull off this reunion between Teddy and the real Gillian, perhaps he would forgive her.

~ ~ ~

TO: champlain25@hotmail.com
FROM: tp@postlethwaites.org.uk
SUBJECT: So sorry ...
May 21, 2013

Darling Gillian,

I'm so very sorry to hear about your friend's passing. I have no doubt you did everything you could to make her last days as comfortable and as happy as possible. I have some news that I hope will cheer you up, my love. I've decided to attend the Home & Garden Expo in Seattle next month … I've always wanted to go there and see what's going to be the next tool or decorating trend you North Americans won't be able to live without! Afterwards, I thought I'd go up to Vancouver, spend a few days there before flying over to Ottawa to finally … finally … hold you in my arms once more. I'm sorry if this is rather short notice, but it seems like the perfect opportunity to kill two birds with one stone and, I hope, it will help you to look beyond your grief. I can't wait! My love, Teddy xxx

~ ~ ~

Georgina didn't, couldn't, reply to Teddy's e-mail. If she ever got around to answering him, she'd simply have to explain that the Internet had been down for a few days, or ask him to understand that she was still recovering from Suzanne's tragic death and wasn't up to a visit yet. She felt the world closing in on her and could see no dignified means of escape. Perhaps she should just blurt out the truth … 'the truth will set you free', they say. Or, perhaps, she should catch Suzanne's fictitious malady and die an expedient and mysterious death. If only she could find Gillian then, at the very least, something good *might* come out of all of this. Of course, Gillian might not even be interested in re-meeting her long lost love ... worse still, Gillian herself could be dead. Then what? Georgina really didn't know what to do.

A few days after Teddy's e-mail, Georgina was working her shift at the Cobden Public Library. It was a Thursday morning right after Storytime and all the parents and pre-schoolers had just left. As usual, the children's 'Listening Corner' looked like a bomb had hit it. The rule was that books taken off the shelves by the youngsters were not to be put back; instead they were supposed to be left on a metal trolley by the window so that a librarian could re-shelve them correctly. Most of the books, however, never made it as far as the trolley and lay, open and exposed, in heaps on the floor, under the stacks and down the sides of the comfy chairs. As Georgina was making her rounds, picking up books and sorting them on the trolley, a slim, hardcover book caught her eye. The front cover depicted an egg-shaped cartoon character wearing navy blue coveralls, waving a Canadian flag and standing in front of a range of jagged blue mountains. *Mr. P Goes To Canada* was the title. Quaint, thought Georgina. Then she noticed a banner printed diagonally across the bottom right corner of the cover. It read: 'Another adventure for the ever popular Mr. Postleth-waite, by Gillian Evans.'

Coincidence? No, thought Georgina! Hadn't Teddy said Gillian always wanted to write children's books? 'Postle-thwaite' and 'Gillian' weren't particularly common names and yet, here they were sharing space on a children's book jacket. Gillian Evans had to be Gillian Mathers!

Georgina sat down abruptly. Her hands were shaking and her mouth was suddenly as dry as a blackboard. Slowly she turned the book over and read the back cover blurb:

'Gillian Evans is the award-winning author of the popular children's series featuring the adventures of hardware store owner, Mr. P. This is Ms. Evans' fifteenth and final book. Ms. Evans, originally from England, currently lives in Vancouver, British Columbia, where she plans to retire and take up water colour painting.'

Georgina was stunned. To think that all this time, 'Gillian' had been right under her nose. Georgina was thrilled, relieved and, on some level, rather disappointed. The disappointment came from the realization that there was, indeed, a real Gillian Mathers and that Georgina's role would soon become superfluous.

In hindsight, she knew that her involvement beyond mailing that long lost letter was wrong. But, oh, what a wonderful journey it had been! She was going to miss her beloved Teddy.

However, there was still plenty of work to do. She had to make contact with Gillian Mathers Evans if Teddy's dream of a reunion was ever going to take place.

Gillian Evans was so easy to find on the Internet that Georgina couldn't believe how much time she had wasted getting absolutely nowhere over the past weeks. Instantly, her search too her to photos of Gillian giving readings at various children's events across British Columbia, excerpts from her newspaper interviews and, most importantly, a dedicated author page on the Harper Collins website.

Georgina studied Gillian's face … it was the mature version of the same face that had appeared in Mrs. Walsh's photographs from years and years ago. She was still that compact little person she'd been in her youth with greying hair cut in a neat shoulder length bob. She had a well-honed, camera-ready smile even though Georgina recognized something vulnerable and tentative behind it. She had the look of someone who had shown up to live the life assigned to her, but hadn't committed to it with any certainty. Perhaps what Georgina spotted in Gillian was something that reminded her of her own life—one lived cautiously on the edges of other people's.

When Georgina selected the 'contact' button, she'd hoped Gillian's e-mail address would be one of the options offered, but instead a standard contact form came up. Obviously, she still had a few more gatekeepers to get past.

She completed the required sections of the form, providing her name, telephone number and e-mail address. From the drop down menu asking the nature of her enquiry, she opted for 'I'm looking to publish', hoping that might take her directly to an agent or editor who would know Gillian personally. Next, in 240 characters or less, she typed the following into the 'additional information' window:

```
To whom it may concern:
I urgently need to contact Ms. Ev-
ans. The real Mr. Postlethwaite, upon
whom her books are based, has asked me
to find her. They were childhood friends
who lost touch years ago. Please help,
it's very important. Georgina Harris.
```

Send.

Out on the west coast, Will Evans opened his front door, stepped inside and dropped his keys on the hall table before draping his overcoat over the newel post at the bottom of the stairs. He marched straight to the kitchen drinks cabinet and poured himself a couple of fingers of scotch. The visits were getting harder and harder to endure. They were always the same and Will couldn't help but wonder if it would make the slightest bit of difference to his mother if he simply stopped going. Of course, he couldn't do that, his conscience wouldn't allow it and, besides, the nurses kept assuring him that his short weekly visits always cheered her up. Frankly, he thought with a grin, it was Nurse Carolyn who really enjoyed his visits the most. She definitely had a bit of a 'thing' for him and he rather enjoyed it. After all, he wasn't a bad prospect. He kept himself in reasonable shape, the two emerging paths heading backwards from his forehead to expose a gradually receding hairline weren't too obvious yet and he was well established in his career. Working against him was his alarming proximity to his fortieth birthday, the fact that he lived in his mother's house (even though *she* didn't) and that he was a bit of a loner. Carolyn was very sweet, probably ten or more years his junior, and he enjoyed her upbeat disposition and the genuine compassion she showed her patients—Gillian included. She'd probably be quite good company, he thought.

"She's writing letters again," chirped Carolyn when Will had arrived at the Home earlier that evening.

Without meaning to, Will groaned out loud. Gillian's idea of 'writing letters' was to scrawl 'Dear Teddy' over and over again in her clumsy handwriting. She could fill an entire pad of pristine white paper in just one day and categorically refused to be fobbed off with recycled sheets or other scraps. Will bought notepads in bulk whenever they were on sale at Staples to keep her supplied.

"Post this for me," she demanded as she tore off her latest 'letter' and thrust it at Will. "Where's your uniform?" she asked.

"What uniform, Mum?"

"Your postman suit, silly," she replied.

Then she'd sat silently for minutes just gazing out of the conservatory window. This was where she spent most of her day, staring at the lawns and gardens and, on a clear day, the backdrop of snowcapped mountains. For the most part, the nurses left her to her private contemplations even permitting her to eat her meals from a lap tray in the conservatory. All other residents who weren't bedbound were required to shuffle down to the dining room for their meals but The Serengeti Nursing Home staff had long given up doing battle with the obstreperous Gillian Evans over such inconsequential things.

"Read it back to me!" she demanded.

This, too, was part of the routine. Will would be required to 'read back' her most recent imaginary letter, the content of which was known only to Gillian. If he got it wrong—which he invariably did—she would berate him. Sometimes he'd be there for a couple of hours trying to get the text of her letter correct. Today had been one of those days and he was completely exhausted by it.

He was relaxing on the couch nursing his drink and absent-mindedly flipping through the channels on his remote when his phone rang. Damn, he thought.

Reluctantly, he picked up the call. "Hello," he sighed into the mouthpiece.

"Hey, Will … so sorry to disturb you. It's Betty. Betty Anderson calling. Have I caught you at a bad time? You sound like I might have woken you up."

"No, it's fine Betty. I'm tired that's all. How are you?" he asked politely. Betty Anderson had been Gillian's editor at Harper Collins throughout her writing career.

"I'm fine, Will. How's your mum?"

"Oh, pretty much the same, I'm afraid. I just got back from there, which is probably why I sound so depleted. It's hard some days and she can be very demanding. She's been writing to Teddy again."

Betty was not just a colleague but, over the years, she'd

become a good friend to Gillian and Will and he was always candid with her regarding Gillian's condition.

"Oh, I'm so sorry to hear that, Will. It must be so difficult to see her like that. Actually, this may not be the best time for me to have called but I don't like to disturb you at work. I wanted to talk to you about an e-mail that was forwarded to me the other day. It could be a crank, but I have a funny feeling there's more to it, although I can't explain why."

"Hey, it's OK, Betty … fire ahead," replied Will.

"Well, it's an e-mail that came to the office. It claims to be from someone who says she knows Teddy Postlethwaite. Her name's Georgina Harris. Ring any bells?"

"Not off hand," answered Will.

"This Georgina woman says that Teddy wants to get in touch with Gillian. If it's a hoax, we'll put an end to it pretty fast, but, if it's real, what do you think we should do?" Betty asked.

"I don't know, Betty, but I'm glad you told me. Can you send me the e-mail?"

"Of course, I'll do it as soon as we hang up. I hope it doesn't add to your burdens, Will. Let me know what you decide to do about it. If it's the genuine article, it could turn out to be the best gift you could possibly give your mother!"

"We'll see," said Will cautiously, "I certainly don't want to put her through anything that could end up making matters worse. Mind you, she seems so far away now that even if it was the famous Teddy, it's probably too late. But thanks for letting me know, Betty. Take care."

Will hung up and went directly to his computer. A few moments later, Will was tapping out a response to Georgina's e-mail:

~ ~ ~

```
TO: champlain25@hotmail.com
FROM: w.evans@gmail.com
SUBJECT: Mr. Postlethwaite
Dear Ms. Harris,
```

My name is Will Evans. I am the son of Gillian Evans. I received a copy of the e-mail you sent to Harper Collins claiming to be a friend of Teddy Postlethwaite. If this is some cruel hoax, I respectfully ask that you put an end to it right now and save us all a lot of bother. If, on the other hand, you really are a friend of Mr. Postlethwaite, perhaps you can provide me with a few more details to corroborate your story. My mother is not in the best of health at this time and I do not intend to tell her about your claim until I am confident that it is genuine. If, as you say, you really know her long lost friend, I'm sure you will understand my wariness.

If you plan to respond, please send all further correspondence to this e-mail address.

Will Evans

~ ~ ~

Back in Cobden, Georgina had been checking her e-mail account almost hourly. She was desperate for some sort of acknowledgement or, better still, a reply from Harper Collins. Time was running out. Potentially, Teddy could be standing at Ottawa's international airport within just a few weeks waiting for his Gillian to greet him.

After a full week had passed without any word from the publisher, she decided that if she heard nothing over the weekend, she'd telephone their offices first thing Monday morning. But, on Friday, she opened up her e-mail and found a message from an unfamiliar address awaiting her. After reading it, she responded immediately.

~ ~ ~

TO: w.evans@gmail.com
FROM: champlain25@hotmail.com
SUBJECT: Mr. Postlethwaite
Dear Mr. Evans,

Thank you so much for your prompt reply. Of course, I completely understand your reticence and I hope that the contents of this e-mail will help put your concerns to rest.

My name is Georgina Harris. I live at 25 Champlain Street in Cobden … the very same house that your mother lived in when she and her family arrived in Canada in 1959 …

~ ~ ~

… Georgina went on to explain about the letter she had found in the desk and her decision to mail it. She then told Will that Teddy had responded immediately and that the two of them had started up a regular correspondence. What she did not bother to mention was that this exchange involved her impersonating his mother! She went on to share some of the things she had learned about Teddy, Gillian and their families and hoped that by doing so Will would be convinced that this was neither a prank nor a scam.

~ ~ ~

TO: tp@postlethwaites.org.uk
FROM: champlain25@hotmail.com
SUBJECT: Our meeting
Dear Teddy,

I agree; meeting in Vancouver would be perfect! We could spend a couple of days exploring the city before flying back here. I'll write again soon with my flight details. I am so looking forward to this … you will not be disappointed!

Love, Gillian

~ ~ ~

TO: tp@postlethwaites.org.uk
FROM: champlain25@hotmail.com
SUBJECT: Our meeting
Dear Teddy,

I've hit a bit of a snag and it looks as though my flight will be arriving several hours after yours. But, don't worry, I've arranged for a young friend of mine to meet you instead and he'll keep you entertained until I show up. His name is Will Evans. He'll be waiting outside the luggage area holding up a sign that will say 'Welcome Mr. P'. I'm sorry I can't be there immediately, but I know the two of you will have plenty to talk about.

Always know that I have grown to love you very much. I sincerely hope that what I'm doing is the right thing … finally.

Your gal, Gill xxx

~ ~ ~

TO: champlain25@hotmail.com
FROM: tp@postlethwaites.org.uk
SUBJECT: Our meeting
Gillian,

I am dreadfully disappointed that your face won't be there in the crowd to greet me tomorrow, but I appreciate you finding a stand in … although I'm a little confused. Who is this chap? Ah well, I suppose I'll find out soon enough.

Are you having doubts about seeing me again? Your last paragraph sounded a bit like you might be having second thoughts. If so, please don't. Stage fright is natural, but you know this is the right thing to do … we've waited most of our lives for this long overdue reunion. Don't be nervous. We're old pals, remember?

See you soon,
Love, Teddy.

~ ~ ~

Georgina read Teddy's last e-mail and closed the lid of her laptop. She would not be replying.

Oh, how she wished she could be a fly on the wall. She'd love to see the look on Gillian's face when the love of her life waltzed into the room. Thank goodness Will had finally agreed to broker the arrangements, although he had not been very forthcoming when it came to talking about his mother. He'd mentioned she was in poor health in his first e-mail but didn't volunteer any further details, nor did he refer to Gillian's husband, so Georgina hoped the coast was clear for Teddy. Teddy would, of course, be a bit shocked to discover Gillian had a son, but she was sure he'd get over it as soon as he held his beloved Gillian in his arms again. Georgina—conveniently forgetting her own shameful role in the matter—congratulated herself on bringing about what she assumed would be one of the most heart-warming and spectacular lovers' reunions of the century. Sad to think that after all her efforts, she wouldn't be there to be congratulated in person.

Chapter 9 - Mr. P Goes To Canada

Will checked his phone to make sure Teddy's flight from Seattle was on time. He arrived at the airport with a few minutes to spare and positioned himself close to the double sliding doors that released passengers from the luggage hall. On the occasions when Will was an arriving passenger himself, he always dreaded that moment when the glass doors automatically slid open and he emerged into a sea of anxiously awaiting faces—wives looking for their returning husbands, children jumping up and down hoping to be the first to spot a weary grandparent. Then, of course, there were those rather conspicuous self-conscious individuals desperately scanning the crowd in search of people they didn't even know. Today, Will was one of those people, standing there awkwardly with his handmade sign at the ready. Too bad he wasn't meeting the real 'Mr. P'; an egg-shaped man wearing dark overalls with bulging pockets laden with tools and humbugs would have been very easy to spot!

Soon there was a constant stream of passengers parading through the doors. Many of them obviously weren't expecting to be met by anyone and walked past, heads down, trying to look as though their uncelebrated arrivals were nothing to pity them for. Others gazed about eagerly hoping to spy a familiar face, eyes lighting up when they were successful, eyes to the floor when they were not.

Eventually, a well-dressed gentleman in a navy blue suit, carrying a grey overcoat over one arm and hauling a smart wheeled suitcase behind him, appeared in the Arrivals Hall. He was a pleasant looking man with a youthful air about him, despite his grey hair and slightly stooped gait. He walked far enough away from the doors to get out of everyone else's way and then paused to take in his surroundings. He'd travelled to America several times before, but this was his first visit to Canada and he knew that he was now closer to his beloved Gillian than he had been in over fifty four years. Soon she, too, would step through those glass doors and he would be waiting there to greet her. It was difficult to contain his excitement.

"Mr. Postlethwaite! Are you Mr. Postlethwaite?"

A handsome young man was walking towards him holding out a sign that read: 'Welcome Mr. P', just as Gillian had promised.

"How do you do? Will, isn't it? I was told to be on the lookout for you. It's dreadfully kind of you to meet me like this."

They shook hands and Will dropped the ridiculous Mr. P sign in a waste bin as he steered Mr. Postlethwaite towards the exit doors.

"Mr. Postlethwaite, I was thinking we could go to my house before you see her. There are a few things I'd like to discuss with you."

"Teddy, please call me Teddy."

"Of course," replied Will, secretly relieved that he wouldn't have to stumble over that awkward surname for the duration of the visit.

"As long as we're not late," Teddy continued, "after all this time, I certainly don't want to be tardy."

"Don't worry, Teddy, she's not going anywhere," Will

answered.

The drive to Will's home took about twenty minutes during which time Teddy and Will made small talk. Teddy told him a little about the Expo in Seattle and what a lovely city he thought Seattle was.

"Of course, I've heard quite a bit about Vancouver too and I'm looking forward to seeing some of the sights. I hope Gillian and I can explore together."

"I doubt that, Teddy," Will murmured but, before Teddy could query him, Will announced that they had arrived.

"Here we are. You'll have to excuse the state of the place. Since Mother left, I've let it become a bit of a bachelor pad," Will remarked apologetically.

"Oh, then we have something in common, my friend. I'm all too familiar with 'bachelor-esque' design."

"I've prepared a room for you, Teddy, but we can bring your suitcase in later after we've had a chat, if you prefer."

"That's very decent of you, Will, but I've actually booked a room at The Coast Plaza. Wouldn't want to put you to all that trouble."

"Whatever you like, Teddy. There's space here if you want it, otherwise, of course, I understand if you'd prefer to be independent."

"I could murder a proper cup of tea," Teddy said, "if you can brew something that doesn't look and taste like last night's washing up water. The Americans can put a man on the moon, but they sure as hell can't brew a proper cup of tea."

"Coming right up," Will replied, although he himself would have preferred something a little more potent. "Please make yourself comfortable in the living room and I'll be right in," he added.

"So," began Teddy feeling immediately restored after a few sips of Will's perfectly brewed loose leaf tea, "tell me,

Will, what exactly is your connection to Gillian?"

Will was taken aback by the question.

"Oh, I – I – I ass-ass-assumed you knew …" he stuttered, "Gillian is my mother."

The mug of steaming tea in Teddy's hand wobbled slightly and a few drops landed on his lap. He fumbled about for a handkerchief to mop them up with and carefully wiped the bottom of the mug before placing it as steadily as he could on the walnut coffee table in front of him.

"I … I'm so sorry … I had no idea," he stuttered back. "How very strange; you see, I was unaware she had a son."

"Well," began Will cautiously, "fifty four years is a long time, Teddy. I imagine there are many things you don't know about one another. I have an older sister too. Her name's Julie, she lives in New Zealand. I'm guessing that's news to you too."

"No … no, I didn't know that either," Teddy answered softly.

Will sensed there was something very wrong. The confident, amiable fellow he'd first encountered suddenly seemed very anxious and unsure of himself.

"Mr. Postlethwaite, er … I mean, Teddy, exactly what has Georgina told you about my mother?"

"Georgina? I don't know a Georgina," he said, looking completely baffled, "your mother never mentioned anyone called Georgina. The only friend she spoke of by name was Suzanne. She died recently, as you probably know. We shared everything with one another, or so I thought. I knew she wasn't married but why on earth wouldn't she have told me she had children? I wouldn't have thought any less of her." Teddy looked up at Will practically begging him for an explanation.

"Teddy," Will began, "when did you last write to my mother?"

"We e-mailed just a few days ago. Why do you ask? Has something happened to her?"

"Teddy, I don't know exactly what's going on here, but I'm beginning to suspect that Georgina Harris has something to do with this. I felt there was something fishy when she first told me she'd found you. But, you see, my mother has never stopped asking for you, so I thought your visit might do her some good. And, to be honest, after all these years, I was curious to see you for myself. You see, Teddy, my mother has been in a care facility for over a year now. She has Alzheimer's disease. She barely knows her own name these days; she's certainly incapable of writing letters or sending e-mails."

Will paused for a moment. "Let me pour you a proper drink, Teddy, and then we'll try and get to the bottom of this together."

Teddy didn't protest and gladly put the tea aside when Will handed him a warmed brandy. After a few sips, the colour began to return to his cheeks and he began to talk.

"You've no idea the joy I felt when I saw your mother's letter. I never stopped loving her, you see. I know it sounds foolish to a young man like yourself, but I couldn't help it …"

Teddy spoke without pause for almost twenty minutes. He told Will about the promises he and Gillian had made the night before she'd left for Canada and then, over five decades later, how easy it had been to resume their friendship … or so he thought. He told Will about the letters he'd received from 25 Champlain Street and how he believed everything they contained to be true. After all, what reason would he have to doubt any of it?

"What a complete and utter fool I have been, Will. You must think me a very stupid old man. I should probably go." He started to rise from his seat.

Will reached out and gently placed a hand on Teddy's shoulder to get him to sit back down. Teddy didn't resist.

"Absolutely not, my friend! You are here now ... and there is absolutely no reason you shouldn't be reunited with my mother as planned. Of course, it won't be the reunion you were anticipating, but it would be awfully sad if you simply walked away after coming all this way and getting this close. She never forgot you either, Teddy. I'll prove it to you, I promise."

Then it was Will's turn to explain how the two of them had been brought together. He told Teddy that it was a trusted family friend who had led him to Georgina. He knew nothing about the woman except that she lived in the house his mother had lived in when she arrived in Canada. He told Teddy about the time his mother had taken him there after his graduation. He said he'd always wondered why that house had made such an impression on her since she'd lived there less than two years but, he concluded, it was probably because of what happened to his grandmother.

By the time Will finished telling his story, he could see that Teddy was suddenly extremely tired.

Teddy spoke first, "I wonder, my friend, if I could take you up on your invitation after all?"

"Of course," Will replied, "you've had a difficult day. There's no need for you to be sitting alone in some strange hotel room grazing from a poorly stocked mini-bar. Let me get your case out of the car."

"I'll tell you what," Will called as he heaved Teddy's luggage up the stairs, "why don't we stay in tonight and bond over a bottle of wine and a bowl of pasta? Like I said before, Mum's not going anywhere. I'll take you to see her first thing tomorrow."

Teddy readily agreed. He settled his belongings upstairs and shed his navy suit in favour of a pair of casual khaki slacks and a pale green cashmere pullover before joining Will at the kitchen table.

After a simple, but restorative, meal, Will and Teddy sat sipping glasses of Shiraz in the living room. They were well into their second bottle and conversation was easy. There were many things they both wanted to know about Will's mother and family.

"How well did you know your grandfather, Will?" Teddy asked.

"Not well at all, I'm afraid. I was only four when he died. I'd met him a couple of times, but he wasn't one of those indulgent grandparents who liked to spoil their grandchildren or bounce them on their knees."

"No, I don't suppose he was," Teddy remarked. "You see, he was always a rather distant and unapproachable man as I recall. I didn't get on with him at all. In hindsight, I suppose I can't blame the fellow. After all, Gillian's infatuation with a village boy with little or no obvious prospects or ambition was not part of his plan. Your grandmother, Mary, was a sweet woman, but she didn't have much of a voice in the family. She was a rather sad soul, I think. Harold obviously thought that if he wanted to keep his family under his control, he'd have to yank them out of their familiar lives and carry them off to the New World. It can't have been an easy decision and it obviously didn't work out as he'd intended. I imagine he felt quite a bit of guilt over Mary's death. I wish I'd known. I'm sure Gillian could have used a shoulder to cry on. I doubt Mr. Mathers thought to offer his own."

"Harold didn't emigrate just to separate you and my mother, surely?" Will asked.

"Oh no, there was much more to it than that. My relationship with Gillian was little more than a petty nuisance to him, I'm certain. You see Gillian's mother was having a love affair of her own. So for poor Harold, both women in his life only had eyes for other men. What Mary was doing wasn't right, of course, but love changes everything. She must have felt overwhelmingly despondent to take her own life and abandon her daughter the way she did."

Teddy paused to take another sip of his wine, "tell me about your childhood, Will. I would imagine Gillian was a very attentive mother. From what I can see, she certainly did a very good job," he added, raising his glass to Will.

"My mother looked after Julie and me well enough, I suppose. We never wanted for anything. I think Julie was a bit more of a handful than I was, so I cruised through with relative ease. But you know, Teddy, she was distant and there was always a part of her that wasn't fully present, if you know what I mean. I mean, she fed us, read us bedtime stories, took us on outings, took us to school, watched us play sports and all those sorts of things, but it sometimes felt as though she was simply going through the motions."

"What about your father, Will? Are you close to him?"

"Not especially. He left Mum right after I left home. It was like he'd been waiting for his moment to escape. He moved in with his mistress and they went on to produce a baby … my half-brother, I suppose. They live here in Vancouver, but I rarely see them. To be honest, my entire life has revolved around Mum for the past few years, at least until she moved into The Serengeti. It's costly. I'll have to sell this place as soon as I get it fixed up, or she could run out of money. I've asked Dad to help but, of course, he doesn't see it as his responsibility anymore. I suppose he's right about that."

"And what about your sister, Will? Does she help you out at all?"

"Frankly, Teddy, I think she was a bit miffed when I put Mum into the Home. She's so far removed from all of this.

She's away on the other side of the globe in her own world of diapers and sheep. She has no clue about how difficult it has been. I think she believes I was just dumping Mum to give myself a break … although I certainly won't deny I needed one. No, I put her there because I really believed that the care she required was beyond my abilities. Besides, it's very difficult when it's someone you know and love and you have to stand by and take their abuse and watch them become someone you no longer recognize. It goes both ways of course; she doesn't recognize me either."

"It's a cruel disease indeed, Will. I'm sorry you've had to cope for so long on your own. I admire you greatly. You are a fine young man and what you have sacrificed in order to take care of Gillian will not go unappreciated. Anyway, you've put up with this old man long enough for one day. I think I'll take myself off to bed. It's been an extraordinary day in many, many ways and I'm suddenly quite tired. I reckon I'll be in the land of nod before my head hits the pillow."

"Wait just a moment," Will said. "I've some books you might be interested in."

"Like I said, son, I won't need to read myself to sleep tonight."

"No, please. Just give me a minute," Will insisted.

He returned minutes later with an armful of thin hardcover books. Teddy glanced at them and was quite sure they were children's books.

"Aren't you a little old to have me read you a bedtime story?" he chuckled.

Will handed him one of the books. On the cover was a jolly looking egg-shaped character wearing blue overalls with a selection of tools, bits of string and a tape measure peeking out from his oversized pockets. The title read: *Mr. P Goes To Work*, by Gillian Evans.

"Oh, my goodness," Teddy exclaimed, "she did it! She really did it! She always said she would become a writer when she grew up. This is amazing, Will."

"Well, there's plenty more where those came from. She wrote over a dozen books about the life of her beloved Mr. P. I told you she never forgot you."

"I'm shocked, Will, I really am. I had no idea. Thank you. Thank you for showing me these. And thank you for welcoming me into your home so graciously. You are a remarkable young man. Gillian must be very, very proud. Goodnight, Will. I'll see you in the morning. May I take a couple of these up with me?"

"Of course. Good night, Teddy. Sleep well."

Teddy slept like the proverbial log and was up and dressed bright and early the following morning. He looked out of his bedroom window and could see the mountains in the distance. Yesterday they'd been shrouded in cotton wool. Today they were magnificent, just like the photographs in the Canadian calendars Audrey gave him every Christmas.

He ambled down to the kitchen where Will was cradling a cup of coffee and perusing the morning newspaper. When Will looked up and saw Teddy wearing his navy suit again, he was a little surprised.

"Oh, I know what you're thinking," Teddy said, "wouldn't I be more comfortable in something less formal? Well, to tell you the truth, no I wouldn't. You have remember, Will, I'm an old-fashioned Englishman courting my special lady friend after a very long absence. I want to make the best possible impression."

It wouldn't matter if Teddy showed up in a track suit or a space suit, Will thought, his mother was unlikely to know the difference, but he decided to keep such thoughts to himself and got up to pour Teddy a cup of coffee.

"Or would you prefer tea?" he asked.

"No, coffee would be terrific," Teddy answered.

"I've called the Home," Will said, "I've explained that I'm bringing a special visitor to see Mum. They're expecting us around eleven, if that's OK with you?"

Will leaned back and watched Teddy apply lashings of butter to a piece of brown toast. Funny how the Brits never seemed to concern themselves with cholesterol and saturated fats, thought Will. He remembered his mother telling him it was all 'American codswallop'; nothing but fear mongering to get people to buy expensive gym memberships they'd never use and over-priced dietary supplements they'd forget to take. However, Will wasn't overly concerned about Teddy's waistline or the state of his arteries; he was far more concerned about his emotional welfare. Today could turn out to be a catastrophe. At best, Gillian might barely acknowledge him; at worst she could become hostile. After half a century spent waiting for this moment, could Teddy really handle it, he wondered.

"You have to be ready for this, Teddy ..." Will began ...

"It's all right, lad, I know what you're about to say. I'm not allowing my expectations to get out of hand. I'm prepared to take her as I find her. Of course, I'd like to find the Gillian I remember, to tell her I never stopped loving her and waiting for her. I'll probably tell her anyway. Perhaps she'll hear me, perhaps she won't. I've grieved the loss of her love many, many times over the years. I'm really quite good at it, so please don't worry about me."

"Have you thought more about Georgina?" Will asked.

"I have," he replied solemnly, "but I'm putting her aside for now. Today is all about Gillian. Georgina—whoever she is—will not spoil this day."

They finished their breakfast in silence and then Teddy

stood up and placed his dishes gently in the sink.

"I need a walk and some fresh Canadian air," he announced, "and I'll need to find a flower shop. Is there anywhere close by?"

Will gave him directions to the little neighbourhood shop that he and his mother had frequented for as long as he could remember.

"Enjoy your walk, Teddy. Remember, this is Vancouver; if Mum was here, she'd insist you 'take your brolly'!"

How many times had Gillian yelled those words at Will when he was setting off to go somewhere with his friends? It was so embarrassing at the time and there was nothing he could do to convince her that young teenage boys did *not* waltz around town toting umbrellas. And now, he thought, he'd give anything to hear those words from her one more time … although he still didn't own an umbrella.

Teddy found it extraordinary to be walking along the very same streets Gillian had walked along time and time again. He stopped at the corner to admire the view of English Bay and the backdrop of gauzy mountains and wondered how many times she had done the very same thing. He strolled through a small park with a playground at the far end. Had Gillian brought her children here? Had she sat on this very bench or pushed them on those swings?

He quickly found his way to the little bodega on 10th Street that Will had suggested. Outside on the sidewalk, there were several rows of white plastic buckets full of tulips, gerbera daisies, daffodils and mixed bouquets. Remembering Gillian's fondness for wild daffodils and Wordsworth, he chose two bunches of fat-stemmed daffodils not yet open.

"Remember to cut the stems off clean at an angle before you put them in water," the shopkeeper advised.

"I'll do that," said Teddy as he handed over a brand new, polymer twenty-dollar bill.

He pocketed the unfamiliar looking change, gripped the flowers and promptly made his way back to Will's house. He was ready now to go and see Gillian and hoped they could set out soon.

As Will tidied up the living room, clearing away the glasses and two empty bottles from the previous evening, he caught a glimpse of Teddy walking up the path to the house. He looked rather out of place in his formal navy suit. Without the flowers in his hand, he could easily have been mistaken for one of those Jehovah Witnesses or member of some other religious sect set on saving the world one doorstep at a time; but with the flowers dangling awkwardly by his side, and his hair blowing in all directions, he looked more like an eccentric Englishman newly escaped from a Monty Python skit.

"The Home is about fifteen minutes from here," Will explained as they headed east along West 16th towards Granville Street, "it's in the West End, right across the bay you see from your bedroom window. I'm glad the sun is shining for you today, Teddy. You look very smart, too. Mum will be pleased, I think."

The Serengeti Nursing Home was a magnificent old building occupying a small, but beautifully tended, estate in a well-to-do residential neighbourhood. From the outside, there was absolutely nothing institutional about it whatsoever. A nefarious shipping magnate, who'd made his considerable fortune as an opium trader, had built it in 1890. Wanting to maintain some distance between his work in Victoria and his private life, he'd chosen Vancouver as the location of his family's home.

"So," Teddy said, "are we likely to see any gazelles frolicking on the front lawns?"

"No, 'fraid not," Will laughed. "The story, as I understand it, is that one of the very first residents here said he couldn't die until he'd seen The Serengeti. It had been his life's dream ... on his 'bucket list' as they say today. Apparently management was very sympathetic to his wishes and named the home accordingly so that this gentleman could fulfill his final dream and depart knowing that he had, in all honesty, seen The Serengeti!"

"What a delightful tale," Teddy remarked. "Is it still a caring place ... would that kind of thing happen today, do you think?"

"Oh, I believe so. The staff is wonderful here. They make every effort to put their charges and their families first. Visiting hours are flexible, the food is edible and there's always some activity or entertainment planned. It's expensive, but I believe it's worth it. There weren't many options available to us that ticked all the boxes ... it's close by, it's clean and friendly, there's a lovely garden and top-notch medical care available as needed. I looked at many places, Teddy. Most of them were rather depressing ... long corridors lined with parked wheelchairs containing dozing, drooling, drugged inmates. You don't see that here. No one here looks abandoned."

Will paused for a moment as he concentrated on making his way around a stalled pickup truck.

"I hope I got it right," he continued, "you read such dreadful things about abused and battered seniors in the care of malicious or negligent professionals. I wouldn't forgive myself if something like that became apparent down the road. But, I'm pretty confident it doesn't happen here," he added as he swung into the driveway.

"Right on time, we have arrived, Teddy."

It was a very handsome three-storey building with an impressive central front door flanked on either side by deep covered porches that continued around the corners and down the sides of the building. The roofline was broken up with gables trimmed with elaborate fretwork. From the street, it looked like any other modest mansion. Behind its gracious façade, however, lay the modern extension that had been added in 1960 when the home had been converted into a girls' school. It wasn't until 1998 that it became a nursing home.

Silently Will and Teddy climbed the ten stone steps that led to the front door. Teddy was feeling excited, nervous and a whole lot of other emotions in between. Will found himself feeling many of them on Teddy's behalf.

"Good morning, Will. Nice to see you," said a bright young nurse seated at Reception just inside the heavy double doors.

As Teddy stood inside the lobby, he realized it wasn't quite what he had envisioned. From the outside, he'd expected to walk into a magnificent foyer with large chandeliers suspended from the ceiling and polished marble tiles on the floor. Perhaps there'd be a seating area with plush, comfortable chairs and a settee in front of a large stone fireplace. In Teddy's mind's eye, he'd seen a luxurious lobby area more appropriate to a hotel than an institution for the soon-to-be departed.

Not that the inside was ugly or unpleasant, but it was definitely clinical. Florescent tube lights hung where he'd imagined chandeliers would dangle and marble-like Linoleum covered the floors in place of the real thing. There was a glassed-in kiosk immediately to the left of the front doors where the perky blond nurse who'd greeted Will was seated. To the right was a collection of cheerful easy-wipe orange and lime vinyl-covered chairs with wooden arms. Music was piped in from somewhere in the walls. An instrumental version of the Beatles' '*Strawberry Fields*' was the current selection. Three wide, well-lit corridors radiated out from the hallway. A tall signpost, contrived to resemble a street sign from years gone by, stood in the centre of the hall indicating the dining hall and library would be found down the yellow corridor on the left, the conservatory and games room down the mauve corridor to the right and residents' rooms and the infirmary lay straight ahead down a corridor painted bile green.

The young nurse at reception—Carolyn, according to her bright pink name badge—emerged and, gently brushing Will's arm, beamed up at him.

"It's good to see you, Will. Your Mum's had a good day so far. She'll enjoy a visit."

Then she turned and looked at Teddy, "and you must be Mr. Postlethwaite. We've heard lots about you. It's lovely to meet you." Teddy shook the small but strong hand held out to him.

"Please, step in here for a moment, so that I can get you both to sign in."

Will scribbled his name on the clipboard provided as he had done many, many times before. Teddy followed.

"One more signature, if you'd be so kind," Carolyn said, smiling up at Teddy.

She reached under the counter and produced a rather tattered copy of *Mr. P Goes Fishing*.

"I hope you don't mind. Will told us you were Gillian's muse throughout her writing career," she said. "This is my nephew's favourite and I know he'd be tickled pink if you wrote something in it for him. He really loves the part where you reel in that angry duck! Did you really do that, Mr. Postlethwaite?"

"I did as a matter of fact," Teddy replied with a shy boyish grin, "Gillian can confirm it," he added, then hesitated, wondering if that were true anymore. "She was right there," he continued, "of course, I'll sign your book. What's your nephew's name?"

"Will, if it's OK with you, I'd rather like to go in by myself," Teddy said after he'd signed his very first autograph.

"She's in the conservatory, Mr. Postlethwaite. Straight down that hall to the end. She's wearing her lilac shawl today," Carolyn explained pointing to the pale mauve corridor on the right.

"I'm just about to go on my break, Will. Can I treat you to a cup of the worst coffee you've ever had?"

"Best offer I've had all day," Will answered with a smile.

Best offer you've had all year, Teddy thought to himself as he watched them walk away down the yellow corridor.

Sunlight, streaming in through the skylights and windows of the conservatory at the end of the hall, cast an alluring, almost mystical glow drawing Teddy further and further along the mauve tunnel to his long-awaited destination.

This is it, he thought, this is the day.

At the entrance to the conservatory Teddy paused to compose himself. Inside there were a few groups of men and women seated around small tables playing dominoes or reading newspapers. One gentleman sat off by himself and appeared to be sketching, or maybe just doodling for the fun of it. Two white haired ladies sat side-by-side engrossed in their knitting. They were so alike, they had to be twins, Teddy thought.

At the far end of the room, with her chair pressed up against the window, a small grey-haired lady sat in a shroud of complete silence and stillness. She appeared utterly absorbed in the amourous dance performed by a couple of robins on the lawn outside. It was as if their performance was just for her. She was slightly hunched over. A lilac wool shawl—not unlike the colour of the corridor Teddy had just emerged from—was draped around her shoulders and she

216

clutched the ends tightly beneath her chin.

Teddy knew it was Gillian. Carolyn needn't have described the shawl she'd be wearing; he'd have recognized her regardless.

He walked slowly across the room hoping that the sound of his shoes squeaking on the well-polished floor wouldn't disturb anyone. He nodded at the two knitting ladies and smiled at one or two other residents. He stopped when he reached the back of Gillian's chair. He didn't want to startle her, but she must have sensed his presence, or perhaps seen his reflection in the window, because she turned round immediately. Her beautiful eyes locked on to the bouquet of daffodils Teddy was holding.

"I'll take them," she said without preamble.

It was Teddy who was startled. The voice coming from this diminutive, diminished elderly lady was surprisingly harsh and demanding, bordering on rude. What had he expected? He'd imagined illness softened—even weakened—a person; he'd not expected her to be so brusque and strident.

Moments later, she spoke again: "do you think I could have one?" she asked. This time, her voice emerged as a whisper. It was the voice of a shy and vulnerable child. "Of course," Teddy whispered back.

Carolyn had given him a vase for the flowers and he placed it on a side table next to Gillian's chair and then pulled out one of the flowers that had obligingly opened during the short drive from Will's house. She took it silently and turned back to the window.

Teddy finally allowed himself to exhale. Cautiously, not wanting to spook her, he sat down on a white wicker chair beside hers.

"I love robins too," he commented. "Spring must be on its way."

Gillian didn't react. Teddy almost said it again, but stopped himself. He knew he mustn't push her. After ten or more minutes passed, it was Gillian who broke the silence:

"My boyfriend's coming today," she said matter-of-factly.

"I know," Teddy answered with a smile, "tell me, what's he like?"

"Who?" Gillian demanded. Her harsh tone had returned.

"Your boyfriend, Gillian. What's he like?"

Gillian turned away from the window and looked directly at Teddy. Under her scrutiny, he daren't allow himself to blink. Those eyes ... he'd never forgotten those eyes ... and there they were looking right into him and yet not knowing him. It was unnerving.

"Like you, I think," she said finally, before resuming her watch over the garden.

Teddy stayed beside her for almost two hours. They exchanged no further words or pleasantries. When he finally noticed Will hovering at the door, he stood up and thanked Gillian for allowing him to visit.

"I'll see you again tomorrow, Gillian."

"My boyfriend's coming today," he heard her say to no one in particular as he walked away.

Teddy walked over to Will. The room was now empty but for the three of them. Funny, thought Teddy, he'd been completely oblivious to his surroundings; all his attention and energy had gone into Gillian. He wondered when everyone else had upped and left.

Will could see Teddy was drained; he seemed to have aged since Will last saw him only a couple of hours before. How sad, he thought. He patted Teddy's shoulder and hoped that Teddy would understand that he understood. Will was all too familiar with the glimmers of hope that came and went like moths drawn to a candle only to be singed and extinguished moments later. He knew just how exhausting it could be.

"Don't take it personally," the doctors would remind him, "remember, she's not herself anymore."

Then why the hell is she still here, Will wondered during his most despondent moments; what's the bloody point?

"Wait here a moment, Teddy. I'll just pop over and say hello to her and then there's something I must show you."

After briefly looking in on his mother who ignored him completely, Will led Teddy back down the mauve hallway and steered him towards the green artery that lead to the residents' rooms. Gillian's room was number 105. It was a rudimentary refuge containing only a bed, a small recliner, chest-of-drawers, side table, and Gillian's trunk. The rose-bud quilt on the bed, matching pink curtains hanging either side of a west-facing window and a pretty embroidered pillow on the chair helped to soften the institutional austerity of the room. A corkboard attached to Gillian's closet door displayed a collection of children's crude and colourful drawings, presumably the work of her grandchildren in New Zealand, Teddy thought. All things considered, the room felt feminine and calming. A small reading lamp stood on the bedside table illuminating a framed photograph of Will and Julie taken at Julie's wedding. Propped up beside the photograph was a rather substantial book containing colour photographs of English country villages.

"Mum loves picture books," Will remarked, "on cloudy days, when she's not taken up her position in the conservatory, she'll sit in here and leaf through that book for hours on end. She's lucky in a way, each time she opens it up she gets to appreciate it for the very first time."

"Lucky? I'm not so sure," Teddy said, "but I hope she is

free from the pain memory can inflict. What is it like to exist in a world without any sense of time or purpose, I wonder."

"I'm not sure, Teddy. I rather suspect it is more frightening for us to contemplate because we still hold most of our faculties intact and our lives still have momentum. When all that is gone, perhaps it's like floating in a perpetually warm pool without bumping into the sides. That wouldn't be so bad, would it?"

Teddy stroked the cover of *The Villages of England* and then picked up the photograph of Gillian's children.

"She looks a lot like your mother," Teddy observed, "a pretty girl."

Meanwhile, Will had lifted the lid of his mother's trunk.

"I brought you in here to show you these," Will said. "I told you I'd prove to you that she never gave up on you."

Teddy replaced the photograph, careful to put it back exactly as it was, and walked over to peer inside the trunk. At first he didn't fully understand what he was seeing. There appeared to be hundreds—if not thousands—of blue airmail envelopes randomly tossed into the trunk. He leaned in closer and allowed his left hand to riffle through them.

"I don't understand," he said looking to Will for an explanation.

"They're all my mother's letters," Will said. "She wrote to you for over fifty years. These are the letters."

Teddy was still having difficulty absorbing it all. He reached in and picked up a handful of the thin blue envelopes. Tentatively, he peeled open the flaps of one of the letters and read the opening paragraph:

July 14, 1963,
My darling Teddy,
It was dreadfully hot here today so my friends and I

spent the day at the beach. It's lovely down there; I know you'd enjoy it. We collected shells and small pieces of smoothed glass. I've put them in a glass vase and they look quite beautiful. I wonder what you're up to today. Perhaps you're working in the shop, or maybe you're walking on the Fells. I wish I knew. I miss you so much …

Love always, your Gillian

For the first time in decades, tears streamed down Teddy's face without restraint.

"How many?" he spluttered, "how many are there?"

"I'm not entirely sure, Teddy, I've never counted."

Will draped a protective arm around Teddy's shoulder. "Come, my friend, that's enough for today. Let me take you home."

The following day, Will went off to work and Teddy returned to The Serengeti. It was another glorious sunny day and Gillian was sat like a sentry in her favourite corner of the conservatory. It was as if she'd never left. Teddy remained by her side for several hours. Again, Gillian told him her boyfriend would be coming that day but that was the extent of their conversation. Before Teddy left for the day, he returned to Gillian's room and helped himself to a handful of the letters. After all, they were addressed to him, so he felt no compunction taking a few with him to read later.

That evening, Will had a surprise for Teddy. He was taking him to his very first ice hockey game. The Vancouver Canucks were taking on the Edmonton Oilers. It would be a thoroughly Canadian experience for Teddy. It was always exciting when two Canadian teams faced off and Will had gone to great lengths to obtain a couple of tickets just three rows behind the Canuck bench. Fortunately, he'd been able to call in a favour from a colleague with connections to Rogers Arena.

At first, Teddy found little enthusiasm for Will's surprise. He'd planned to spend a quiet evening at home reading Gillian's letters, but he could tell that Will was very excited about showing his English guest a bit of Canadian culture and Teddy wasn't about to disappoint him. Besides, the change of pace and the distraction would probably do him good.

And it certainly did; Teddy couldn't help but get caught up in the excitement as he and Will made their way down the steps to their seats in the magnificent arena. Once settled, he struggled to take it all in, with all the noise and colour and movement both on and off the ice. He found the huge screen suspended from the rafters absolutely mesmerizing and probably spent more time looking at that than at the ice. The screen provided the score and other details about penalties and time remaining and so forth along with glimpses of outrageously enthusiastic fans with their painted faces and silly signs. He was equally intrigued by the banter between players on the bench just below him and the melodramatic antics of their coach, even though he couldn't really hear what they were saying over the background noise. Everything was loud and bright and energized, he didn't know where to focus his attention first. One of his favourite moments was when the Zamboni took to the ice. He told Will it reminded him of a gigantic snail slowly making its way around the ice leaving a perfect trail of blemish-free 'slime' in its wake. He said he thought it was quite graceful and provided a refreshing break from the frantic stick-clacking and skate-gnashing of the actual game.

Will laughed, "I'm not sure there's time to make you into a proper Canuck fan, Teddy, but I'm glad you're enjoying the spectacle."

With Will's help he was beginning to understand the rules of play by the second period and, by the third period, he was on his feet cheering every goal, no matter which team scored. The final score was 7 to 3 for the Oilers. Vancouver fans were despondent, but Teddy was exuberant.

"That was splendid!" he told Will as they fought their way through the crowds and out to the street. It was a cold, damp evening and Teddy, suddenly far from tired, suggested they find a warm pub and enjoy a nightcap.

"So, you enjoyed that, Teddy?"

"Oh, I most certainly did. What an experience, Will. Thank you so very much! I'll never forget it for the rest of my days."

"How was the rest of *this* day, your visit with Mum?" asked Will, after their drinks arrived.

Teddy's face immediately shed its smile and became serious and reflective: "she was very quiet today, Will. We didn't talk. I just sat with her. I know it's not a lot, but it's more than I've enjoyed for such a long time, I really don't mind the silence."

"Will you go again tomorrow?"

"Yes, I'd like to. I hope it's OK with you if I stay a few more days. I could always move into a hotel if you prefer. I doubt you expected me to take roost for a whole week."

"I enjoy having you," Will replied honestly, "please, stay as long as you wish. You're an easy guest and I like knowing that Mum is having regular visits for a while. By the way, I've asked Carolyn out."

"That's great, Will. I am pleased. She's a lovely girl and it's time you gave yourself a chance to live a proper life. If there's one thing I've learned, it's not to postpone things too long."

The next day, Teddy found Gillian sitting in the armchair recliner in her room. Carolyn told him that she didn't like to sit in the conservatory on rainy days.

"You are a lucky lady, Gillian, your handsome gentleman caller has returned," Carolyn said as she led Teddy into the room. "I'll fetch you an extra chair."

"Good morning, my love. I have some letters for you today," Teddy said.

Gillian lifted her head from the picture book she had been staring into, "are you the new postman?" she asked.

"In a way," he answered gently.

He took the chair Carolyn had brought in and moved it closer to a position directly opposite Gillian. Until now, they'd always sat side-by-side and Teddy wasn't sure if this proximity would alarm her, but she didn't flinch.

"I have some letters for you," he repeated. "Would you like me to read them out to you?"

Teddy took Gillian's almost imperceptible nod to be a 'yes'.

"Are you sitting comfortably?" he asked, like the children's storyteller on the wireless so many years ago. "Then I'll begin …"

Teddy spent the next four and a half hours 'reading' replies to some of Gillian's letters:

"Darling Gillian,

I'm so sorry I wasn't able to attend your mother's funeral. I wish I could have been there to hold you and comfort you. Please know you never leave my thoughts. I treasure every letter and every moment. It will get better. Time absorbs pain.

Love, Teddy."

"Dear Gillian,

I don't think you should worry about Will. I'm confident he will grow up to become a very fine young man. You are a great mother. He will overcome his shyness in time. You mustn't compare him to Julie. If we'd had children, I wonder what they would have been like. I hope they would have inherited your beauty, your creativity and your kindness ..."

"Dearest Gillian,

How I wish you could have been here for Pa's wedding. Plain old 'newtless' Frobisher was a radiant and beautiful bride. They say all brides are beautiful, but I never expected Audrey to polish up so well! I couldn't be happier for them. They are sharing a joy I once hoped you and I would experience. Perhaps we still can someday. I'll wait for you, my love ..."

And so he continued with only a short break for a cup of tea and a shortbread biscuit. He read his made-up letters until his voice gave out. He was exhausted both by the physical effort and the emotional toll it took. Gillian remained quiet throughout. Once in a while, she would look up at Teddy and smile. For those brief seconds, Teddy was certain she knew exactly who he was but then, just seconds later, she would revert to staring down at her lap and fiddling with the fringe of her shawl as though the man pouring out his heart just inches away from her didn't exist.

Teddy 'read' letters to Gillian for the next three days and, each evening, he returned to Will's house with another batch of hers. Slowly, page by page, he was putting the pieces of her life together, not necessarily in the correct order, but that didn't matter. Before bed each night, he would sit bathing his raw throat in 'medicinal' scotch, listening to Will talk, or watching mind-numbing North American television with him in companionable silence.

"I wonder," said Will one evening, "if she'd had a happier life … I mean, if she'd been more present in her life, would she have left us this way? When I first discovered all those letters, I thought back to the times when she'd disappear to her room to 'do a bit of work', as she put it. My dad always said she had an imaginary friend upstairs. It really annoyed him. I don't know if he ever knew you were real, but he was well aware of Mum's preoccupation. They were both lonely. As a teenager I kept my distance from her because often she made me feel like anything she had to do for me was a great inconvenience to her. Back then, I thought she was just selfish … in fact, I still do, but I don't believe it was ever her intention. Since she became ill, I've often wondered whether being so disconnected from us for all those years made crossing the line into the realm of total disassociation easier. Perhaps she even welcomed it."

"I'm sorry you and Julie felt neglected once in a while … if that's the appropriate word to use," Teddy replied, "I do feel partly responsible despite knowing nothing about it at the time. It makes one wonder about the power of thought. I mean, for all those years, neither one of us really knew what the other was thinking, but it was as if the sheer strength of our thoughts was enough to limit the scope of our lives and damage the lives of those around us. Perhaps energy alone was all it took to create and maintain this extraordinary bond between us."

"'Bond', or excuse?" Will asked.

Teddy didn't respond immediately and Will wondered if he'd overstepped the boundaries.

"I'm sorry, Teddy, that didn't come out quite right."

"Oh, I think perhaps it did, Will. You are not a person who is careless with his words. You make a good point. I can't speak for your mother, of course, but I do know that in my own life I shied away from certain commitments and responsibilities because I still had an ace up my sleeve ... or so I thought. I don't regret the decisions I made or, rather, avoided; I liked my cushion of hope, if you will. I'm sure both of our lives would have been very different if we'd cut the ties back in 1959 when your mother first came over here ... but we didn't and I can't apologize to you for that, I'm afraid."

"I'm not asking you to, Teddy. I have no regrets either and to speculate on an endless compendium of 'what ifs' is a pointless pursuit ... that much I completely understand. I'm very glad you're here Teddy, I sincerely mean that."

The following evening, after Teddy and Will had taken up their post-prandial seats in the living room once more, Will decided to broach the subject of his grandfather and asked Teddy if he'd ever forgiven Harold for taking Gillian away.

"Oh, I was right royally pissed when your grandfather whisked your mother away to Canada—I was a teenager, it was my job and my God-given right to be angry ... or so I believed at the time. I thought Harold's decision was both cruel and cowardly, but I can look at it differently now. Besides, who can say what would have become of us had she stayed in Hawesdale. Perhaps our relationship would have run its course within a few months. Or, perhaps we'd have stayed together and spent the rest of our lives running the shop and living in the flat above it just as my father would have liked. Who knows how it would have all turned out? But, what I do know for certain, and what I have learned to be very grateful for, is the fact that your mother's departure made mine not only possible, but necessary. At first, I simply wanted to escape the memories and the confines of my life as mapped out by my father. But I soon discovered there was so much more to me than I'd realized before. It turned out that I had a genuine capacity to learn, to achieve and to make a difference. Perhaps, indirectly I should be grateful to Harold for that."

Teddy paused for a moment, focusing on his hands as if seeing them for the first time.

"The experience formed me, Will. It made me who I am today. I needed to unload the chip on my shoulder that was nothing more than a sack of tales I'd grown up listening to. I'd heard it all: 'you're just a lad from the village ... you won't ever be wearing fancy clothes and driving fancy cars ... don't waste time thinking above yourself ...' I proved them wrong and, more importantly, I proved myself wrong. I've not forgotten where I came from and I am grateful every time I return there. But, more than anything, I'm grateful that I found other places where I could belong. Like I say, Will, I might never have stepped out into the world had Gillian and I remained together and settled for the Postlethwaite tradition of hard graft, grim resignation and acceptance. I only hope that Gillian's journey has been as rewarding and fulfilling as mine."

"Probably not," Will answered, "at least, that's what I've come to realize. Before I discovered the hidden letters, I would have assumed that raising me and my sister and writing a few books was more than enough for her. But, it wasn't, was it? And now I get it. No one's to blame; it's just the way things turned out."

For the next two days, Teddy continued to 'read' letters to Gillian. On the third day, he decided to alter the routine and brought along a copy of *Swallow And Amazons* he'd found in Will's house. Perhaps it was the very same book that he and Gillian had read from over a lifetime ago.

"Do you remember us reading this together?" he asked Gillian.

Gillian studied the book he'd placed in her hands.

"I've read this before," she said matter-of-factly.

"Yes, Gillian, you have. I'm so pleased you remember. Would you like me to read it to you now?"

"In the garden," she answered.

"In the garden it is then," he replied.

With Carolyn's help, Gillian was bundled up and, gently supporting her elbow, Teddy led her to a cedar bench beside the pond in the garden. This was the first time he had touched her in over fifty years. He would have walked to the ends of the earth if it meant he didn't have to relinquish her arm, but she made a beeline for the nearest bench and their stroll came to an abrupt end. The sun shone again on this day and it was a very pleasant sensation to feel the sun seeping through their layers of clothing to warm their backs. Teddy began to read.

Pages 17 to 21 were stuck together at the top corners and there was a faint patch of yellowish discolouration on the outer margins. This was definitely Gillian's original copy, Teddy was sure of it! He remembered the day she had been reading to him in the back of the shop. He'd leaned over to plant an unexpected kiss on her cheek and had knocked over her glass of Orange Squash in the process.

He looked up from his reading and contemplated repeating the behaviour—minus the spilled drink—but, looking at Gillian, he decided it might do more harm than good. She was in her own little world and whether she was rowing a boat across a lake like the characters in the story, or she was somewhere else entirely, Teddy had no way of knowing.

After a couple of seconds, Gillian's eyes looked accusingly at Teddy and then at the book in his hand as if to say, 'why did you stop?' Despite her limited verbal communication, Teddy couldn't help but marvel at the power of her authority even now. In fact, this revealed to him a whole new side of her. As a young girl, she had been anything but assertive or demanding. Teddy wondered where and when the more forthright Gillian had come into being. He wasn't sure he would have liked it necessarily. What else about Gillian might he not have liked had their connection never been broken, he wondered. He'd never know. Perhaps that was a good thing.

When the sun disappeared behind a large horse chestnut tree, there was an instant chill in the air. Gillian became restless and so Teddy suggested they return indoors to enjoy a nice hot cup of tea.

"Hot chocolate," Gillian said.

"Hot chocolate," he conceded.

"Gillian," he began, after they'd finished their steaming cups of cocoa; he'd been dreading this moment, but he knew he had to tell her whether or not she understood or even cared, "I have to go away, my darling. I have to go back to the shop, back to England."

Minutes passed and neither of them spoke or moved. Teddy wondered if Gillian had even heard him. Then, unexpectedly, Gillian reached out her hand and gently placed it on Teddy's forearm. It would have been an unremarkable gesture between friends in any other context but, in this situation, it took Teddy completely by surprise. He stopped breathing. He wished the moment could last forever. He would gladly cease to be right there and then if it were at all possible. He felt he'd come far enough.

"I know," she whispered.

Teddy looked up and saw she was looking directly at him. She was really seeing him, he'd swear on it. They held their gaze for seconds—maybe minutes—Teddy had no idea but, all of a sudden, he saw a tear meander down Gillian's left cheek and come to rest in that little crease beside her nose.

Teddy didn't know what to do. Should he comfort her, or pretend he hadn't noticed? I didn't matter in the end because, seconds later, Gillian simply stood up and, without a word, shuffled off down the green corridor. Teddy's final image of the love of his life was that of a small, frail creature, walking away, back to the safety and familiarity of the secret life and memories she much preferred. Teddy truly believed Gillian had stepped into the real world with him for a few moments that day but, as before, she couldn't stay.

No one could or would ever know what had passed through Gillian's mind during those few moments. It wasn't that she had no memories; it was that normally she couldn't recognize them. All day memories would bubble up from the black abyss of her mind like shadows shrugging off the night, but they were inscrutable slippery strangers to her. All too soon, they'd re-drape themselves in shrouds of darkness and disappear without a trace. She watched with her inner eye as this particular shadow melted into the darkness beyond her reach and, this time, she knew she'd seen the last of it.

Chapter 10 - Tidying Up Loose Ends

"Promise you'll come and see me in Hawesdale someday?" Teddy said to Will as they shook hands at Vancouver airport.

"Of course I will," he answered.

Teddy knew that such open-ended invitations made during sad farewells were rarely acted on, but he had plans to ensure that one day Will would come to England and see the places where this remarkable story of love and loss began.

A few hours later, Teddy's plane landed like a jittery toad, practically hopping its way down the runway at Ottawa's international airport. Emerging into a damp and drizzly evening, Teddy was reminded of the sheer size and diversity of this vast country, Canada. When he'd left Vancouver that morning he'd been in his shirtsleeves and now, here he was, five hours later, fumbling around in his luggage in search of a jumper.

From his window seat on the plane he'd watched as they'd left Vancouver's beautiful city skyline behind and climbed higher and higher into a mystical world above the clouds. From there he'd looked down on the almighty Rocky Mountains with their jagged snow-capped peaks puncturing the clouds as they thrust upward from the earth's mantle. Shortly after that they'd plunged into thick clouds for the duration of the journey except for a brief glimpse of the Prairies and, later, Lake Superior, as they made their way across to the nation's capital. If he'd had the time, he would have loved to have made the journey by train, or even by car, but it would have taken far too long.

Teddy had tried to take a nap on the plane, but it was impossible, his thoughts were scurrying around inside his head like ants trying to regroup after their nest has been disturbed. What an extraordinary few days it had been, falling short of and exceeding his expectations in equal measure. Soon he would be home, but he had one more loose end to tie up first. In truth, he was looking forward to returning to his flat in Leeds and to the demands of a normal workweek. Emotionally, the past week with Gillian had been like herding cats. One minute he thought he'd got a grip on his feelings and the next minute they were careening about all over the place with their claws out! Teddy was keen to get back to a world defined by familiar demands, deadlines and spreadsheets. Funny, he thought, the very things that often drove him crazy in his job were the very things he longed to return to. He guessed Gillian must have felt much the same as she trotted off back to her room on their last day together. It was, in a sense, her place of business for the time being.

It had been difficult saying goodbye to Will. Teddy had grown very fond of him. But it felt very good knowing that he had been able to help him in some way. Last night, he'd given Will an envelope. Inside was a printed out e-mail from Teddy's bank explaining that, from that day forth, all Gillian's expenses at The Serengeti would be taken care of. Funds would transfer directly to the Home each month for as long as Gillian lived … even if she outlived Teddy. Will had been overwhelmed by Teddy's gesture. He'd told Teddy it would free him from the financial pressures that had been weighing him down for so long. He felt he might finally be getting his life back and Teddy's financial contribution, along with his friendship, were jointly responsible for that.

"You've helped me too, Will, you've no idea," Teddy had said. "Anyway, I hope this will take some weight off your shoulders and you'll start living your life like a normal man about town. I reckon Carolyn is a very good place to start! One more thing," he'd added as he passed a second envelope across the table, "Will, I don't know whether you'd like to remain in this house, or whether it's time you sold up and moved on but, either way, you're going to need to do some work on it. I've been in the trade a while, Will, so I know what I'm talking about. Anyway, this will help get you started. If you want my advice, I'd replace that roof as soon as you can. I don't think I'd sleep comfortably with it over my head for another winter."

The envelope contained a cheque for $50,000.00 made out to Will Evans.

Teddy, having retrieved his luggage, was just completing the paperwork for his rental car. He'd chosen a compact Chevrolet Sonic with an automatic transmission and air conditioning—although he was fairly certain he wouldn't need the latter. He'd made a reservation at a Quality Inn in Arnprior, just north of Ottawa, so he had an easy drive ahead of him as long as he remembered which side of the road he was supposed to be on.

The following day, Georgina Harris was busily dusting shelves in her living room when she saw a dark grey Chevrolet pull up in her driveway. She wasn't expecting anyone. Hastily, she retreated behind the curtains and peeked out in time to see a grey-haired gentleman wearing a grey overcoat step out of the car.

"Oh no," she mumbled out loud, "not another one. I

wonder what this one's selling."

The man looked around and studied the front of the house for a few moments then walked up the front steps and knocked on the door.

Georgina ran her fingers through her unwieldy hair, brushed a bit of dust from her pink tracksuit trousers and went to unlock the front door.

She opened it just a few inches, "can I help you?" she asked.

"Miss Harris? Georgina Harris?"

"Yes," she replied warily, "I'm Ms. Harris."

"I wonder if I might have a few words with you, Georgina. My name's Teddy Postlethwaite."

Teddy wondered whether the sturdy-looking woman blocking his entry to the house was going to collapse on the floor at his feet. He was quite certain he wouldn't be strong enough to pick her up if she did. Her face had suddenly turned an unnatural shade of crimson and beads of perspiration were sprouting from her forehead like miniature geysers.

"Let me come in, Georgina," he urged gently, "I'm not here to hurt you. I just want to talk to you."

Numbly, Georgina stepped aside and Teddy entered the house.

"Let's sit in the living room, shall we?" he suggested, as if the role of guest and host had been completely reversed.

Georgina obeyed silently.

"How about a cup of tea?" Teddy asked. "I'm really quite thirsty," he added, knowing that the act of brewing tea and fussing with cups and saucers would give Georgina an opportunity to compose herself.

"Of course," she spluttered, "what kind of a hostess am I? Of course … whatever the occasion, the English make tea, don't they?" She smiled, tentatively.

While Georgina tended to things in the kitchen, Teddy looked around the living room. It was a comfy, old-lady kind of room with piles of magazines, books and half-finished mending littered about. It was by no means a tidy room, but it was clean. In fact, there was a feather duster recumbent on the windowsill as if it were taking a nap in the midst of its duties. There were a couple of photographs on the mantelpiece, including an old family portrait of a man and a woman and a rather chubby child. Teddy assumed the child was Georgina.

It had been a bit of a shock when he'd first laid eyes upon her just minutes ago. After all those months of corresponding with someone who, in his mind's eye, resembled Gillian, it was strange to discover that this woman was nothing like her at all in looks or body type. She was a large-framed woman for whom sloppy track pants and a saggy top were far from flattering. She wore no make-up and her hair looked as though she had just got out of bed. But, thought Teddy, her eyes were quite beautiful, windows into warmth and vulnerability.

There was a second photograph on the mantel and this one was even more of a shock. It was the picture Teddy had e-mailed to her. She'd had it printed off and put into a cheap acrylic frame. Teddy wanted to remove it. He didn't like the idea of being in the home of a stranger who might be misrepresenting him to her friends. He was about to grab it so he could get rid of it when he left but then Georgina returned carrying the tea tray into the living room. She was looking much better. She placed the tray on the low coffee table.

"I'm sorry," she said, "I didn't recognize you when you came to the door. How do you like it?" she asked.

Teddy was about to reply that he didn't like it one little bit until he realized she was referring to his tea, not the photograph.

"Milk, and plenty of sugar," he replied.

"Do you think you should?" she mumbled as she watched Teddy shovel three heaping teaspoons of granulated sugar into his cup. She felt her face flush when she realized that it really wasn't her place to show concern over Teddy's diet or health. A few weeks ago it might have been perceived as solicitous, but everything had changed since then.

With the ritual of tea serving complete, they sat down—Georgina in her blue chair and Teddy on the sofa opposite.

After a few minutes watching Georgina fiddle with a piece of blue thread that had attached itself to her sweatpants, Teddy broke the silence.

"Aren't you curious about why I'm here?" he asked.

Georgina looked up at him struggling to read the expression on his face. She had no idea whether he was pleased with her or angry; she chose the former.

"Well, I assume you were finally reunited with your sweetheart, so I imagine you are here to thank me."

"To *thank* you?"

Teddy was shocked by the nerve of the woman! He stood up abruptly and began pacing back and forth in front of the window. It was a habit he employed on those rare occasions when he was tempted to blow his stack. He found the constant motion helped to absorb any extraneous energy and prevent him from doing or saying things he might regret later. He'd almost worn out the carpet in the Postlethwaite boardroom over the years.

"I don't know about that! After all, your motives weren't exactly altruistic, were they? You chose to insert yourself into a situation that was none of your business, without any thought for the consequences and the impact they might have on other people. I'd already lost her once and now, thanks to you, I've lost her again. You're a common meddler, Georgina Harris. Not only that, you deceived me without hesitation and I find that especially difficult to forgive. When, exactly, were you going to own up, or are you a coward as well?"

The colour rising in Georgina's cheeks almost matched the raspberry pink of her tracksuit. She stared at Teddy in disbelief ... after all that she had done for him.

"Well?" he demanded, "this is your chance to explain yourself."

"Teddy, you don't have to speak to me like I'm a child. First of all, I took a leap of faith when I posted that first letter, the one I discovered in the bureau. I had no idea what kind of Pandora's Box I was opening. But, Teddy, let me assure you, my intentions were not to cause anyone any pain."

"Well, you did! And, I think we all know where that infamous path ultimately leads, don't we!" Teddy interjected.

Teddy took a very deep breath and, reining himself in, returned to his seat. He leaned forward resting his elbows on his knees and supporting his head in his hands as if it weighed a ton or two.

"Why didn't you just tell the truth from the beginning?" His voice was softer now as if his pacing had worn him out. "You could have explained the situation right at the start instead of engaging in such an unforgivable deceit and allowing me to believe I'd re-found the love of my life. Did it never occur to you that one day you'd be exposed for the fraud you are?"

"Teddy," Georgina began, "I never set out to deceive anyone but, when I read your response to that first letter, I could feel the joy and love in it and I didn't want you to be disappointed again."

"But, I am disappointed, Georgina. I am very disappointed and it needn't have happened. What were you going to do if you couldn't find Gillian, or if you discovered she was already deceased? Were you going to keep up this charade indefinitely and assume that, if or when we met, I was old and dotty enough not to notice that you bear no resemble to my beloved Gillian in any way whatsoever?"

"I never meant it to go this far," she answered. "I didn't think ahead. I got caught up in the romance and, I confess, there were times when I fantasized about us meeting one day and you falling for me as you'd fallen for Gillian. I thought that perhaps you could find her in me if we continued to get to know one another. I know I'm not Gillian, but I'm not a bad person, Teddy."

"Oh, you're right about that, you're definitely not my Gillian, not even close. She would never have done something as underhanded as this. And all that nonsense you told me about working in a dairy and having an affair with a married man ... none of that sounded like the Gillian I knew. My mistake was in wanting it to be true. But Georgina, do you have any idea what it felt like to be met at the airport by a young man claiming to be Gillian's son ... a son you'd never bothered to mention? And the next thing I discover is that I have been carrying on a correspondence with an imposter. How do you think that felt, Georgina?"

"Look, Teddy, I didn't have to go to all the trouble of tracking down your teenage crush. I could have simply stopped writing to you at any time and that would have been the end of it. I know that what I did was wrong, but you must see that I tried to make up for it by reuniting the two of you."

"Oh, I see," said Teddy, "this is the part where I'm supposed to thank you, is it? Well, let me tell you something else, Miss Harris, I saw Gillian, but she didn't see me. All I got to meet was an empty shell. Perhaps I'd have been better off never knowing. But, thanks to you, I no longer have the luxury of that option, do I?"

"I don't believe you mean that, Teddy. I understand that your reunion wasn't as you'd imagined it for all these years—life seldom is—but at the very least you must have some sense of peace now that you know what became of her. Perhaps you can finally let her go. It's not too late for you to find someone else. We could still be friends if you wanted to. We got on well, didn't we?"

"Oh, don't be absurd, woman! I don't even know you. Listen," Teddy said rising from his seat, "it's time I left. I only came to see the house where Gillian had lived and to meet the woman who turned my life into a shambles. Maybe I'll be grateful to you one day, Georgina, but for now, I'd prefer to leave it, and you, alone. I'm tired and I'm grieving. Seeing you sitting there wrapped in your own self-pity and trying to justify your selfish actions isn't helping one little bit. Goodbye, Georgina Harris. I'll see myself out."

While Teddy had been staying with Will, he'd made a conscious effort to keep his true, raw emotions under control. Will didn't need, or deserve, to have Teddy's grief, anger, disappointment and frustration added to his own. But, Georgina? Well, she was a whole different kettle of fish. Teddy needed to release his pent up feelings and she seemed like the best person to unleash them on … in the heat of the moment.

But, as he drove back towards Ottawa, he did wonder if perhaps he'd been a little harsh with the poor lonely Georgina. After all, meeting Will had turned out to be a bonus and discovering the stash of Gillian's letters had, at the very least, confirmed she never forgot him.

Forty-eight hours later, Teddy was back in Hawesdale. He was relieved to be at home again, sitting in the flat above the shop. Everything looked just as he had left it. He could almost convince himself that the past couple of weeks had been nothing more than a dream. In retrospect, it had been a good dream for the most part. But, with time to think on the flight home, he realized that what he felt most uncomfortable about was his encounter with Georgina, particularly when he'd said that Gillian would never have done some of the things she'd done. What did Teddy know? Honestly, he had no idea who Gillian had been beyond the age of sixteen. Her letters told only part of her story. In truth, he knew very little about her. She was hardly likely to have written to him about things that put her in an unfavourable light. For all he knew, she could have had a multitude of lovers outside her marriage, or misrepresented herself in any number of ways, intentionally or not. He didn't even know the simplest things about her, like whether she put the top back on the toothpaste tube after she'd used it, or if she had icy feet in bed. Did she use a pen or a pencil to do a crossword puzzle (did she even do crosswords)? And so on and so forth. He had to admit to himself that the only Gillian he knew was the one he'd wanted to know and his getting taken in by Georgina in the first place was further proof of his romantic self-deception.

~ ~ ~

TO: champlain25@hotmail.com
FROM: tp@postlethwaites.org.uk
SUBJECT: An apology
Dear Georgina,
You probably didn't expect to hear from me again. I want to apologise to you for my behavior the other day. I know you are not a bad person, Georgina. I think you and I are more alike than perhaps I'd like to admit. We're both loners and I

think we've both lived much of our lives in our imaginations. I've spent most of my years dreaming about Gillian despite the obvious fact that we had no contact and couldn't really know one another. You inadvertently brought her back to life for a while. And then, you took her away. But we are both at fault for allowing ourselves to get caught up in it all. I don't believe you set out to do harm and I am sorry if that is the impression I left with you.

I don't imagine we will stay in touch, but I did want to make amends to the best of my ability. Please accept my apologies. I had no right to judge.

Warmly,
Teddy

~ ~ ~

TO: tp@postlethwaites.org.uk
FROM: champlain25@hotmail.com
SUBJECT: An apology
Thank you, Teddy. I'm very sorry too.

Georgina

~ ~ ~

Teddy and Georgina never exchanged e-mails again.

Teddy returned to work with a copyright release signed by both Gillian's literary agent and Will, who had power of attorney over all things to do with his mother. The document allowed Teddy to use the Mr. P character in any advertising and promotions related to Postlethwaite's Home & Garden Centres. The first life-sized Mr. P cutout was unveiled in the Kendal shop in the autumn of 2013. Although Mr. P was made from a plastic-core material, his two-dimensional stand-in always wore a real canvas navy apron with huge pockets bulging with flyers and informational pamphlets. Before long, Mr. P cutouts were greeting shoppers in every Postlethwaite store in the country and appearing in television ads, on billboards and even, on special occasions, as a costumed mascot at special events. His commercial debut lead to negotiations that eventually resulted in the distribution of Mr. P books in England. Teddy took it upon himself to update some of the stories for new young audiences. There was even talk of an animated cartoon in the works!

Will and Carolyn were engaged on New Year's Eve, 2013. Teddy promised to fly over to attend the wedding planned for the following summer. Unfortunately, he never made it. Teddy died from a massive heart attack on April 14th, 2014, exactly 55 years to the day since Gillian had left for Canada. Will learned about Teddy's death when he received a formal letter from one Angus Bosworth *LLP*, a solicitor with Bosworth, Bacon & Newman in Leeds. The letter expressed Mr. Bosworth's sorrow for Mr. Evans' loss and then went on to explain that Mr. Evans was named in Mr. Postlethwaite's will.

Will was both shocked and saddened. He and Carolyn had become very fond of Teddy and had kept in touch regularly since he'd left. Will suspected his indulgent lifestyle had finally caught up with him, but perhaps it was more likely that now, stripped of the dreams and fantasies surrounding his beloved Gillian that had sustained him over the decades, he'd simply run out of enthusiasm.

Teddy didn't have any direct heirs, although Will knew that he'd remained close to his father's widow and to the family that ran the Hawesdale shop. However, he was completely unprepared when he learned that Teddy had left him the flat above the shop; it seemed like a very odd and rather inconvenient bequest. And, it came with a caveat … Teddy's will stated very clearly that Will could opt to keep or dispose of the flat at any time on one condition, and that condition was that he come to Hawesdale and stay in the flat for at least a fortnight before making up his mind.

"You old schemer," thought Will out loud, "you always said you'd make sure I got there some day! Well, you're on. Carolyn and I are delighted to accept your invitation; in fact, we will spend our honeymoon in your precious Hawesdale."

There was a second sealed envelope inside the solicitor's. Will's name was handwritten on the outside. He tore it open immediately and found a personal note from Teddy explaining exactly what he'd like Will to do with Gillian's trunk of letters after she died. Like the Hawsedale flat, it was another unusual bequest, but Will was confident Teddy had his reasons.

Having refused food since the beginning of April, Gillian died just days after Teddy. They couldn't have planned it any better. One of the nurses discovered her asleep in her favourite chair in the conservatory wrapped in the afternoon sunshine. She was dreadfully thin and frail beneath her purple shawl, but death bestowed a child-like innocence to her face that implied that this was finally a happy day, not a sad one.

It was hardly a surprise to anyone that she had gone. Will was not overly upset—not because he didn't care—but because he'd ceased grieving for his mother long ago. He had a strange dream not long after Gillian's death. Hundreds of people were crowded together on a railway platform, all of them frantically looking for their friends or loved ones. It was a chaotic and rather alarming scene in Will's dream but, all of a sudden, the crowds parted and there stood Teddy. He was wearing a suit even though he looked like a young lad in the dream. He walked straight forward with his arms extended. And then, out of the crowd, Gillian appeared. She was wearing a 1960's style dress and dragging her mauve shawl behind her. Just as she and Teddy were about to collide, Will's alarm went off. Nonetheless, his nocturnal ramblings had left him with a strong feeling of peace and acceptance.

Julie, of course, went to great lengths to make up for what she saw as her brother's callous detachment. She wailed and sobbed over the phone on multiple occasions without any consideration for the time difference.

"How could this have happened? They let her starve to death! You said she was well cared for," she cried accusingly, "you have no idea how much I'm going to miss her. It's hard for a daughter to lose her mother."

"The mother you never bothered to visit in … how many years …?" Will thought. It was two o'clock in the morning Vancouver time; he had no intention of allowing a squabble with his sister to fully awaken him so he kept the question to himself.

Julie also demanded to know what Will was planning to do about the house and contents.

"Mum would have wanted me to have some of her things, you know. What about that trunk she loved? I could have that."

Oh, that damned trunk, thought Will. Will had never told Julie about meeting Teddy and he wasn't entirely sure how to explain that the trunk was already spoken for.

"Well, she didn't mention anything specific in her will, Julie. But I don't care. You can have whatever you like if you're willing to come and get it. Most of her stuff is boxed and ready as it has been ever since she moved into The Serengeti. Just let me know when you'll be dropping by," he added bitterly.

"Will, you're being so cold. What about the house? I'm entitled to some of the money from that."

"Sure you are. I had it evaluated before we began the repairs and renovations so we could get a mortgage in our own names. Carolyn and I will buy you out based on that appraisal. But, we're staying here. I've put in a lot of dollars and sweat equity. This is our home, Julie. But, I'll make sure you get your fair share."

Not once did she ask how her mother had spent her final days. Not once did she thank Will for all the years he'd taken care of her, or ask him how he was coping with her death. Not once did she ask about Carolyn or show any interest in their upcoming wedding.

Following Teddy's death, Georgina had also received an envelope from Angus Bosworth Esq. In it, was a second smaller envelope, still sealed. Georgina opened it with shaking hands and discovered a note in Teddy's all too familiar handwriting:

Dear Georgina,

If you are reading this note, it is because I have gone. I have given much thought to our unusual relationship and must confess that those few months, before it went so awfully wrong, were among the happiest of my life. I know it was all built on rather unsound and spurious foundations but, nonetheless, we were both complicit and I refuse to burden myself with regrets. As a belated gesture of my gratitude for those few months and for the great lengths you went to in order to engineer my reunion with Gillian—even if it was only to save your own hide(!)—I would like you to become the custodian—curator, if you will—of the collection of letters Gillian wrote to me over the years. It was both heartwarming and tragic to discover that she had written to me regularly ever since leaving England. However, the letters were never posted. She kept them stored in a large trunk that accompanied her as far as her final earthly destination. They were all intended for me, so I have no qualms in determining their fate after Gillian's and my deaths.

I have become very fond of Gillian's son, Will, but do not feel that the letters belong with him. He is aware of my wishes and, although it is ultimately his prerogative to decide what becomes of them, I believe he will honour my unusual request after Gillian's death. You have my permission to read as many of them as you like. I never managed to read them all, but someone should. At the end of all this I do believe you will know and understand my Gillian better than anyone—how extraordinary is that! I'm laughing out loud as I write this. I hope you enjoy the irony too.

Take care of my precious Gillian. Perhaps you'll discover that the two of you have more in common than I dared to consider.

Yours affectionately,
Teddy Postlethwaite

~ ~ ~

A Bit About Kate Bridger

Kate Bridger is a writer, an award-winning Fabric Artist, and an interior consultant. She grew up in northern England until moving to Canada in the late'60s. Currently, Kate lives in the picturesque town of Nelson in the interior of British Columbia, Canada. This is her second work of fiction.

Books previously published by Kate Bridger:

Nest Building: A Guide To Finding Your Inner Interior Designer (2011) – a lifestyle guide

The Fabric Of Nelson (2013) – an art book

Talking To Myself (2014) – a novel

To know more about Kate, visit: **www.katebridger.ca**

You can also follow Kate on Facebook at:
www.facebook.com/WordsAndStitches

To contact Kate: kbridka@yahoo.ca